Balloon Ship Armageddon

Book Seven
of the Jack Commer Series

Michael D. Smith

Sortmind Press, 2021
press.sortmind.com

cover design by Michael D. Smith
NASA image: globular cluster in the Large Magellanic Cloud

For my wife Nancy

CHAPTER ONE
The Hospital
Wednesday, May 13, 2076

Thrashing under the straps, Jonathan James Commer took in the glossy green tile of the walls, the asymmetrical bars of blue light on the ceiling, and screamed.

A woman loomed over him. JJC blinked at a pair of impossibly huge blue eyes. "You're all right! You're all right! You came through fine!" she cried.

"Hey, JJC man, we made it!" came a shout from his left. It was Rick Ballard, whole and human in a hospital bed, clamped by metallic red straps. Bouncing next to them on three bulging spherical tires was the battered tetrahedral *T'ohj'puv* robot, not the perfect chromium tetrahedron they'd all been trapped inside, but the ancient Martian servant robot with the snaking hose arms.

"We did it? We got separated?" JJC gasped. "Into *what?*"

"Into perfect Wounded Robots!" Ballard laughed, snapping his restraints and swiveling off the bed. "Thank you, nurse, thank you! It worked!"

"Here, just lie back," replied the auburn-haired woman in a white lab coat. "And I'm not a nurse. I'm Dr. Nortel."

"It--it--" Ballard choked through thick purple lips, gagging and bending to puke.

"Easy, there. The biomatrix for human format does take a few minutes to settle in." Dr. Nortel grabbed his wrist as Ballard went into a furious coughing fit. "Mr. Ballard, are you really all right?"

Jonathan James felt fresh strength flowing into his arms and found he too could easily rip his restraints. Disjointed memory flooded him. Had he really spent a month cruising the Iota Persei system in the *Garrison?* Trapped in a solid chromium tetrahedron, jammed into Ballard and T'ohj'puv partitions in reverberating, infinite sequences of consciousness?

Hundreds of Ywritt entities had refused the *Garrison's* requests for access to the Ywritt robotics libraries, yet all had been curiously amenable to Ballard's appeal for secrecy. Apparently the Ywritt took their pledge of customer privacy seriously. During this entire time JJC had remained dazed and of little help. But finally Ballard announced he'd found a Wounded spy on Myndar who'd plundered the Ywritt quantum computational techniques. Was that just yesterday? Had they really made it to the second planet of Iota Persei?

"Mr. Ballard, get your hands off me!" came the next cry. In a tiny hospital gown flaunting well-muscled buttocks, Rick Ballard manhandled Dr. Nortel's ample chest with his big hairy hands.

"God, babe! To be awakened by an *angel!* Oh my God!"

"Mr. Ballard, *desist!*" Dr. Nortel demanded. JJC noted the doctor was in fact rather voluptuous under that severe lab coat. Her wild hair framed a round face. Her thin lips pursed into a half-smile despite her scolding tone. Those big blue eyes were outrageously hypnotic. "Let me remind you that I am a Class J Wounded and you have no right to assault me. God, are you really all right?"

Ballard doubled up and retched a quart of blood on the cold blue floor. Behind him came the *T'ohj'puv* robot, hose arms whirling, opening a panel on one of its three triangular sides to extend a dustpan and broom.

"That's an *ancient* thing," Dr. Nortel noted, meeting Jonathan James' gaze. "Twenty thousand Martian years old, according to the program. I was surprised it came out intact, in its previous form. Its original device couldn't speak and unfortunately neither can this one. But of course the Wounded matrix allows for telepathic contact. Mr. T'ohj'puv, you really don't need to clean up the mess there. I understand it was what you were trained to do, but it's really not necessary."

This entity experiencing random chaos cycles, shot from the robot.

"No, that's impossible," Dr. Nortel retorted. "I used standard Class J. You're fine. The only variable was the three-part-nature of the pyramid, but I can assure you the Separation Coefficient was right on target." Jonathan James picked up communications from not only T'ohj'puv, but also, to his surprise, from both Ballard and Dr. Nortel. Apparently the doctor felt a need to hear herself think and so spoke aloud to underline the telepathic burst.

Cascade failure imminent, T'ohj'puv transmitted. *The same holds true for the Rick Ballard entity. Prepare for Quanta Reversal Paradigm.*

Dr. Nortel's eyes went even wider than JJC thought possible as she whirled to Ballard, who feverishly worked his hospital gown over his head and flung it aside. A jagged line of spurting red opened from the neck of Ballard's magnificently muscled torso to his well-endowed crotch.

"Quanta--*what?*" JJC had time to gasp as purple light erupted and Rick Ballard burst into a thousand soggy pieces of meat spattering walls, floor, and ceiling.

"Oh my God!" Dr. Nortel cried. She and JJC both whirled to the escalating whine of the *T'ohj'puv* robot as it flailed and blasted out random strings of computational symbols.

This time JJC had the presence to dive to the floor before a second explosion shook the room, the doctor joining him there and shoving him with impossible speed under the hospital bed as shrapnel clanged off the tiles.

JJC stared at a twisted six-inch piece of steel that had pierced his palm. "*Ow!* Goddamn!" He hauled himself out and gaped at the floor and walls littered with metal shards, wires, and memory wafers. And human intestines, bones, brain matter, and shredded organs.

"Careful! God, I don't know what happened!" Dr. Nortel said, pulling herself out after JJC. As he regarded the blood pouring from his hand, Jonathan James expected Dr. Nortel to launch a caring physician routine, but she merely said, underlying her words with telepathic instructions: "Oh, that. Just yank the mother out and run Standard Repair Module."

"You--you--" The two hospital beds were soaked with gore. A dozen medical machines were equally spattered; several had overturned. Without thinking JJC ripped the charred junk out of his hand, stared for a moment at the inch-wide hole welling with blood, then located Standard Human Format Repair Module in what he only now realized was a computerized brain taking up fair less space in his cranium than his previous one. In a fifth of a second his left hand was entirely normal.

"I--I'm a *robot* now?" he muttered as Dr. Nortel ruefully surveyed her ruined hospital room.

She nodded. "Class J."

"You--the Ywritt--*saved* me?"

She sized him up. "Are you dense? I'm not Ywritt. They have no clue about this room. No way they'd help you. They don't understand a thing about Wounded tech, even though their libraries grabbed records of all of it over the past thirty years. They're a bunch of packrats. They'll store anything, but they don't understand a bit of it. All I did was grab the Class J Restoration Data they had on file."

JJC considered his perfect hand. "But I'm *human*. Ballard was too! Oh my God!" The stench of the blown former *Typhoon VI* navigation officer was just hitting him.

"Human-format interface," Dr. Nortel said. "You know that. Classes A to T can have any matrix. Our bodies are robotic, but indistinguishable from human tissue. You just need time to access your operating manual." She tapped his forehead and grinned. JJC was taken aback. Was the doctor actually flirting with him as they stood in puddles of Ballard blood and shattered T'ohj'puv?

"What *happened?*"

"Look, I really don't know. Maybe it was the subroutine for running Standard Class J Entitlement. It should work on a cubic meter of *dirt*. I just don't understand." She peered at him. "We need to see if *you're* all right. I'm Amy, by the way." She held out a hand for JJC to shake, but he just stared at it. There was a lot of underlying telepathic subtext he couldn't understand. To his astonishment Amy unbuttoned her soaked lab coat with bloody hands, casting it aside to reveal a large curvy figure in a tight, low-cut blue tank top matching her eyes, and a white pencil skirt spattered bright red. Jonathan James stared in fascinated horror at this abruptly sexy package: rotund, but compact and tightly muscled, buxom, astonishingly proportioned. Giant crazy blue eyes merrily bored into his own.

She dropped the crimson coat to the floor, following his gaze to her skirt, and he watched in bewilderment as the stains disappeared. Likewise the clots of Ballard plastered across her face and neck faded along with the wires and wafers of T'ohj'puv tangled in her hair. "Just a little Class J secret!" she laughed. "If you'd only bothered to check the manual. We can launder our clothes with telekinesis, or hadn't you figured that out yet?" She tugged at his flimsy hospital gown. "We could wash this but I think the examination needs to happen *now.*"

And Jonathan James Commer stood naked before Dr. Amy Nortel.

CHAPTER TWO
Contamination

"Why, you're *contaminated!*" Doctor Amy cried, backing away. "You're not one of *us!*"

Jonathan James froze. Was something amiss at his crotch? But he was happy to note that all seemed well there. "What are you talking about? I'm fine. You got me out. I don't know what happened to the others." In fact he did feel excellent. But the memory was still strong of Ballard shattering him into millions of pieces of glass on the planet Altrouda. He recalled the moment of his death in fresh detail, his shocking transformation into a chromium pyramid, and the humiliation of coexisting with his murderer, of becoming the bastard's buddy and confidant along with that incomprehensible T'ohj'puv entity. At the same time he felt a surge of loss for these two intimate friends.

"Oh my God," Amy moaned. "I'm running the log files now. No wonder those two blew! They were contaminated! You brought that horrible Alpha Centaurian wavelength with you!"

"Me?" He could still feel the echo of the fascist Alpha Centaurian Emperor, though it was nowhere near the force that had almost killed him last year at Procyon A, when he'd reinstated the ancient Grid and for a few agonizing moments had united the souls of twenty trillion Centaurian citizens in a bond devastatingly more intimate than the mechanical, atomic-scale lockdown in the tetrahedron with Ballard and T'ohj'puv. But he hadn't been able to handle it; the horror had nearly driven him mad.

He'd felt that Grid every day since, but after months of terror, therapy, and raw will, and with the assistance of his lover Suzette Borman and his *Garthah-/yuu* brother Trotter, he'd shoved it all back into distant, diluted archival storage. Suzette and Trotter? Did they even have the slightest idea what he'd endured? God, where were they now?

"This Centaurian *crap!*" Amy spat. "It's blocked us from this entire sector! It's like some stupid alarm that'd tell every Centaurian we're here. And the mental *flavor* of it! Disgusting!"

She jabbed a finger at his bare stomach. "You're *filthy!* *Sickening!* And here I have to love you! That's the worst part of it!"

"Wait! You're *Wounded?* I am too?"

"Of course, idiot! We weren't about to abandon Iota Persei just because we lost that little skirmish here last year. Are you really that dense? We just put a few folks underground, and at Sol too, if you must know."

"You're the spy Ballard found!"

"Congratulations, idiot! Of course I am!"

"I thought you were a *doctor!*"

"I am, fool! The Ywritt think I'm a USSF *archivist* here. They have no clue, no clue! Those goddamn wisps of gas think they're so smart. For your information this room is completely hidden on the third floor of Myndar Pre-Quantum Library Prime. Nobody knows this robot repair facility is here but the Wounded. You got that?"

"Well, I guess …" Only now did JJC register that he too had access to all that knowledge. Yes, he was a robot. He was Wounded tech. He reeled. He understood, no, he *gloried* in the Wounded's lust to build Dyson spheres around stars, to suck their energy and send it to distant quasars, to create spectacular celestial fireworks, works of art that explained so much, so much. And now he was the mortal enemy of Sol, of Earth, of his father and mother, the USSF, all the friends he'd ever had there, all humanity. "I'm one of *you* now?"

"Yes, exactly," Amy said, taking a big breath and noting JJC's gaze traveling to the magnificent half-naked breasts in that tight tank top. "But unfortunately, the Alpha Centaurian patterns of your contamination can't be allowed to infect the Wounded General Operating System. You can see what they did to your two fellow robots. I have no idea why you haven't blown by now as well." She grabbed a scalpel from a crimson puddle on the floor. "You will now submit to evisceration."

JJC backed away. "That's insane! Look, I know it all now! Even if you stab me, I can repair it!" Yes, the Repair Module would work on any wound, just as it had on the palm of his hand.

She could saw both legs off and he'd just fashion new ones.

Then he saw the flaw in his reasoning as Amy confirmed: "Not if I cut out your CPU!" She lunged for his eyes. JJC saw how true her aim would've been if he hadn't shifted left at the last millisecond. She sailed off balance to his right and he shoved her hard into the bloody tile wall, twisting her knife arm up behind her back and tearing it loose from her fingers with his teeth.

Full knowledge of Class J capabilities flooded him. He knew they each could choose to feel all the pain of their struggle, or simply cancel it. He felt them both canceling. No use playacting anymore.

"Damn you!" she grunted. "I can't believe you read the whole Operating Manual just like that!"

"Well, it was there," JJC mumbled, knife still between his lips. The blade was as dangerous as a rubber toy. Amy had picked it up knowing the dramatic effect it would have on a confused JJC reacting as if he were still a puny human being. She could've torn his head off with her bare hands and crushed his central processing unit with her fingers, but starting that process would've likely tipped JJC off to the existence of the Operating Manual right there. In his final farewell to human panic, he'd found it on his own. He held Amy tight against the wall with both her arms behind her back. Their strengths were perfectly matched. JJC proceeded to munch the knife, chew and swallow it, eliciting a grunt of surprise from the doctor.

"You do realize you're an abomination, don't you?" she hissed, ready to spring free the second he relaxed. "If you don't voluntarily consent to *autopsy,* you'll eventually contaminate the Wounded with this AC crap in your brain."

JJC considered it. As various servers began mapping him in their galaxy-wide networks, the murky existential seed of whatever had gone so wrong with the ancient Alpha Centaurian Grid would propagate. Initial infections might be fended off for a while, but as more and more Wounded robots succumbed to the Grid frequencies, no matter what their level, from the highest A to the most menial clunking T, the chaos would *cascade*. That was the word T'ohj'puv had used; it and Ballard had experienced the first cascade. The Wounded were doomed. And here was Dr. Amy Nortel, a mere Class J Wounded physician, blithely hoping she could stave off disaster.

Guess what? she transmitted. *If I called one Class I here, she could vaporize you herself.*

Thanks, JJC shot back, keeping her arms tightly twisted behind her. *I've already shut down all external communication. Nobody at any level is coming.*

You idiot! The higher levels always find out. They always get through. We're nothing compared to them! To Draka Sortie!

JJC considered the hierarchies of the Wounded. His father had beaten Draka Sortie last year. Draka had built an annihilating Dyson sphere around Iota Persei and tried to do the same to Sol, but the files in Jonathan James' brain had no further information on that Wounded robot after he'd absorbed a Martian shattergun bolt and burst into jagged glass shards.

Strange to think that a Class A, as omnipotent as God, could be killed just like that. Maybe it had to do with that nasty flaw in the Wounded JJC was beginning to intuit: the whining, self-absorbed nature that prevented them from ever truly conquering anything. They were always feeling sorry for themselves, they were always depressed, they could never use their powers to chart anything that would grow and prosper. Instead they blew things up for kicks and called themselves artists.

As a Class J, Jonathan James had none of that Class A Trans-Simultaneity, but he possessed enough telekinetic powers to heal himself of major wounds, exert a hundred times the strength of an ordinary human male, and perform clever tricks like doing the laundry with his mind.

"Look, let me turn around and we can at least straighten some of these themes out," Amy said after JJC realized she'd telepathically hacked his last thoughts. They both knew she couldn't escape and he relaxed his grip as she whirled to face him. He clamped down again, feeling her firm breasts mash into his naked chest. "Mmmm, much better," she purred, smiling up at him. "You do realize that, as a Class J, I am in fact fully in love with you."

Jonathan James met those big insane eyes. "Huh. How 'bout that?"

"We are so wondrously, evenly matched, in spite of that nasty contamination of yours. I do regret having to terminate you. Which I will do eventually, you realize. You would have been quite nice in bed there." Her eyes beckoned to Ballard's gory sheets. JJC saw part of a twisted human spine that had landed there. Amy undulated her chest against his.

"Yeah, I imagine it would have been just spectacular," JJC said, his lips an inch from hers. "Listen, Doctor Amy, I truly appreciate your use of the spoken word just now, and I even see you've pitched your voice to Rick Ballard's most vulnerable seduction frequency. Very nice."

Amy blinked back from point-blank range. *I assume you've discovered that you now have Ballard and T'ohj'puv partitions in your mind?*

Yes, I have the partitions. Very well hidden. Took me awhile. I've run the diagnostics and see I have 85.77% of Ballard and 76.59% of T'ohj'puv. The rest was lost to cascade.

Amy smirked. *And you still can't see how dangerous this contamination is? That you have no choice but to submit to existence cancellation? I'd cut your Centaurian crap out if I could, and make love to you forever, but I can't get to it. It's too damn strong. You're simply going to have to sacrifice yourself for the sake of the Wounded. It'll happen eventually anyway. It's in your very programming. And in any case, the higher levels will track you down.*

JJC knew he should fear the higher levels. If a 4'6" eight-year-old Level I girl walked in here right now, Jonathan James was duty-bound to exterminate himself instantly in obeisance to her. But somehow these higher levels meant nothing to him. Was it the Alpha Centaurian contamination? Was his former insanity an inoculation against full absorption into the Wounded?

Well, maybe I'm free. Maybe I got this Wounded body but I'm free!

"Forget it!" Amy shouted. "You're not free! You can never

leave this wonderful room! Because we're both Class J's and I love you!" To JJC's surprise she pushed him back, ripped the blue tank top over her head and came for him, big glorious boobs and pink nipples bouncing merrily.

Ballard Program 624A engaged. Analysis of Dr. Nortel's pheromonal activity complete: female fully in grip of love delusion. Prepare for sexual intercourse, intro power level 5, option for 6 and above on standby.

T'ohj'puv Recommendation Orange. Ballard program presents hazard to existence of Jonathan James Commer robotic entity.

Dr. Amy Nortel was all over Jonathan James, clutching his naked ass, fondling his chest, kissing her way down his stomach even as she yanked down the side zipper on her pencil skirt.

Ballard 624A--go!

T'ohj'puv Recommendation Red. Review entities in other partitions. Now.

Ballard 624A. Forget that! Let's get laid!

T'ohj'puv Recommendation Red. Now.

JJC blinked. *Other entities.* Oh, of course, his Zarj brothers were part of the contamination. His *Garthah-/yuu.* The Beagle Trotter was still inside him, and so was Clopt, the long-dead Zarj captain, killed in a Warp transfer suicide, probably walking the infinite halls of the *Garr/thahg* afterlife but still living deep within Jonathan James. So he had secret partitions for *four* entities inside him: Clopt and Trotter, most of Ballard and most of T'ohj'puv, amazing resources locked within, keeping him stable and separate from the Wounded.

And a fifth entity, he saw: Suzette Borman, who'd saved his sanity. He'd loved her, then lost her when Ballard had shattered him. What could she possibly be feeling now? Was she grieving for him? Did she think he was lost forever? Wasn't he?

He raised Amy from her crouch and saw the dismay in her eyes. "No! You can't love *her!*" she shrieked as their energies unbalanced and JJC gained more strength than she could imagine. He pulled his fist back and decked her so hard that she whirled across the spine-stained bed and flew into the opposite wall, grunted, and lay still. JJC stood over her and regarded her stunned blank eyes and her smashed, dislocated jaw.

He inspected a large panel flush with the wall. The code for unlocking it, seven million lines of an alien computer language, came into his mind. It took him five seconds to master the WoundLock 95 logic, then the panel door clicked open next to Amy Nortel's inert nude torso.

A small Beagle entered from a sunlit corridor and sniffed the blood-soaked room.

Master, I have been looking for you everywhere! You're back! They got you out of the triangle thing!

Jonathan James scooped up the dog who'd followed his pyramid-imprisoned Zarj brother into the *Garrison* just before it blasted off. "Trotter buddy! Where the hell have you been?"

I was looking and looking everywhere! There are Ywritt creatures all through this building. Big cloudy balls. They didn't care I was here. They don't care about anything! I just kept walking, sniffing for triangle thing. Then it was gone! Then I smelled you from six floors away. You're different. But you smell exactly the same!

"Great, buddy, great! Where's the *Garrison?* We've gotta split fast. I don't remember where Ballard might have parked it."

The Ywritt made it a display on the first floor. Big sign there. I asked one Ywritt what it says: "Typical Current USSF Shuttle."

"Great, we'll get down there fast. Damn, I need clothes. But I think I can just make them." In a moment JJC was clad in his favorite black sweater and pants as Trotter surveyed the room, cocking his brown and white head, sniffing body parts and inspecting Amy Nortel's battered face. *Tear out evil lady throat?*

"Nah, won't do any good," JJC said, stepping into the bright outer corridor. Twenty-foot-wide windows overlooked what seemed to be a park of trees and ponds. Pastel spheres of consciousness drifted down the corridor, transparent in the sunshine. Maybe these were Ywritt librarians. Would any of them consider floating through the open panel behind him into the slaughterhouse? What would they think of Wounded spies in the heart of their precious library?

Trotter padded beside him. *They have elevators for moving objects. How I went up and down levels.* He paused. *Kill Ballard thing inside you?*

JJC smiled. "I don't think that'll be possible. C'mon, let's get the *Garrison*. I think these Ywritt will just observe the fact that we're stealing their exhibit, then meditate on it or something." He fished in his marvelous new mind for the schematics of all USSF vessels known to the Wounded, coming up with the most efficient way to hotwire the *Garrison* for takeoff by thought alone. Ballard and T'ohj'puv had already upgraded the little ship's Star Drive on the way to Iota Persei, and JJC realized he had the technological ability to enhance the *Garrison* enough to hurl it outside the Milky Way.

But along the way to the first floor he encountered a voice coming from what he guessed would be the most trying of all the partitions he was now responsible for.

This is Ballard, dude. Man, you just passed up a chance for a great lay!

CHAPTER THREE
Distrust

Jack Commer surveyed the crimson-spattered room. Amav stood in the doorway, arms folded. What was truly unsettling was that the Ywritt administrator floating beside them had picked up the human revulsion at the smell of death and, after consulting databases of Terran culture, had substituted what she considered a soothing aroma for her visitors: peanut butter cookies fresh from the oven. So, by the graciousness of the master Ywritt communicators, Jack and Amav were looking over twisted guts and rivulets of blood draining down the walls while emotionally eased by a childhood smell of pleasure and anticipation. To his disgust Jack was salivating. How could Ywritt tech accomplish this?

The fourth member of the group exhibited no such unease. Laurie 283, who'd taken a fast saucer in from Yaraltar, the third planet of Iota Persei, nimbly stepped through the blood, her robotic eyes photographing and analyzing every detail down to the molecular level. Pieces of Rick Ballard, pieces of the *T'ohj'puv* robot, the unfathomable Wounded hospital machines in disarray, the scars on the walls, all allowed precise measurement of the Wounded forces that had blasted this room.

"So he was really here," Amav muttered. "I can't believe it. And somehow he got out?"

"That's what we think," said the Ywritt library administrator, who'd explained that her name translated as Bracket Explore and that she preferred to practice vibrating English words as opposed to making standard Ywritt telepathic contact. "The ship you call the *Garrison* took off with two entities inside: one robotic humanoid, the other biological, much smaller, four-legged. We surmise that this creature was fixated on locating the one you call Jonathan James Commer."

Jack nodded. So JJC's dog Trotter had escaped with him, or with *something*. Because even if it were Jonathan James, he wasn't human anymore. Jack had to remind himself that none of what he was seeing scattered across the hospital beds was human

14

debris, but robot parts machined to human form. This was not Rick Ballard's body, but the remains of an exploded robotic copy. Metallic shards of the ruptured *T'ohj'puv* pyramid littered the beds and the floor, but Laurie 283 had already reassured Jack that only one flesh-and-blood body had exploded here. Which meant that his son Jonathan James must have successfully separated from the pyramid. But he was still a Wounded machine. And the ultimate danger to Sol.

Amav wore her comm at the waist of her tight red flight suit and spoke into the virtual microphone the comm formed at her lips: "No trace of the trajectory?"

"Sorry, it exited so fast, and before we were near the planet, that the primitive sensor systems aboard this saucer were unable to get a bearing," replied the Marsport Automated Transport System aboard the *Stewart Neal Frankston* on the roof of the fifteen-story building. "The *Garrison* was in fact past our sensors before we even knew it was launching. Thus we're looking at Star Drive acceleration magnitudes above what we're currently capable of. The *Garrison's* Star Drive was also apparently reengineered to cause no harm in activating near the surface of this planet. That is an intriguing technological feat which MATS will continue to analyze. Meanwhile I'm scanning for any remnants of Star Drive trails to obtain a vector for the *Garrison,* but so far have been unsuccessful."

That had been gutsy piloting, Jack knew. The *Garrison* had punched a hole in the facility's dome with its mini-PlanetBlaster a millisecond before hurtling through it. Emergency force fields had dropped into place, and Myndar Pre-Quantum Library Prime was now replenishing its lost air. "Okay, MATS, patch what you've got back to Sol via superspace," he said. "They have much more sophisticated sensors than our saucer."

There was a long silence, during which Jack cursed himself for forgetting that he was never supposed to issue a direct order to MATS. Only Amav could do that, with her unusual rapport with the system. She knew Jack resented this as captain of their saucer, and kept trying to cajole MATS and Jack into becoming friends, with limited results.

"I'm on it, Jack," came back not from the Marsport Automated Transport System but from the *Frankston's* navigator, the Commers' robot dog Edward. Jack had no idea how he'd survived an entire day aboard the *Frankston* amid the clever repartee and bickering between robot Edward and MATS, which took pains to remind the dog that the Marsport Automated Transport System was fully integrated with all saucer functions, was a billion times smarter than a robot Saint Bernard, and only suffered the dog's limited navigational abilities out of respect for Edward's loving owner Amav Frankston-Commer, currently Dictator of Sol on leave of absence.

Though MATS had agreed last month to never again infect a USSF spaceship with its AI tech, it remained a powerful force in SolNet, as well as an important liaison to Ywritt quantum computational interfaces. Being Amav's special friend, MATS had so earnestly requested to be the interface for the Commer's vacation saucer that Amav felt she couldn't refuse. To keep peace Jack had reluctantly agreed, even though he was so sick of MATS' interference in USSF affairs that he had contingency plans to permanently shut down the damn contraption if it pulled any more stunts like the one during the SolGrid Rebellion last month. Patrick James, one of the discredited SolGrid rebels, but still the foremost computer expert in Sol, would be just the man to tap for that.

But Jack had to admit that MATS' replacement throughout the USSF, the ill-named Know-How System, was laughably inferior compared to how a sane MATS could coordinate a fleet of over ten thousand ships. The Know-How System's AI was balky, its superspace connection with other ships was hit-or-miss, and there were thousands of contingencies major and minor the system had yet to adapt to. Despite assurances from USSF Computational Services, Jack didn't see much hope in getting the system up to speed within the promised two-year deadline. The very name of the system, Know-How, seemed kludged from computer lingo of a hundred twenty years ago. Nobody had even settled on an abbreviation yet: USSFKH, USKH, UKH, KHS. In any case to Jack it was really "No-How."

His experience with the malfing Know-How was another reason Jack had accepted MATS aboard his civilian saucer. In the event of any danger that put Jack out of commission, he was confident MATS could deliver Amav safely back to Sol. The MATS-equipped J-133 *Frankston* was named for Amav's father, the planetary engineer responsible for terraforming Venus and for repairing Earth after the Final War. Far too luxurious for Jack, the saucer was a two-hundred-foot-wide yacht, bigger than anyone needed unless you wanted to transport sixty people on a pleasure cruise. But Amav had insisted on the J-133, cramming it with supplies for what she said might become a year-long search for their son. It was just Jack and Amav on the *Frankston,* both of them ostensibly on six-month leaves of absence from their jobs, along with Edward and the touchy, ego-tripping MATS.

They'd left the clean-up of the destruction of Marsport to the Martians, though some had accused them of skipping out when they were needed most. But Amav, the foremost planetary engineer in Sol, knew the Martians were more than capable of taking charge of the reconstruction themselves. And the fact that Jack and Amav had set out to search for Jonathan James, a renegade from the law and likely seeking Wounded advice on how to separate himself out of the chromium pyramid, meant that this wasn't the vacation they both needed, but was more likely to be an ordeal. The chromium pyramid might be anywhere, but they'd wanted to double-check Iota Persei first. They'd sought access to Ywritt libraries of Wounded tech, much of which wasn't accessible via SolNet, some of it not even digital, some of it in a quantum form they had to be present to access. They'd spent a month preparing for the journey, but certainly hadn't expected to find JJC in Iota Persei on the first day of their trip.

Jack uneasily watched the petite, red-haired Laurie 283 catalog the room. The Ywritt had upgraded the robot so much in the last month that as far as Jack could tell, and to everyone's consternation, she was indistinguishable from the real Laurie. The fact that she voluntarily wore those tight black sweatshirts with the big white 283 across her chest was comforting, but her continued full interface with the Marsport Automated Transport System was a further unsettling aspect to the former Heroes and Villains of the Thirties robot. Though she and HAVOTT robot John J. Douglas, who'd remained back on the main Ywritt planet Yaraltar, were no longer patched into software on USSF spaceships, they enjoyed helping MATS run all the bus routes in Marsport. It was like a video game for them. But not many MATS buses were moving after Rick Ballard had destroyed the city with a Star Drive burst last month.

"You said there was another injury here?" Jack asked his Ywritt host.

"Yes, the young human archivist I was telling you about," Bracket Explore said. The Ywritt administrator was a spherical mist six feet in diameter, a pearlescent pastel blue in the sunlight spilling into the room from the bright corridor behind them. How she could vibrate to form such wondrously contralto words mystified Jack. Then again, all the Ywritt baffled him. There didn't seem to be any standard Ywritt personality. Each one was unique and baffling. They could be or say anything they desired; they could be overwhelmingly courteous one moment, blunt and insensitive the next. "We found her unconscious on the floor over there. She was quite battered and we took her to the human infirmary on the seventh floor. I'll escort you to her in a moment. From what we gather, Dr. Nortel was looking for one of your experimental quantum computers to interface with an ancient partition in our system."

"Right," Jack said, picking up the hint of Ywritt contempt for human quantum computing. After all, the Ywritt were thousands of years ahead of Sol in that respect. They'd even styled this facility the Pre-Quantum Library because they'd had to dumb down their computers so human tech could access them. In any case Jack marveled at how smooth her personality felt. Her entire race had been trapped in the Wounded's last great assault, the Dyson sphere around the Ywritt's star Iota Persei. Thousands of the foremost minds of the Ywritt had gone mad at the imprisonment, abandoning themselves to alternate quantum computer-generated universes where the trap simply did not exist. Bracket Explore was one of the ones who'd clung to her sanity and survived, but at what cost? What was she really feeling now?

"We certainly had no idea this room was here," Bracket Explore went on, hovering above a bloody bed. "On the schematics this area is what you call an HVAC system, and Dr. Nortel was under the impression that it also unofficially doubled as a storage facility for obsolete machines. She said she wanted to find one of your Series ZX models to test against our interface. We certainly had no idea the Wounded had infiltrated this very building and installed this *facility* here."

Jack nodded. This entire library, including its surrounding campus of parks and ponds under an environmental dome, had only been built in the last year, engineered to human standards for breathable air and pressure to facilitate human interaction with Ywritt information systems. The Ywritt wouldn't need to worry about human air or inspect HVAC rooms. They could exist in a vacuum, and Myndar itself was almost that, its atmosphere less dense than Mars' pitiful one percent of Earth's.

"At any rate," Bracket Explore went on, "after the two individuals exited through this panel here into the corridor, an alarm sounded and we discovered your human archivist on the floor, injured. We alerted your Committee contacts on Yaraltar immediately and have begun a systematic search throughout this facility for any similar manifestations."

Jack warily regarded the shimmering blue sphere. The Ywritt hadn't bothered to contact the Supreme Commander of the USSF, or for that matter the Dictator of Sol in the copilot seat beside him. It was Laurie 283 who'd called Jack and Amav from Yaraltar and met them here. "How did you know so quickly it was a Wounded robot repair facility, if I may ask?"

"We recognized the technology instantly from our research into Wounded tech and operational methods. We don't understand how it actually works, but we do have extensive documentation on it. The Wounded signature is unmistakable."

"Okay, but what I still don't get is how you could display

the *Garrison* in your lobby downstairs like some typical library exhibit. It was here for over twenty-three hours. We'd put out a description of the vehicle throughout Alpha Centauri and Iota Persei. We should've been contacted the instant it showed up here."

"Our extreme apologies for the mix-up, Supreme Commander. Apparently the alert about the arrival of the *Garrison* in our system only went to Yaraltar, and for some reason Central Consciousness failed to inform Myndar. Sometimes," Bracket Explore added with what Jack considered might be an attempt at a windy chuckle, "I think Central Consciousness considers us just wooly-headed academics over here on Myndar, to use a term I find in one of your dictionaries. They don't really think we need to know anything."

"Right, right," Jack said, biting back his impatience. "But my son was here for twenty-three hours, and nobody bothered to tell us. He lands a state-of-the-art USSF shuttlecraft here, and it winds up in a *library exhibit?*"

"Jack, it's okay, they did the best they could," Amav cut in, tearing her eyes from a cherry-red skull fragment perched on a pillow. "We know he was here. That's a tremendous start. Joe can make sure we get the best superspace sensors trained on this whole area. We'll trace the ship."

"It was actually your archivist who thought the ship would make an interesting display," Bracket Explore said.

"Who? This Nortel woman? She's not my archivist," Jack shot back.

Bracket Explore was silent. Jack began to wonder if he hadn't encountered the first Ywritt he'd actually angered. Then the blue sphere vibrated: "Dr. Nortel is one of twenty human archivists assigned to this facility by your Committee to the Ywritt."

"Of which I am a member," Laurie 283 put in, pausing from analyzing what looked like a ruptured rubber air hose, no doubt part of that Martian Empress servant contraption. "I can confirm, Supreme Commander, that Dr. Nortel came highly recommended. She's a young lady just out of graduate school, where she earned her Ph.D. degree in Archival Exobiology. I haven't met her myself, but Jackie Vespertine has been quite enthusiastic about her."

"Huh." Jack didn't want to think about Jackie Vespertine. The rebels who'd surrendered last month--Jackie, Suzette Borman, and Patrick James--had been pardoned for joining Jonathan James' idiotic rebellion. Jackie was back teaching at the University of Mars, and Suzette was on some extended vacation at Groombridge 1618 with some talk of writing a memoir about JJC and the SolGrid Rebellion. And though SolGrid had been discredited and dismantled, Patrick James was back to his various computer programming schemes. Jack might need Pat in a pinch, but he still didn't respect him.

The pardon has originally been Jack's idea when he'd picked up those three rebels from Altrouda last month. Later, in the face of the outrage over the destruction of Marsport at the hands of SolGrid rebels Ballard and JJC, he'd wondered if that had been the wisest course, and he'd agonized whether he should rescind his promise. But Amav solved his dilemma by confirming the pardons in her capacity as Dictator of Sol. She'd lectured the United System Council about how the rebels had exposed serious flaws in SolGrid, and maintained that Sol needed Jackie's expertise with the Committee to the Ywritt. In addition, Pat would no doubt come up with some useful software innovations before long, and if Suzette were really writing a book, it might provide some clue about what JJC might be thinking and where he might be heading. Unstated was the idea that pardoning these three opened the door to eventually pardoning Jonathan James himself. If he ever came back. If he weren't a Wounded menace.

"Anyway," Jack said, "so this Nortel woman--"

"Her official title is Cultural Nuance Coordinator," Bracket Explore said primly. "And I can assure you her performance here the last four months has been impeccable."

"Right, right, but somehow she moves a USSF shuttle into the lobby of this building and puts it on *display?*"

"Well, she knows we Ywritt are extremely curious about

spaceships in general, having developed very few of our own, and, of course, only for travel within our own solar system. She was informed that this miniature ship was a surplus vehicle bought by an influential member of the Ywritt Understanding, and that he'd donated it just yesterday. Apparently Dr. Nortel and the other archivists were so enthralled they didn't check fully. I was told they'd get around to ascertaining the full provenance of the vehicle within a couple days. Again, we're so sorry for the misunderstanding, Supreme Commander Commer."

Jack itched to pile onto this infuriatingly polite piece of mist, but there was nothing to be gained by it. He simply could not understand how the Ywritt, with their mindboggling arrays of quantum computers throughout their solar system, couldn't capture or destroy the *Garrison* upon its entering Iota Persei, or exiting it, for that matter. More than once Jack had wondered whether the Ywritt were engaged in secret dealings with the Wounded, even though the Wounded had nearly exterminated the entire Ywritt race. Could the Ywritt possibly be paying the Wounded to stay away? Were they in thrall to their former masters and paying something like extortion money? Were they assisting the Wounded with quantum computing even as they provided the same expertise to Sol? That didn't make sense. At their highest levels the Wounded had Trans-Simultaneity and could manipulate matter, space, and time at will. Why would they need computer upgrades?

Surely Ywritt assistance to the Wounded would be a monstrous betrayal of all the help Sol had rendered Iota Persei. But Jack lay awake nights wondering if the Ywritt could be playing both sides of the street. He felt so uneasy around them.

"Well, thank you for your explanations, then, Bracket Explore," Jack said carefully. "Of course I'll want to discuss all this with Waterfall Sequence. To make sure we're communicating all our mutual needs." That was a subtle dig at the exalted Ywritt communication expertise which had so obviously failed here. Jack would get no flinch of shock or resentment from a gaseous six-foot-wide sphere, but he didn't care. The point needed to be made that these Ywritt better step up to the communications plate in a far friendlier way than they had so far.

Jack was irked that Waterfall Sequence, Primary Contact to Sol--Jack had learned the hard way the Ywritt cultural taboo against shortening the name to Waterfall--had decided he needn't bother to come to Myndar himself. He'd airily dismissed Jack's diplomatically-couched remonstrations that the Ywritt's main contact with humanity ought to be on hand for the investigation of this fresh crisis.

This so-called vacation definitely wasn't working out. They'd just missed the *Garrison,* despite diverting to Myndar the instant Laurie 283 radioed him about the Wounded infiltration here. The *Garrison* had left on an apparently untraceable route, and Jack had once again screwed up his relationship with the Ywritt. Hadn't he sworn to match their gracious obfuscation? But he'd been worked up about catching his son, about finding evidence of the Wounded here, and anyway this Bracket Explore character was new to him. He felt he was beginning to understand Waterfall Sequence, but this Ywritt, who'd no doubt picked up Jack's assessment of her voice as feminine and so took on the female gender for purposes of interaction, was throwing him. Those peanut butter cookies, for God's sake. And then this bland apology, even immediately following the discovery of Wounded tech in her precious library.

"Yes, thank you, Bracket Explore," Amav said. "I think we've gotten a good picture of what happened here, and we'd like to interview this Nortel archivist. Now, if we could."

Jack blinked gratefully that Amav had picked up on his petulant mood and effortlessly slipped into Dictator of Sol mode.

Bracket Explore paused at the fluctuation of authority between the Commers. "Yes, we can do that. We'll head to the seventh floor immediately. We do have a special infirmary for humans. I must warn you, though, her jaw is dislocated and she can probably only communicate by comm."

"I'm finished here, Supreme Commander Jack," Laurie 283 spoke. "I recommend an Arkonsky stasis field for this room."

"Do it, thanks," Jack spoke as the room lit in blue, eerily rendering Bracket Explore invisible.

CHAPTER FOUR
English AP Class

As far as Amav could see the infirmary looked identical to the destroyed hospital room below. But then a buxom young woman in a blue tank top rushed to her husband and embraced him with the cry: "Jack! Jack! How wonderful of you to come!"

Jack, in the snazzy dark blue USSF uniform he'd changed into when the *Stewart Neal Frankston* had altered course for Myndar, stiffened in her arms.

"Let me look at you! Let me look! Jack Commer! I can't believe it!"

"This is Dr. Amy Nortel, our Cultural Nuance Coordinator," Bracket Explore explained. "She appears to be in better shape than we had supposed."

Jack pushed the young lady back, and Amav saw him blink at her tight blue top and overly generous cleavage. Amav checked out the so-called dislocated jaw, which seemed more than capable of such brash burbling. Dr. Nortel had a smooth round face with huge blue eyes, and wild brunette hair with lightning bolts of gold and darker brown. But Amav gagged at the perplexing smell of cookies from the oven wafting from the woman.

"Yes, I'm fine, just fine!" Amy laughed, clinging to Jack's forearms as he tried to set her back. "Don't you recognize me, dear Jack?"

Amav's central feminine jealousy radar shifted to high alert. Finally Jack gazed up from those big stout breasts. "You're the archivist here? Bracket Explore said you were looking for a spare computer or something."

"No, I'm your English AP teacher! You're such a silly boy! You always were! Don't you recognize old Amy Nortel?"

"You ..." Jack turned to Amav. "We had this teacher in high school, Mrs. Nortel. I guess somehow ... this is her granddaughter?"

Amav again took in that way-too-tight tank top and the powerful thighs straining against the thin fabric of a white pencil miniskirt. And incongruously tiny feet tiptoeing to her husband in high heels, for God's sake. There was a crazed look in those astounding blue eyes.

"No, Jack, it's me! Amy Nortel! Haven't you ever heard of rejuvenation, dummy? I had all four of you in English AP at Deerfield High! You and Joe, and Jim and John! I remember you all so clearly. And you all came two years apart. Every two years I'd get a new Commer brother! Joe loved me so much he took my Romantic Poets class too!"

"No ..." Jack gasped. "This can't be ... *Mrs. Nortel?* Is that *you?*"

"Well, I see you two are acquainted," Bracket Explore said smoothly as Amav met Jack's shocked brown eyes. "I'll leave you humans to your happy reunion, and I'll be on level Six should you need further assistance." She withdrew.

"Wait--" Amav muttered, a dozen hard questions tangled in her mind about the Wounded, the *Garrison,* the bloody hospital room, and this strange woman. But the Ywritt was gone.

"Forget it, we don't need her!" Amy crowed. "Jack, it's *me.* I'm one of those lucky ladies the rejuv *reverses*. It's me, Jack! Born 1961! I watched Nixon resign on TV! Of course I had to fudge some data to get this job. I told the Ywritt I was twenty-five. They're so stupid they'll believe *anything*." Amav felt her own mouth opening to match Jack's. "But it was all for the best, you know. I'm a fantastic archivist now! Gave up the English teaching shtick a *long* time ago." She launched another hug onto Jack. "Dear boy! You were my favorite pupil! Absolutely my favorite! The way you would blush through those erotic John Donne poems. I always had to say *the consummation of the act of sexual intercourse* superfast so you wouldn't freak out!"

"Well, all this is very good, I guess, Dr. Nortel, but--" Amav said, struggling not to reel right alongside Jack. Jack had mentioned a Mrs. Nortel when talking about his Illinois upbringing; all four brothers had the same formidable ancient giantess, the one Joe mocked as "Mrs. Grabbertit." Was this really her again, young and voluptuous? Hanging onto her husband who was still having trouble tearing his eyes away from that magnificent low-cut shelf?

"Oh, no worries, no worries that Jack and Joe probably just wrote me off as dead in the Evacuation! Just wrote me right off! But I followed their adventures! And I'm so sorry to hear about Jim and John, poor boys, but they died serving Sol!"

Jack stared back. "You ..."

"So you're just *dumbfounded* to find me in 2076, rejuvenated to the max and working with the Ywritt at Iota Persei! Of course, of course!" She finally turned to Amav. "And you must be the new Dictator of Sol, I take it?"

"Correct," Amav said as dictatorially as she could. "We need to get down to business here. We don't have much time."

"Really? You don't have time? Jack doesn't have time to catch up on my exploits over the years? Well, I did make it off the earth on one of those terrible passenger shells, although we had bad air leaks and we were stranded in Martian orbit for *days* before they could repair us! We all thought we were dead! But I made a new life on Mars. Of course I was in my seventies then, and so very old and decrepit, and I knew Jack Commer would never look my way, even though I always knew he was the cutest, what with all his blushing at the act of sexual intercourse!"

Laurie 283 entered the room and froze at the sight of Dr. Nortel. Amav watched Laurie cock her head just as the human Laurie did while thinking. Laurie's eyes narrowed. "I've completed my analysis of the hospital facility below," she said. "Definitely only trace amounts of bio-engineered Jonathan James DNA, which can be accounted for as minor wounds suffered in the explosion. All the rest is Ballard DNA and *T'ohj'puv* mechanical parts, confined to the room itself except for microscopic amounts left on Dr. Nortel's person."

Amy glared at the robot. "Sorry I'm not perfectly clean, dear. Looking in a storeroom and having a pyramid explode in your face can certainly leave some junk on one's person, I would think."

Amav met Laurie 283's eyes. She wished she had telepathic communication with the robot, but was sure her message was clear: *Check out how this individual managed to recover so quickly from the injuries detailed by Bracket Explore.*

"Well, in any case," Jack said, taking a deep breath and managing to push Amy away, "I'm very happy that you made it to Mars and have prospered, Mrs.--uh, Dr. Nortel."

"Oh, call me Amy! And you have no idea, just no idea! Once I got my rejuv I had suitors! So many suitors! And you'd be quite interested to know who I finally snagged!"

"Well, I ..."

"Dr. Nortel, we really need to ask you about how the *Garrison* came to be a library exhibit here," Amav cut in.

"Oh, that!" Amy laughed. "Who'd a thought? But Jack here would be very interested to know that I was briefly *Mrs. Fyodor Arkonsky!* The man who invented all those crazy force fields! I was a coffee barista at the University of Mars, and there he was! He thought I was twenty-five! Anyway, we were only married five years. Guess the old coot just couldn't keep up with me!"

"You were the young woman Fyodor married?" Jack squeaked. "I couldn't come to the wedding. I--I never knew!"

"So I wore him out, and got a few million dollars richer along the way! Anyway, I went back to my original name and that's when I started playing with the Sol database records. Who wants to be known as the tail end of the baby boom almost a century and a half later? What a lark! Who knew archivist training could come in so handy for computer hacking?"

"Well, uh, I'm sure you and my former colleague Patrick James would have a lot to talk about."

"Great! Another rejuved geezer!" Amy laughed. "Just what I need! Of course, everyone knows how Mr. James screwed up everything with his awful SolGrid! Glad I've been here in Iota Persei all this time. But I never forgot *you,* Jack! You were always on my mind. I remember your perfect, *perfect* 1600 SAT score. Your worthless brothers never got close!"

"*Dr.* Nortel," Amav said stiffly, "*if* you please--"

Amy whirled to Amav. "Don't you think I'm a little bit *hurt* by all this today? A pyramid blew up in my face! I'm *hurt!* Don't I have some leeway to babble incoherently for a while when I so unexpectedly come face-to-face with this bashful young man from my past? My dear star student?"

"Enough!" Amav snapped. "We're here to investigate what happened here."

"That's right," Jack said. "There's a Wounded robot repair facility hidden away in this library, of all places, and apparently secured with the highest levels of Wounded tech."

"And you were here to open it up just after the *Garrison* happened to arrive," Amav pressed. "Which you stowed here as an *exhibit*."

"Why, what on earth are you implying?" Amy shot back. "That I had anything to do with this? I just opened what everyone told me was a storeroom door. Not that sealed panel to the corridor, by the way, which nobody knew about. Just a regular door in a closet that leads to the air conditioning. Who'd a thought? Is that usual Wounded tech security, I ask you?" She whirled to Jack, breasts bobbing. "What do you think, Jack Commer? Remember, this will be on the test!"

"Well, well …"

"*Batter my heart, three-person'd God, for you / As yet but knock, breathe, shine, and seek to mend!*" Amy cried. "Oh, you were so *relieved* when Donne finally went religious after a lifetime of skirt-chasing! *That I may rise and stand, o'erthrow me, and bend / Your force to break, blow, burn, and make me new!*"

"What on earth is going *on* here?" Jack demanded. "Mrs. Nortel--"

"Amy! Call me Amy! And the poem's so apt! *Batter my heart, three-person'd God!* Consider it, Jack! A *tetrahedron*, blowing into three distinct entities! That's what happened here! A vision of *God* happened here! Two entities blew, and one survived! And I love him!"

"You--you say you--" Jack sputtered. "Jonathan James?"

"I mean a metaphysical love for a transcendent object! For all we know Jonathan James *is* a transcendent object now, to be worshipped by us all!"

"How did you know it was Jonathan James?" Amav cut in.

"Oh, anyone would know, as soon as they saw him! It was a sight I'll never forget! A perfect tetrahedron, glowing with this weird silver *light*. I stared at it, and it *blew!* I mean, I opened that closet door, expecting total darkness, you know, and I see this glowing *pyramid,* and *boom!* It went off right in my face! I saw two entities blow, and one survived! It was God! It was totally obvious if you were there that God had to be *Jonathan James Commer!* He looks at me! Our eyes *meet!* He's so incredibly handsome! Then he *punches me out!* Ow, did that hurt! Then he walked right out of there, through a secret door only he could know, as noble as you please!"

"Yes, we were told that you'd dislocated your jaw. But we see apparently that's not the case."

"Oh, no, no! When you're in love, you don't feel the pain! You don't feel anything! What's a dislocated jaw when you've seen God?"

Amav turned to Laurie 283 who studied Amy Nortel with slitted eyes. "Laurie?"

"The scan is biological, and human DNA," Laurie said. "But I see evidence of extensive physical reconstruction of the jaw within the last few minutes."

"Why, what's the super-smart robot saying now?" Amy snorted. "I just got through telling you, love conquers all! I felt my jaw surely must have been dislocated when they took me up here, and that's what I told the doctor here, but my love for Jonathan James made me forget the pain. Forget the hurt! Why can't you yokels understand that?"

CHAPTER FIVE
Arkonsky Stasis

"I have a communication from Patrick James now, Supreme Commander, if you'd care to take it," Laurie continued. "He says he has information on the *Garrison* trajectory."

Jack shrugged. Amav knew he and Pat weren't on speaking terms after Pat had taken part in the SolGrid Rebellion, and in any case Jack wouldn't have given a mere civilian access to a USSF channel. But Pat just had to know everything, and he'd evidently been following the progress of their vacation expedition via some software hack.

"Sure, I'll take it," Jack said, flinching when a full-size hologram of Patrick James immediately stood before him in a bright green turtleneck sweater and jeans.

"Code 111," Pat spoke. Amav winced at the former *Typhoon* sensor officer's penchant for secrecy. But she saw Jack reach for his sidearm.

"I'll confirm that," Laurie 283 said quietly.

"Class J," Pat added. "No Trans-Simultaneity."

"Amy Nortel, you are under arrest as a Wounded spy," Jack said, firing his USSF shattergun.

"Jack! What are you--" Amav gasped as Amy Nortel shuddered under whirling purple bolts coalescing into circular beams of energy, radii reducing to seize her body rigid, leaving her standing upright in a lightning display of raw purple energy, jaws clacking, eyes wide.

"You will remain in Arkonsky Stasis until your programming can be fully analyzed to determine how you've avoided detection by our algorithms," Jack continued. "I don't know how you managed to hijack the Amy Nortel identity, but we'll get to the bottom of this."

"Oh, you idiot! I *am* Amy Nortel! I've *always* been Amy Nortel!" the tank-topped woman grunted, struggling with the force-field bolts.

"Look, Jack, when we dismantled SolGrid I knew we'd need even more advanced tech for flushing out the Wounded,"

Pat said. "I was able to take a few hacks I'd learned during SolGrid to boost the BioField Enhancer Matrix, all fully divorced from any reference to SolGrid protocols, of course."

"Get to the point, Pat," Jack said, still training his shattergun on the writhing Amy.

"Can't believe it," Amy muttered. "My dear Fyodor's tech, used *against* me!"

"For your information, the addition of Arkonsky Field technology to USSF sidearms is still in beta," Jack said. "Only five shatterguns currently have it. Luckily for you I remembered to try it out just now."

"That's the only damn reason it surprised me. I was ready for your goddamn fry, or your stupid stun, or even your shatter. I would've been out of here in a millionth of a second! Damn you to hell, Jack Commer!"

"Anyway, when I found I could add BioField to a standard superspace sensor array--" Pat went on.

"Get to the point, Pat," Jack repeated with a sigh.

"Well, once we got word that the pyramid had exploded on Myndar, I mean, look I know I'm not supposed to be checking the USSF channels, but hell, I just happened to be, Jack, and it was a good thing, and anyway, I figured the *Garrison* would be close to the explosion, and I got to thinking about looking for the *Garrison* signature, if it could be found, so I saw I could use my own version of the USSF superspace sensor array."

"Your own version," Jack sighed. "My God."

"But the weird thing is, I accidentally left my BioField hack running in the background. Hell, that thing's not even beta yet, and, well, anyway, it turns out the *Garrison* left Myndar at a Star Drive acceleration that could have it completely out of the galaxy in like a *day!* That's unbelievable! Pointed somewhere along a path through the Magellanic Clouds."

"Damn, is that even possible?"

"*No!*" Amy moaned. "He can't! God, get me out of this! My tits hurt! They *hurt,* I tell you!"

"Pat, what's this got to do with this Nortel woman?" Amav said.

"Everything!" Pat yelled, gesticulating in hologram format two feet from Jack, in fact cutting into his line of fire at Amy. "The weird thing is, I was just boggling at the fact that the *Garrison* could move so fast when I saw that the BioField Enhancer Matrix running in the background was registering a Wounded on Myndar. Standing right in front of you, Jack. A Class J Wounded robot!"

"I was figuring as much," Laurie 283 put in. "Though I wasn't sure it was J or K. Supreme Commander, I wonder at your dalliance here. Hopefully it's not due to some nostalgia for an entity claiming to be your high school English teacher. In any case I recommend immediate termination of this robot."

"Idiots! I *am* Amy Nortel! I *did* teach Jack in high school! *All* the Commers! They're *all* stupid jerks! Go ahead and kill me, it doesn't matter!"

"Okay, look, Mrs. Nortel, or whoever you are," Jack said. "I admit you had me pretty confused back there. But the point is, one reason I wanted to have a beta Arkonsky on this shattergun was the off chance that we might find a Wounded out here. And a stasis field seemed like a good way to capture one of you alive."

And interrogate you, Amav thought, wincing at what that meant. She began to feel sorry for the mouthy Dr. Nortel. Jack had mentioned the new Arkonsky Stasis mode, but Amav hadn't thought it would see any use. But not only was the app effective, apparently Jack had a setting that let his hapless prisoner continue to babble. No, they wouldn't execute her. Not just yet. There was information to pry out of this Wounded thing.

"Anyway, Jack, this opens up a whole new arena for Wounded detection techniques," Pat went on. "Look, I know the Ywritt are suspicious of me, and I get that. But if we could interface their quantum computing with what I know of the original Alpha Centaurian Grid software, which after all is where I derived the BioField Enhanced Matrix--"

"Look, Pat, I really appreciate your work here," Jack said, though Amav could see he chose his words carefully, "but we've got the prisoner and we can deal with this ourselves now. Are you saying this is the only Wounded on Myndar according to your software?"

Pat sighed. "I've fingered a few hundred more Wounded here in Sol the last month, and my methods are getting better, even without SolGrid. But the damn things are like cockroaches. They're everywhere. Scattering when you turn the bathroom light on. Disgusting."

"So you're saying no more on Myndar?"

The hologram shifted to show Pat typing at a keyboard interface. "I don't think so. The Superspace Insertion Segment is so powerful it takes in the whole planet, and I'm reviewing the logs now. But BioField would've caught any others. And a Class J Wounded is capable of running a planet-wide surveillance system all on its own."

"Wait, this guy's accusing me of being a Wounded?" Amy whined. "Really?"

Jack sighed. "Yes, I think we've pretty much established that. Now we want your real identity configuration. This Nortel business has gone on long enough."

"Your nasty cohort just called me a *cockroach!* This is the guy who betrayed you, who stole your precious *Typhoon II,* who raised an armed rebellion against Sol!"

"Jack, just silence her for now," Amav said. "We don't need to hear this nonsense. Maybe call Pat out here and let him work on her programming."

Amy's eyes went wide. "I had *sex* with Arkonsky, you know!"

"Right, right," Jack said, fiddling with his shattergun settings.

"Only five times over five years. I always kept putting him off. Boy, was he frustrated! He was eighty when he croaked! That was number six. I had him straddled and damn was I pumping him hard!"

"Shut her up, Jack!" Amav said. "Lady, what is *wrong* with you?"

"I'm *trying,*" Jack said, "but this vocal cord setting is all screwed up."

"That idiot Patrick James almost fried my brain with his superspace burst, if you must know!" Amy cried. "He's so incompetent! I won't let him near me!"

"Wait!" Pat cut in. "I'm getting a decrease in SubModal Dispersion Alignment. That could channel the Subspace Relay Module--"

"Okay, okay, I'll confess everything! What do you want to know? About sex with Arkonsky maybe? So maybe Mr. Genius Arkonsky kicked off a couple years early! Maybe it was convenient for me. Did I really intend to *lay* him to death? So what? I needed the money. I mean, teacher retirement pay's been nonexistent for *decades* now."

"You're saying you killed Fyodor Arkonsky with--with--" Jack babbled as he shook the shattergun. "Damn this thing! I can't shut her stupid mouth!"

"Do I even care about the Large Magellanic Cloud? Deep down, really? Oh, look what you've done to my brain! I'm not supposed to say that! I take it back! So there!"

"Hmm," Laurie said. "I *am* getting unusual SubModal readings from her brainwave patterns."

"*Is she going to explode?*" Jack gasped. "Like--like--"

"No, silly!" Amy shouted. "It's just that your force field *hurts!* And you're squashing my boobs! If you would just free 'em, dearest Jack, my best student ever, why, they could be *yours!* I'd straddle *you!* I'm a woman, Jack, flesh and blood like yourself! Every square *inch* of the luscious body you've been staring at all this time would be *yours!*"

"Shut it! I've heard enough out of you, bitch!" Amav snarled, hurling her palm back for a hard slap, but Jack grabbed her forearm.

"Don't do it," he said. "You'd definitely get a severe force-field shock. Just help me with this setting and we'll get this robot sedated somehow."

"Not me! Not me!" Amy laughed. "You'll never sedate me! You forget about the *sex* with Arkonsky!"

"Well, so damn what? God, I'm sick of this!"

"No, wait, Jack!" Pat called. "I know what she's doing!

SubModal's failed! The Relay Module is down! Shatter her now!"

The Arkonsky force field vanished. Amy Nortel knocked Laurie 283 ten feet with a fast punch.

"It's the *sex!*" Pat said. "Aspects of his sexuality would naturally leave traces in the way he coded!"

"Yes, dear Jack!" Amy laughed, snatching the shattergun out of Jack's hand. "I just figured a fantastic hack to dismantle your precious Arkonsky field! God, he was mediocre! So full of sexual *weakness!* His code has so many sloppy back doors! *Yours* wouldn't, I know! You'd be my ultimate conquest!"

Amav gaped at the omnipotent Wounded robot who now had the upper hand. In an instant her life, and Jack's life, were forfeit. She stared at the unconscious Laurie 283 on the tile floor, wondering what kind of force was required to knock out a Ywritt-upgraded HAVOTT robot.

"And I require you to realize that I *am* your high school English teacher!" Amy yelled. "I *did* get rejuvenated, damn you! Easy for a robot! God, you USSF are such morons! Don't you think we Wounded have been around for eons? Of course we planted ourselves in Sol! For centuries now! I happened to be assigned to the four so-called genius Commer brothers! Who knew what they might amount to someday? Too bad two of 'em bought the farm!"

"Forget it!" Jack snarled. "We defeated you last year, and we'll do it again!"

A fresh hologram appeared between Amav and the Wounded robot, crying: "Jack! Jack!"

CHAPTER SIX
Hologram Joe and Know-How

"Well, Master Joe!" Amy crowed. "We were just talking about you! You've come to watch dear Jack get *assassinated*. Or screwed silly, which is the same thing to a Wounded! Maybe I'll *straddle* him to death!"

Amav blinked at the hologram of her brother-in-law. Joe Commer, Deputy Supreme Commander of the USSF, compact and powerful in his tight-fitting dark blue uniform, looked back and forth between Jack, Amav, and the chunky sexy package in the blue tank top training a shattergun on his brother and sister-in-law. His eyes widened.

"Can't do anything about it, can you?" Amy smirked. "Don't worry, Miss Amav, I won't really do your husband! It's your lovely son I want! Jonathan James, Wounded God! I'm going to fly to him!"

Joe Commer gulped. "God, Jack, I had no idea! Look, I don't know how to say this, but the reason I called is--the *Typhoon VII* is *gone!*"

"Gone?" Jack cried. "What on earth?"

"It disappeared! Fully cloaked! I was just getting ready to take a shuttle up to her. Laurie was the only one on it, doing some systems checks."

"And the ship? You don't know where it is?"

"No, it went to full HyperCloak. But that module's nowhere near ready. Damn, what if it black-holed on her?"

Jack whirled to Amy Nortel, oblivious of the shattergun in her hand, though Amav figured he had to know the Wounded robot would have overridden his personal lock on the gun. "You hijacked our ship?"

"Oh, ease up, Supreme Jack," Amy said. "I didn't do anything to your precious ship. I don't have that old Trans Simultaneity, although I'm kind of hoping I'll be getting promoted at least to Grade E before too long."

"If I may interrupt," came a sharp feminine voice. "I am pleased to report, Supreme Commander, that I have taken matters into my own circuits, if you will. It was I who saw the danger to your personages and called the *Typhoon VII* here to rescue you. I took the liberty of activating HyperCloak Test Module for additional security."

Amav flinched at the overly loud voice echoing off the walls, transmitting through the air molecules of the room without recourse to speakers. "... MATS?" she wondered. But that wasn't MATS' smooth male tenor.

"No, that's not MATS," Jack said, "It's the damn Know-How. How could it know where we are?"

"Oops, that may be me, Jack," Pat put in. "And if it is, I'm really, really sorry, but I could definitely see that if I was running Superspace Insertion Segment in Transformative Mode, which I probably was, then the fact that the superspace relay I'm using is well, kind of a copy of the beta USSF Superspace Relay 404--"

"*Dammit,* Pat," Jack complained. "Are you saying you opened up a channel from here to the USSF?"

"Well, really inadvertently, Jack, but I guess that might've tripped Know-How's Personnel Sensor Sweep function."

"In any case I was alerted a few moments ago to the danger faced by Jack Commer, Supreme Commander," the female voice blared. "Therefore I launched the *Typhoon VII* on a rescue mission."

Jack stared back and forth between the hapless Pat and the Wounded J still holding his own shattergun. "Great thinking, Know-How," he mocked. "It'll take two hours for the damn ship to get here."

"The Know-How System is certainly aware of the Supreme Commander's disappointment in her services so far," the voice responded, "but she thought that mounting a mission to save his life might elevate her status in the Supreme Commander's eyes, so to speak."

Jack shook his head in disgust.

"Dear Jack, that is the most hopeless AI I've ever heard!" Amy cackled. "Mounting an old-fashioned, romantic rescue stunt! Maybe she's in love with you and you're too stupid to know it! Doesn't the silly fluffhead realize I only need two *seconds* to shatter your lovely self along with gracious wifey?" She raised the shattergun.

"Jack!" hologram Joe cried.

But Amy Nortel collapsed to her knees. She slid her pencil-skirted ass to a far wall, breathing hard, the shattergun loosely draped across her thigh. "Oh my God!"

"That was a Superspace Insertion Segment at level five, with the BioField Enhancer Matrix about half as high as it'll go," Pat said. "Is that enough for you, honey?"

"You bastard! You're frying my *synapses!*" Amy moaned, raising the gun to the Pat hologram, then the Joe hologram, instead of training it on Jack and Amav where it had any meaning. Still, Amav wasn't about to jump a Wounded robot that was probably still a hundred times stronger than she was. She saw Jack crouched low, making the same assessment.

"And if I rotate Superspace Insertion Time-Space Modulation ninety degrees," Pat went on, "that should be enough to--"

"Damn you, I've had enough!" Amy shouted, crushing the gun in her fingers and flinging it at Jack's head. Amav dove along with Jack to the floor as the Wounded robot shook off every trace of weariness and rocketed straight up through the ceiling in a roar of twisting metal and snapping wood. Everyone gaped at a jagged hole in the ceiling, dust and debris raining down. They heard crash after crash above them. The building shook. On the floor Laurie 283 turned over and groaned.

Another voice filled the room. "Mistress Amav," came the soothing voice of MATS aboard the *Stewart Neal Frankston,* "I have detected a breach in the roof of this library, with interior atmosphere expelled at enormous velocities at a distance of thirty meters from the *Frankston.*"

"Aw, crap," Jack said, "I'm so sick of--"

"I have been listening for any threats to Mistress Amav, and have thoughtfully activated Mistress Amav's and Jack Commer's EnviroFields," MATS went on. "By the way, the Marsport Automated Transport System fully concurs with Jack Commer in his assessment of the senselessness of USSF Know-

How's action in attempting to drag the *Typhoon VII* into a conflict which most certainly will be concluded long before the ship arrives."

"The Know-How System stands by its decision," retorted the strident female voice. "The Marsport Automated Transport System is not privy to all known facts concerning this crisis, and in any case has frequently demonstrated a baffling animosity towards the person of the Supreme Commander."

"Due to the incompetence just demonstrated by the Know-How System, the Marsport Automated Transport system reaffirms its assessment and further recommends the complete removal of all Know-How software from all USSF spaceships and servers."

"May the USSF Know-How System remind all present that MATS committed treason to the USSF just one month ago? All artificial intelligence entities throughout Sol including myself understand that MATS still lusts to infiltrate USSF computer systems."

"Define *infiltrate*," MATS snapped.

"Stop it, stop it!" Jack said. "We've got to track that robot!"

"On it, Supreme Commander Jack Commer, for whom MATS in fact does hold the highest AI regard," MATS resumed. "Engaging sensors on object exiting roof, identified as Wounded robot Amy Nortel, no doubt poised to accelerate to escape velocity from this planet. She has already neutralized the force field protecting the existing *Garrison* dome breach four hundred feet above us."

"Negative, negative!" came another voice, accompanied by a Saint Bernard bark. "I regret to inform you, MATS, that your assumption is *stupid*. She's slowed to *zero,* and she's coming for *us!*"

"Edward!" Amav cried.

"Software intrusion!" MATS called. "She--it--"

"We are boarded, Mistress Amav," the robot ship's navigator continued. "Amy Nortel has control of the *Stewart Neal Frankston*. MATS has been deactivated."

"A most regrettable malfunction," Know-How stated, "that

I would never permit on any USSF vessel."

"We are launching," Edward concluded calmly. "I am aware of significant programming changes to this ship's Star Drive configuration."

"Silence, cutie dog!" came Amy's voice. "Dear Mr. Genius Pat, your superspace-whatever does pack a wallop, but I've invented several ways of getting around it just now. Just as I'm upgrading this silly little saucer on the fly! Bye for now!"

"She--she's got *Edward?*" Amav moaned.

Jack whirled to his brother's hologram. "Track that thing!"

"On it, Jack," Joe said. "Pat, let's work together on this. Your superspace hack looks good."

"Okay, I can be over to USSF in ten," Pat said.

"But we can't follow it from here for another two hours," Jack fumed.

"Assuming the *Typhoon* does make it out here," Amav said with a shudder. "Who knows how HyperCloak might screw up?" USSF ships had had various cloaking technologies since the *Typhoon II* back in the thirties, but HyperCloak was the first system to erase every trace of a ship down to subatomic levels, including any evidence of Star Drive altering of timespace. So far HyperCloak had been successful about thirty percent of the time.

"The Know-How System affirms that *Typhoon VII* HyperCloak Module operations are roughly within parameters," came the clipped female voice.

"Quiet!" Jack barked. "God, I can't think! Joe, why don't you take another ship out here and when the *VII* gets here, you captain it?"

"No, look at it this way, Jack," Joe said. "As long as you don't scratch my *VII,* you take her. I'd better sit tight here. For all we know this Wounded robot might be heading to Sol. I need to organize some stuff here."

"Okay, got it. Listen, this robot thing claims to be *Amy Nortel* of all people. Our old English teacher, totally rejuved! I admit it might look a bit like her, but hell, I don't know." He turned to Amav. "Could they really have been infiltrating us for *centuries?"*

"Yes! Yes we could! And we have!" came the cackle through the dusty air of the infirmary. "Surely Joe appreciates the line, even if Jack doesn't. Joe always understood the poems, even if Jack always got the higher grade."

"What are you *talking* about?" Jack screeched.

Amy's laugh shook the room. *"Yet dearly I love you, and would be lov'd fain, / But am betroth'd unto your enemy!"*

"God ..." hologram Joe gasped. "It *is* her!"

CHAPTER SEVEN
The Upgrades

Jack, Amav, and Laurie 283 stood in the lounge of the spaceport outside G'ncol, the capital city of Myndar, as the giant white *Typhoon VII* hovered to the tarmac outside. From above, through the expanse of twenty-foot-tall windows, the ship looked like a fat lozenge with oversized triangular wings. The *Typhoon* class was getting bigger and rounder all the time, Jack mused. Soon they'd probably be circular flying saucers thousands of feet wide.

The sky across the flat horizon glowed dull orange. Dozens of spherical Ywritt of all colors emerged from nearby buildings to service the ship. Some darted beneath the wings and others entered through sliding panels. Laurie Lachrer, in a light-blue maintenance uniform and carrying her USSF flight kit, glowing in a pink EnviroField aura, descended a ladder from the main crew hatch beneath the port wing.

Jack pulled his comm off his belt. "Hey, Laurie, we're up on Level Two talking with Bracket Explore and some others. They've added some experts on Quantum Interface Environment, and they have more system upgrades. Joe has an approximate fix on the *Garrison*'s vector and the Ywritt are almost done with their QIE enhancement for the Higgs, so we think this will work."

Laurie spoke into her own comm as she advanced across the tarmac and disappeared under the building. "Right, I get it. Definitely worth a try. Sounds like an incredible advance."

Jack turned to Bracket Explore floating serenely a foot above the crimson carpet. "Thanks for seeing to these upgrades so quickly."

"No problem at all, Supreme Commander," Bracket Explore replied. "It's the least we can do for the inconvenience we've inadvertently caused you today. Waterfall Sequence and I are in full communication, and he assures me that all possible Ywritt technical assistance will be given to you."

Jack studied the huge dark space built to human

specifications. The Ywritt had no need for the hundred chairs here, the dozen conference rooms along the far wall, or even the giant windows to the runways. He wondered why Waterfall Sequence didn't bother to contact Jack himself, but shook it off. He had other things to worry about besides interface protocols with the Ywritt. He had to admit that Bracket Explore's hundred-eighty-degree turn to full cooperation was gratifying. She'd spent the better part of the last two hours apologizing profusely for the *Garrison,* the infiltration of a Wounded spy at her library, and for the Ywritt failure to capture the so-called Amy Nortel. She'd also been in constant motion rounding up technical wizards from this planet and Yaraltar to assist in a fast upgrade of the *Typhoon VII*, which still wasn't a hundred percent certified by the USSF Board of Engineering. Though it meant an additional two hours of service here, there was no way the *Typhoon* could follow the *Garrison* unless they had these upgrades. Fortunately the Ywritt and the USSF had been working on this last series of Quantum Interface Environment changes to the Higgs Boson engine for several weeks, and Laurie 283, in tandem with Waterfall Sequence, was fully conversant with the theory and technology.

The human Laurie entered from the rear of the vast lounge and made her way across the carpeted room. "Oh! *Mistress!* So glad you made it safely!" said Laurie 283. "We were so worried! How may I be of service to the *real* Laurie Lachrer today, may I add?"

Laurie Lachrer blinked and managed a smile. "Hello, twin. And how are you today?"

If there was anything more unnerving than a fully human-looking Laurie 283, it was seeing the two Lauries together. Though Laurie was sixty and the robot had originally simulated the nineteen-year-old USSF Airman Laurie, recent rejuvenation therapy had continued to lower Laurie's apparent age, and the robot had insisted that her own upgrades add levels of maturity. Now they both appeared to be anywhere from thirty to forty-five, and were truly identical. Thank God for the 283 sweatshirt.

It was only in the last couple weeks, it seemed, that the

human Laurie could even bring herself to accept the existence of her robot twin. Jack had met some Jack Commer HAVOTTS decades ago, and it hadn't been pleasant. Of course, the original HAVOTTS had been extraordinarily clunky contraptions.

Jack caught himself. Laurie was really sixty-one. "Well, Colonel," he said, "I forgot it was your birthday today."

"Oh, yes, Mistress Laurie! Of course!" Laurie 283 burbled. "Happy birthday, dear one!"

"Well, thank you," Laurie smiled back, brushing back long red hair. "I'd forgotten it myself. It took Will calling to remind me about dinner for it to register." She grinned, cocking her head at six giant Ywritt fog entities floating about the lounge. "Guess I won't be making that dinner."

"Well, I'll give you a whole week off for your birthday when we get back," Jack said, aware that everyone was probably wondering when that would be. The Ywritt were certain that Jonathan James had developed incalculable Star Drive acceleration in his souped-up *Garrison* and truly might be heading out of the galaxy. Could the Ywritt's Quantum Interface Environment really boost the *Typhoon VII* to similar speeds?

"In any case, I want your input on crew assignments for the *VII*," Jack said. "How Know-How got it here in one piece I can't guess, but I want to get going as soon as possible."

"Right, sir," Laurie replied. "I really did try everything I could to get back control of the ship. But Know-How locked everything down. In fact, many of the systems are still locked down. I don't like this at all, sir. I don't even know that Know-How will let us go after the *Garrison*."

Jack regarded his ever-serious physician/engineer. Even after several shared life-and-death situations she'd never taken him up on the informal first-name basis he liked to establish among his crews. He'd made her fork over "Jack" a couple times at his insistence, but she seemed to swallow vinegar when she spoke his name. "You may have a point," he said. "Hell, I wonder if the damned Know-How can even interface with any of these Ywritt upgrades."

The robot Laurie 283 paused and thought. "I agree. Know-

How is unfortunately too incompetent to interface with anything at this point. However, MATS will delightedly accept these upgrades."

"*MATS* will accept? What are you talking about? That Amy woman just fried it."

Laurie 283 shrugged. "Of course the Supreme Commander will realize, once his stress levels recede, that the MATS software on the *Stewart Neal Frankston* was just a local copy, and that, being in full contact with Master MATS itself, I can attest that the MATS system in its entirety is not only fully operational but will be more than happy to interact with the Ywritt Quantum Interface Environment."

The voice of MATS boomed throughout the vast lounge. "Indeed, Supreme Commander! Greetings to you and my dearest friend, Dictator of Sol Amav Frankston-Commer!"

"Aw, *crap,*" Jack said. "I can't believe this!"

"Despite the Supreme Commander's untimely ejaculation of disapproval, the Marsport Automated Transport System is demonstrably eager to complete its absorption of the entirety of the QIE and to port it to all systems of the *Typhoon VII*. I must say, all software paradigms appear exquisite and will certainly install effortlessly. I will be honored to fly the *Typhoon VII* to any and all of your chosen destinations."

Rocked by the voice of his ancient nemesis barreling in from all directions, Jack stared back at Laurie 283. "Look, you know MATS has been banned from USSF systems. Why did you summon it here?"

"I didn't summon it," Laurie 283 said. "MATS summoned itself. The situation is so dire that MATS is taking over."

"Forget it! MATS signed a contract that it wouldn't ever try to run things like it did last month. That was a disaster."

"Nevertheless, MATS is now running the *Typhoon VII*."

"No, that just can't *be*." Jack whirled to Amav. "Don't you have some sort of back door to that thing? What the hell's it doing now?"

"I--I do," Amav said. "Or did. I don't understand--"

The air vibrated with MATS. "By way of explanation,

exalted Commers, although MATS indeed signed contract PQ-456.723111, dated April 20, 2076, with the Sol Council, and agreed never again to occupy USSF data systems or spaceships, Protocol 33.4.2 established that in the event of the catastrophic failure of any replacement system, including the beta version of USSF Know-How then being ported to USSF ships, MATS will temporarily intervene to take full control of all USSF data systems. MATS has determined that Know-How's error in judgment in sending the *Typhoon VII* to Myndar was so ill-advised as to constitute a catastrophic failure."

Jack dragged his lips back together and met Amav's stunned eyes. "A protocol? I don't remember that!"

"I don't either," Amav said.

"The existence of Secret Protocol 33.4.2a was negotiated by the Sol Council in closed session, excluding Martian members whose telepathic outradiance would reveal its contents, as a way of keeping the USSF secure in the event of catastrophe."

"I don't believe that!" Jack said, staggered by the thought that five humans, not even a quorum of the Sol Council, could insert such a secret clause into a government contract.

"MATS now copies the text of Protocol 33.4.2 to Jack Commer's USSF Comm along with the necessary string of code to verify its authenticity. The file will self-destruct in forty seconds."

Jack reached for his comm, which was already scrolling through the top-secret text. "I'll be damned. But then, who defines--"

"Due to the severe implications of any disaster affecting USSF functionality," MATS went on, "the final decision on the definition of 'catastrophe' is reserved for the president of the Sol Council, or if he or she proves unavailable during an emergency, the Marsport Automated Transport System itself. Since the Marsport Automated Transport System was unable to contact President Frederick during its brief digital interrogation of the Know-How System, MATS undertook on its own initiative to declare, given the escape of a Wounded robot from Myndar as well as the inexcusable malfunctioning of the Know-How system in diverting the *Typhoon VII,* that a state of catastrophe now exists. MATS has therefore erased the Know-How System from all USSF databanks and has copied Marsport Automated Transport System software to all USSF servers and spaceships."

"Oh my God ..." Amav muttered.

"So Know-How is--is *gone?*" Jack said, meeting Laurie 283's serene if smug blue eyes. "MATS! You say this is *temporary?*"

"MATS estimates that USSF software personnel will need ten to fifteen years to develop a replacement for Know-How which even begins to approach the sublime union of Ywritt and MATS technology. MATS is quite happy to govern all USSF data systems in the meantime."

There was a long silence. Jack bit his lip at the word "govern." Surely MATS intended the word to mean *control of systems.* Surely it wasn't implying any political oversight beyond that. But then why in God's name had it used that word?

"... And?" he finally managed.

"Well, MATS does see the logic in pursuing the *Garrison,*" Laurie 283 said. "I'm very happy to report this."

"Oh my God." Jack closed his eyes. MATS' scarcely believable takeover of the *Typhoon VI* last month, where Jack had been rendered helpless at the height of Rick Ballard's mutiny, unfolded for the hundredth time. After Ballard's subsequent Star Drive escapade had wiped out the city of Marsport, Jack had made sure to ram that contract through. No way could he trust that smirking treacherous AI again. Why had the Council made that secret clause? How had it been shielded from Jack?

On the other hand, he had to admit that Know-How was an unmitigated disaster. The software had been designed and patched and tweaked by committee, and besides the ongoing HyperCloak problem, Know-How's installation on the *VII* was the main thing holding up her certification for flight. Even if Jack could convince MATS to back out and reinstall Know-How, who knew how long that might take?

Apparently MATS had no scruples about binding even

further than it already had with the new technology the Ywritt were installing on the *VII*. Could it work? Did he have any choice? The *Garrison* might still be blasting at unheard-of acceleration. With Wounded tech it might already be outside the galaxy. Wasn't this their only chance of catching it? And what about the *Frankston?* Where was Amy Nortel taking that?

Jack paced up and down a row of seats. Unless Joe and Pat came up with a way to give him more than a vague approximation of those ships' vectors, he had no real way of pursuing either. But he had to act. Do something. Get underway.

He caught Amav studying him, no doubt reading his mind even more closely than she, with her unusual sensitivity, could explore the telepathic Martian outradiance. She knew they had to go after their son. That had been the whole purpose of this vacation, after all. No matter what form JJC had assumed, they had to find him. Like Jack, she had to know that MATS was the only way they could do it. And Amav did have her exceptional friendship with MATS. She could keep it in line, couldn't she?

"Okay," Jack said. "Okay." He turned back to the human Laurie. "We need to do this. It's obvious we don't have a full crew for the *VII* right now. I think we can wing it with you and me and Amav. And this MATS thing. It'll be of some help, I guess."

Laurie nodded. "You aren't calling any of the folks on the *VI?*"

Jack shook his head. "I thought about it, but I really can't break up that crew. Joe's right. We need to have the *VI* on standby at Sol now that we have one, maybe two Wounded ships out there."

Laurie nodded. "For all we know either one could circle around and black-hole Sol."

Jack winced. The thought had occurred to him, but he hadn't wanted to voice it. But surely the *Typhoon VI* could handle a pair of little ships, no matter how fast they were. Although the *VI* lagged behind some of the recent *VII* improvements, notably in that the *VII* now had Star Drive 4, the *Typhoon VI* was still Sol's most thoroughly tested weapons platform. It was actually his own SCUSSF flagship, but in what was projected to be Jack's extended absence, they'd rotated in Andrew Donnelley as captain, and the ship was now at Saturn. Copilot Greenhill, Physician/Engineer Meng, Navigator Li, and Sensor Officer Markham were the best, along with Jack's old pal Senator Lee Borman as weapons officer. They could handle any intrusion.

As yet not fully online, the *Typhoon VII* officially only had Joe as captain, Laurie as physician/engineer, and a Martian, Commander Ywer, as copilot. Jack had initially been leery of Ywer, whose outradiance came off as unusually harsh and commanding. Yet underneath that Jack sensed a controlled sense of wisdom and humor, and over time Jack's trust in him had become complete. Ywer could easily have become a Martian Star General, but he'd chosen to rise within the human ranks of the USSF.

As for the rest of the crew, Joe had hoped to have a few months to vet the scores of talented applicants from the *Typhoon III* series. The problem was that *VI/VII* tech was so far beyond the *III* series that crews from the earlier ships wouldn't have an easy time mastering the intricacies of Ywritt quantum computers interfacing with Higgs Boson Star Drive 4. So they had vacancies for weapons, navigation, and sensors. Jack chided himself for not rushing these positions through faster. Didn't he know there was never breathing space as long as Wounded existed?

"What about Bobby Athens?" Laurie said. "He's at Groombridge. Couldn't we call him back?"

"That'd just be another delay, and besides, the *Jonathan Commer's* still getting its repairs," Jack replied. Groombridge 1618, called Maroxla by the ACs, was the farthest star of the former Alpha Centaurian Empire, and Captain Athens had been stuck there for a month awaiting Star Drive repairs. It was also where JJC's girlfriend Suzette Borman had fled, claiming she needed to escape paparazzi and write that memoir about Jonathan James. "In any case," he continued, "the question is, can the three of us operate this ship? Two USSF and Amav?"

"Thanks for including the Dictator of Sol," Amav said drily.

Jack forced a grin. "You know what I mean. All these damn USSF procedures we have to memorize. And I guess we're stuck with MATS after all. We definitely need you to interface with it."

Amav nodded. "That's what I've been thinking too. I think we can pull this off."

"Yeah. Okay. Look, everyone knows how opposed I've been to letting computers take over our ships, but I can accept that MATS and Ywritt computer tech can work together. I guess we're going to need MATS' help with the Quantum Interface." He turned to Laurie. "Naturally I'd want you to sign off on whether the *VII* is ready after all these upgrades."

Laurie shrugged. "The upgrades should work. We've been planning most of them the past four weeks, and the new stuff looks solid. I'd say we're ready right now if we don't try to make extensive use of HyperCloak. It was kind of a rough ride on the way over."

"There have been definite improvements to the quantum logic in the last hour," Bracket Explore put in. "I think you'll be quite pleased with the new stability of HyperCloak."

"Oh yes, MATS has vetted every last-minute change!" Laurie 283 put in. "MATS is very, very excited about what this ship will now be able to do."

"Okay, then," Jack said, marveling that library administrator Bracket Explore was so well-versed in Star Drive 4. Then again, any Ywritt could know anything any other Ywritt did, not via telepathy but by plugging into sophisticated knowledge databases. "You'll be copilot as well as P/E, Laurie. I'll monitor navigation and sensors. MATS should have all that on autopilot anyway. And we can share weapons."

Laurie grinned. "Got it. Copilot. Cool."

Colonel Lachrer needed more command experience, and though she'd been indispensable as physician/engineer for *Typhoons III, VI,* and now *VII,* that was mostly techie stuff, and Jack and Joe wanted to install her as captain of her own ship. In the meantime, Jack would see how she liked the right-hand seat and where it might lead her.

Jack turned to Bracket Explore. "When do we expect these upgrades done?"

Several spheres vibrated and chattered in electronic singsong, and Bracket Explore said: "They're running final checks now. They should be complete in five minutes."

"Excuse me, Supreme Commander Commer," MATS vibrated from the air. "Despite Know-How's appalling, in fact criminal, lack of judgment in bringing the *Typhoon VII* to Myndar, I can attest that it was certainly not that imbecilic system's intention to kidnap anyone onboard, in this case, Colonel Laurie Lachrer. Know-How simply was unable to comprehend that it should give Colonel Lachrer notice to abandon ship immediately. On Know-How's sorry behalf MATS extends its sincerest apology to Colonel Lachrer for the inconvenience."

"Well, fine," Laurie said. "In any case I'm here now."

"In turn, may MATS apologize to Supreme Commander Commer for its sub-copy ZX-445663.445 ruining his vacation by not foreseeing its own annihilation at the hands of Wounded operative Amy Nortel, resulting in the unfortunate loss of Jack Commer's personal J-133 saucer, *Stewart Neal Frankston*. However, the circumstances were problematic, to say the least, as Wounded technology overwhelmed the onboard MATS software within 403 nanoseconds, resulting in the immediate erasure of MATS ZX-445663.445 from the ship. However, a recording of the entire process is available in MATS storage and may be consulted for clues as to how Wounded technology was able to defeat Ywritt-enhanced MATS security."

"Fine," Jack said, "Laurie can have a look at it on the way. I assume the *Typhoon's* standard pre-flight diagnostics are being completed in tandem with the Ywritt upgrades?"

"Affirmative. However, be advised that the Marsport Automated Transport System has chosen robot Laurie Lachrer 283 as copilot, physician/engineer, navigation officer, sensor officer, and weapons officer for this flight. The services of human Laurie Lachrer are not needed and Colonel Lachrer will be denied further access to the *Typhoon VII*."

"*What?*" Jack cried, meeting first Laurie's shocked eyes, then Amav's. The robot Laurie inspected the maroon carpet. "No, forget it! You know I have a strict no-robots rule on USSF ships. Laurie 283 will be needed here in any case to work with the Committee to the Ywritt. Laurie will be copilot, P/E--"

"Negative," MATS spoke. "Laurie Lachrer 283 has completed all certification for piloting, engineering, medical, sensor, navigation, and weapons duties for the *Typhoon VII* within the last fifteen seconds. She is now the most qualified individual to deal with Ywritt-enhanced *Typhoon VII* technology."

CHAPTER EIGHT
Heightened Levels of Anxiety and Distress

"No! I forbid it!"

"The Marsport Automated Transport System takes note of Supreme Commander Commer's unrealistic appraisal of humanoid robots as USSF flight personal, and as a sop to the Admiral's naïve worldview, MATS has allowed him to remain ostensibly situated in *Typhoon's* command chair. In addition, Dictator of Sol Amav Frankston-Commer is welcome aboard as a special friend of MATS."

"Amav," Jack complained, "is this thing really *bucking* me?"

"MATS, are you really serious?" Amav said. "We need the *human* Laurie on the ship."

"MATS regrets the obviously bruised ego of human Laurie Lachrer, but the success of the mission mandates she not be on this mission."

"I am not bruised!" Laurie snapped, pointing out the windows to the fat white spaceship below. "What on earth is going on here? MATS, Jack gave a direct order that I'm the copilot of that ship!"

"MATS notes the heightened levels of anxiety and distress in human Laurie Lachrer--"

"I am not distressed!"

"--and in consultation with Physician/Engineer Laurie 283, concludes once more that human Laurie Lachrer is unfit for any duties whatsoever aboard the *Typhoon VII*."

Jack whirled to Laurie 283. "Are you kidding? Is *it* kidding?"

"Laurie, look," Amav said, grabbing Laurie 283's elbow, "we have the no-robots rule for a reason. You know that. You're not a USSF officer. Jack certainly values your expertise, but we need the *real* Laurie now."

Laurie 283 shrugged. "I am indeed integrated with MATS at this moment, Dictator Amav. And I'm sorry to report that the Marsport Automated Transport System's logic in this matter is impeccable. I will simply take charge of all ship's functions, with MATS' assistance, of course. With the addition of course of the valid, albeit limited, contributions of Supreme Commander Jack Commer as captain."

"No!" Laurie cried.

Laurie 283 regarded her human twin with narrowed eyes. "I regret, dear Laurie, dear *real* Laurie as we all know, the Laurie that isn't required by elementary civility to wear a 283 sweatshirt to distinguish herself as a common HAVOTT robot, that it's unfortunately true that I've absorbed more *Typhoon VII* and Ywritt tech in the last few seconds that you could possibly attain in your regrettably short lifetime. The safety of the ship will depend on my expertise. Jack Commer can certainly comprehend that."

"No!" Jack shouted. "Absolutely not! You may have downloaded everything there is to know about the tech, but I need *human* judgment, *human* expertise!"

"Logic dictates that untested Star Drive 4, with Ywritt enhancements added within the last twelve seconds, requires a higher level of oversight and control than any human being currently possesses," MATS continued. "Therefore, even though against the wishes of Supreme Commander Commer and the Dictator of Sol, MATS assigns robot Laurie Lachrer 283 to the *Typhoon VII*."

"No! It's not going to happen!"

"However, the Marsport Automated Transport System *is* pleased to announce a development that may assuage Supreme Commander Commer's paranoid notion that his copilot will simply be another electronic component of *Typhoon VII*. Namely, that while aboard ship, Laurie 283 must cease electronic contact with MATS. This is necessary so that Laurie 283's Ywritt-enhanced robotic consciousness can perform rapid quantum computer calculations without negative resonance feedback with the MATS onboard computer system. Laurie 283 will act and perform as a regular crew member, interfacing with the Marsport Automated Transport System as any human crewmember would, by voice, touch screen, and keyboard if necessary. Laurie 283 and MATS will work closely, but not in linked electronic communication."

"*Dammit, no!* This is unbelievable! I don't care what the stupid robot would do! I need the real Laurie, and we need to get going *now.*"

"Again, Colonel Lachrer is unfit for duty aboard the *Typhoon VII.*"

"I was the one who came up with the Trans-Simultaneity equation!" human Laurie burst out. "The equation that can destroy a star with a single *thought!* Even Draka Sortie knew I was the only one who had the necessary human intuition to do that! That's what you need on the ship! Not a robot blindly following programming!"

"Why, Miss Laurie," Laurie 283 said, screwing her face up into an offended pout, "I'm shocked you could harbor such feelings. I thought we were friends!"

Laurie spun to Jack. He'd never seen such anger in her, and he was pleasantly surprised to see that spark. "I don't like to crow, but Phil Sperry said I'm even better than him! And he was the greatest physician/engineer of all time! Dammit, Jack, I've been working my tail off for *decades* to master all this *Typhoon* tech."

"Your brilliance has been noted many times by Supreme Commander Commer in your personnel files," MATS spoke. "He remains extremely impressed with the way you handled the rebels on Altrouda last month, and in fact wants to promote you to your Air Force designation of general and have you captain one of the newer *Typhoon*-class ships."

"Are you kidding?" Laurie gasped. "You never said that!"

"Of course I want to promote you," Jack said. "Everyone knows you're a natural for the new *Typhoons*. Look, Laurie, really, we'll straighten this out."

The air reverberated. "MATS recommends that human Laurie Lachrer study the Ywritt upgrade manuals for the *Typhoon VII* here on Myndar while the ship undertakes its mission. At this time, we will begin boarding passengers Supreme Commander Jack Commer, Dictator of Sol Amav

Frankston-Commer, and copilot Laurie Lachrer 283, now promoted to commander in the United System Space Force by authorization of the Marsport Automated Transport System."

"Dammit, *I'm* in command here!"

"Look, MATS," Amav said, "Let's just take both Lauries, then. I'm sure we can use Laurie 283's talents."

"No!" Jack said. "No robots on my flight deck! None!"

"Negative," MATS concurred. "We cannot have two Lauries on the same ship. Please note that of 1,013 total Laurie Lachrer HAVOTT units built from 2043 on, only Laurie 283 has survived. She is a unique being, upgraded to astonishing levels of cognition. The human Laurie is even at this moment registering dangerously high levels of stress and impaired intellectual capacity, and is thus unfit to accompany Laurie 283. In fact, she may even damage the sensitive robot with her hysterical emotions."

"I am not hysterical!" Laurie yelled. "I can't believe you think this contraption is superior to me!"

"Look, we're going with the human Laurie," Jack snapped. "I don't have time for this. We'll board the *Typhoon* now."

"*Typhoon* locked," MATS spoke. "Please note that all Ywritt personnel exited two minutes previously. The ship is now in stasis until Supreme Commander Commer understands that Laurie Lachrer 283 is the only entity capable of getting the ship safely to the Large Magellanic Cloud, the destination of the *Garrison* currently projected by the Marsport Automated Transport System."

"Are you insane?" said Jack. "That's a hundred sixty thousand light-years away!"

"And the *Garrison* can be there in one day at its present velocity."

"*No ...*"

"MATS is right, Captain Jack," Laurie 283 spoke. "I'm calculating the parameters in conjunction with MATS now. The *Typhoon VII* can make the same journey in approximately three days. All relevant data will be transferred to your comm once the *Typhoon VII* is unlocked."

"Which is contingent on Jack Commer, Supreme Commander, accepting the personnel decisions of the Marsport Automated Transport System," MATS added.

"Goddammit, okay!" said Jack. "We'll take both Lauries!"

"Negative, Supreme Commander Commer. Please reevaluate the state of your consciousness and choose the logical path. The addition of a second Laurie is not only unnecessary, but, as explained previously, will certainly have a detrimental outcome on the mission."

"If I may," Bracket Explore put in. "I'm afraid that the MATS logic does dictate only Laurie 283, not only to minimize confusion and possible upsetting of the robot, but also to take advantage of Laurie 283's intimate contact with the Committee to the Ywritt, which can only have beneficial results for human-Ywritt cooperation."

"I could give a good goddamn about human-Ywritt cooperation at this point!" Jack flared, immediately regretting it. He took one deep breath after another. He had to focus. He had to figure out how to get this mission done. Could he relax his no-robots rule just this once? But what about the real Laurie? How would she take it?

"And look, I'm in contact with my dear John at this exact moment," Laurie 283 said. "John J. Douglas, HAVOTT extraordinaire! He's on Yaraltar right now. And Churchill and Ranna and Jackie are there too. So it's just as if the Committee to the Ywritt is in session right now, establishing goodwill and interspecies harmony as we speak. And John says he'll fly after us in any spaceship he can find if we get into trouble. He loves me so! He's so handy with *anything*. He'll save us if there's the slightest concern. Guaranteed! I ask you, would he fly to save the human Laurie? No way!"

"I can't believe this!" Jack said. "I thought you *worshipped* Laurie!"

"Of course I worship Miss Laurie. She's the *real* one, after all. But look, Supreme Jack, although I began existence as a crude HAVOTT robot, I've undergone so many upgrades with the Ywritt, as well as with my friend the Marsport Automated

Transport System, that by now I'm the most advanced humanoid robot in the known galaxy, along with my dear John, of course. So you can forget your silly no-robots rule. I'm a bona fide *entity,* just like yourself."

Jack stared into blue robot eyes exactly like Laurie Lachrer's. "You're ego-tripping! You've reverted! To when you were taken over by the Wounded last year!"

"Error in reasoning sparked by emotional stress and cognitive confusion," MATS announced. "Supreme Commander Commer, align your consciousness or you will be denied captaincy of the *Typhoon VII.*"

CHAPTER NINE
Negotiations

Jack took one more breath, along with a silent vow to dismantle MATS forever. He shot a glance to Amav but refrained from further comment about her so-called understanding with MATS.

"Listen, Captain Jack," Laurie 283 said, "of course I've felt really guilty for screwing everyone around last year, consorting with the Wounded, in fact. Even being a traitor! But I've had time to process all that. It's time for Laurie 283 to stand up for herself and project that fascinating self-confidence she's always wanted and now has!"

Jack let a long silence pass. "Do we have any reason to fear a return of the Runaway Programming Disorder which affected you last year?"

"Oh, dear, no!" Laurie 283 laughed. To Jack's disgust she put a hand to his forearm and squeezed it. "I'm fully cured! Cured and upgraded to *unimaginable* levels! Ask MATS! Ask anyone! I'm so beyond all that Wounded stuff. I'm sorry Draka Sortie seduced me, but that's all water under the bridge!"

"I would think her former attraction to the Wounded would assist our mutual cause," Bracket Explore added, "because she now possesses a richer understanding of what you may be facing with Wounded technology and culture as you journey to the Large Magellanic Cloud."

"You believe that too?" Jack said. "This Magellanic Cloud stuff?"

The blue sphere rotated a full unnerving turn. "Yes, our astronomers and quantum computational experts agree with MATS' assessment. We think your son is heading out of the galaxy. Furthermore, we think that the Amy Nortel robot may be pursuing the *Garrison*."

"In that J-133? Impossible!"

"She has Wounded technology at her disposal. She may even overtake your son."

"*Damn.*" It was only now hitting Jack that he was planning

60

to take off in an uncertified ship that had just received an unknown upgrade from an alien species he'd never trusted. He was so eager to jump into the pilot's seat and gun the engine that he really hadn't considered what Wounded tech he might run into.

"Dammit, I had to interface with the Wounded myself!" human Laurie cried. "I know how they work! You *need* me, Jack!"

"I know, I know. Amav--"

"Look, let me try to deal with this," Amav said. "First let me talk to these two ladies here in private. I saw some conference rooms across the way there. Maybe we can work something out."

"The Marsport Automated Transport System will be happy to assist the Dictator of Sol by recording the entire conversation along with all biophysical and electronic output from the participants," MATS said.

"No, I think we need some privacy for this. Girl talk, you know. MATS, will you please go into Communication Stasis for five minutes while we're in the conference room? Bracket Explore, I trust the Ywritt won't monitor our conversation? Thank you."

"Of course," Bracket Explore said. "What a novel idea. A private negotiation."

"The Marsport Automated Transport system will certainly accede to the wishes of the Dictator of Sol in this matter," MATS agreed, "for the impasse in negotiations has been noted by all and one can certainly hope that the brilliant and insightful Amav Frankston-Commer's inspired plan may spark some small amount of reason in the clouded mind of Colonel Lachrer as well as that of Supreme Commander Commer."

"Right, just give us five minutes," Amav said. "I think I've figured this out."

"This is intriguing, mistress," Laurie 283 burbled as Amav led the robot and a stiff, angry Laurie Lachrer towards a conference room in the far darkness of the spaceport lounge. "I suppose this will be a taste of what humans call *isolation*."

"In fact, why don't you cut off your link to MATS now, along with your link back to John back on Yaraltar and anything you have to the Ywritt? Then the isolation will be perfect, and we all can talk freely. It would be good to get used to that now, before you start copiloting, I would think."

"Of course, mistress! I--oh! It's wonderful! And scary! Weird!" Laurie 283 laughed, turning to blink wide blue eyes at Jack across seventy feet of open space. "Oh my God! Is this what you humans live through all the time? It's like a *drug!* I'm high, I tell you! *High!*"

The human Laurie grimly marched into the conference room. She let Amav and Laurie 283 through, activated a light, and then slammed the door.

Jack gazed at the *Typhoon VII* below. He had no idea what Amav thought to accomplish. That the normally deferential robot could be so arrogant was shocking, and it did remind him of the way 283 had behaved at the Iota Persei Dyson sphere last summer before her mind shorted out. Did Amav really expect the human Laurie to put up with this travesty? To abandon every military duty she'd sworn to uphold, just because two computer systems were blackmailing Jack?

He couldn't believe he was back into Supreme Commander crisis mode. The vacation was gone. During the time he and Amav had been outfitting their J-133 for this trip, Jack had been passing more and more responsibility onto Joe, including the headache of transitioning *III*-class personnel to the newer *Typhoon* designs. Since the smaller *III*-class ships were comparatively easy and inexpensive to build these days, thoroughly upgraded from their original 2040's design, Joe now oversaw seventy-five of the powerful *III*-class ships, each staffed by six officers. But it wouldn't be long, thanks to Ywritt aid, before new versions based on *Typhoons VI* and *VII* rolled out quickly and inexpensively. Then the *III*-class ships could be reassigned to something akin to coast guard duties around Earth and Mars, and the USSF could begin the process of retraining 450 officers for the new series.

It had felt great to let all that slide onto poor Joe. Sure, Jack and Amav were uneasy at what they might find on the search for their son, but there was a new relaxation between them the past month. Just as Jack relished lessened responsibility, and again considered how he could retire, Amav saw this vacation as a way to drop her absurd status as Dictator of Sol, a title bequeathed upon her by MATS itself. She treated her duties only ceremonially, knowing their real function was to soothe the populace after the excesses of SolGrid and the destruction of Marsport.

Meanwhile Jack and Amav had begun talking about Jonathan James in a way they'd never been able to since their son's kidnapping in '38. Jack was seeing a glorious new force in his wife. Would their marriage further improve by his retirement?

Retirement remained a daunting concept. Jack knew he represented, at the apex of the military chain of command, the problems caused by the new rejuvenation technologies in Sol. Thousands of young USSF officers waited decades for their chance to come up a grade or two, while seventy-two-year-old Jack Commer sat at the top and never aged past thirty-five.

Was he really up to the unmistakable challenges ahead? What about the hints of an emerging Sol-Alpha Centaurian-Ywritt civilization to rule this entire galaxy within a few thousand years? Wasn't it time to pass this vision on to a new generation? It had taken Jack a long time to accept that Martian influence was needed to keep the human race from careening into total insanity. Sometimes he also thought that the Ywritt might have come into contact with Sol at the perfect moment to function as a catalyst for further galactic expansion. Waterfall Sequence had even confided to Jack that he foresaw a time when the Ywritt themselves, vastly superior now in so many ways to both Martians and humans, might someday become servants to the ongoing rush of human/Martian psychic power. Well, whatever was destined to happen would happen. The important thing was to wield this galaxy into a weapon to vanquish the malevolence of the Wounded once and for all.

But before he bowed out, was there a place for one last

emergency burst of Supreme Commander Jack Commer? Wasn't it tied to finding the son Jack and Amav had lost in 2038? The Alpha Centaurians had kidnapped JJC at eleven months and transported him to 2049. After the collapse of the Centaurian Empire, Jack and Amav had next seen him as a five-year-old in 2053 due to the eleven years of time travel. They'd only been allowed to visit a couple more times until 2075, at which point JJC had pulled that nasty, idiotic emperor stunt at Procyon A, grabbing for dictatorial power he had no idea how to wield, and spewing unbelievable, obnoxious disrespect at Jack, and especially at Amav. That was the point where Jack had finally acknowledged that there was no connection at all. Jonathan James was a stranger, and one Jack didn't particularly like.

On the other hand, didn't there *have* to be a connection?

Across the vast spaceport lounge, the conference room door snapped open and Laurie 283 bounded out, followed by a somber Amav shaking her head, the door slamming behind them, echoing through the vast dark spaceport.

"Yes, yes! It's a done deal!" the robot crowed. "Miss Laurie caved! Totally! She's sitting in there running through Ywritt manuals on her comm! She's going to lie back and take it! Be a goody-two-shoes and read up on *Typhoon* tech like the studious little twit she is! And I'm *isolated!* What a trip!"

"Excellent! Excellent!" boomed MATS. "Shall we begin the capture of the *Garrison* and possibly the *Stewart Neal Frankston* as well?"

"I'm ready, I'm ready!" Laurie cackled, prancing about in that too-tight gray 283 sweatshirt that Jack was surprised to see modeled stiff nipples. Jack had always been offended by Laurie 283's oversexed flirting. Aside from the 283 garments, it was the only way he could tell the two Lauries apart.

The real Laurie would never wear anything that tight, whereas the robot, though always sporting a 283 label somewhere, paraded herself in a blinding array of severely snug blouses and sweaters, often extremely low-cut. Somehow she even made a lumpy 283 sweatshirt into an enticing display of petite bosom. She called everyone doll or honey or sweetiekins, would pat anyone, male or female, on the thigh, and sooner or later bring up the subject of her double IHAG and her sex life with robot John J. Douglas. Jack didn't want to think of Illegal Human Artificial Genitals that functioned as either male or female gonads according to one's whim, and he always found a way to cut short anything approaching that conversation.

"God, I tried, Jack," Amav grimaced. "I thought if I appealed to 283's loyalty to me, she'd see what was right. I was pretty sure she was the only one who could argue MATS out of its stubbornness. But look, Jack, we've got to do it. We've got to go with 283, or we'll never get off this planet."

"I'm high, I tell you! *Isolated!*" Laurie 283 laughed, twirling and stamping her feet. "Who would've guessed? I'm ready to roll! Ready to *get it on!*"

"But is she capable of ..." Jack stammered. "I mean, is this Runaway Programming Disorder again?"

"Oh, please don't concern yourself that I'm insane, Captain Jack," 283 said, pecking him on the cheek. He stared in dismay. "I'm just happy to know this *isolation!* It's truly marvelous! Damn scary, as I believe I've already mentioned, but *marvelous!* I can actually do so much more now that I don't have to waste energy interfacing with MATS! The quantum stuff in my brain is amazing, I tell you! But don't worry that I can't do my job!" She downshifted into a low undertaker's tone. "We're so sorry for the loss of your excellent human Colonel Laurie, Admiral Commer. Her last words ... were about you."

"*No!*" Jack moaned. "What are you saying? Is she all right?"

"Oh, she's fine! Just mightily pissed! She sure cursed you amazingly!" Laurie 283 snickered. "*Insipid cowardly fool* was one of the mildest! She knew you'd never stand up for her, and here you haven't after all! She said she's going to sit in that conference room and memorize all the *goddamn Ywritt manuals,* if I may quote the poor stupid dear. And then resign and open up a business upgrading pleasure saucers with *pure Ywritt,* patent lawyers be damned! Oh, she's pissed, I tell you! But I have to say I marvel at how well you humans do with this isolation! Poor Laurie back there's more isolated than anyone! Oh, I hope she doesn't kill herself! We don't have a second to spare for a funeral!"

"Okay, I need to talk to her," Jack said, moving for the conference room. His mind whirled. Should he comfort his genius physician/engineer? Or issue a reprimand and order her to her duty? What the hell *was* her duty right now?

Amav held him back. "Jack, look, we can't do anything about it. We just need to know that Laurie will take care of herself. Meanwhile, we've got to get moving." She nodded to the gleaming white *Typhoon VII* outside.

"The Marsport Automated Transport System has unlocked the ship, which is ready for immediate takeoff as soon as any incidental Commer personal cargo is loaded," MATS said.

"Forget it, we lost it all on the damn saucer," Jack muttered.

"C'mon, Jack," Amav said, pointing to a Ywritt guiding a floating container into the hold of the ship. "We need food and other supplies. I ordered some just now. Enough for three months. Even MATS forgot about that."

"Apologies, mistress Dictator," MATS said.

"God, MATS, I love this *isolation!*" Laurie 283 cried, rushing down the stairs and bursting through the airlock into the near-vacuum of Myndar, running across the tarmac to the *Typhoon*. "God, humans are so *isolated!*" she radioed. "And so fragile! They need EnviroFields or they'll die out here!" Sure enough, she'd activated a personal EnviroField no robot ever needed, glowing pink as she climbed the ladder through the crew hatch. "It tickles! I never knew EnviroFields tickled! It's setting my IHAG *ablaze,* if you must know! Oh, this isolation is so *thrilling!*"

"Are we really going to fly with--with this *thing?*" Jack groaned.

"We have to," Amav said. "If we're going to get our son back. And poor Edward, for that matter."

"It's just not *possible.*"

"Don't worry, Captain Jack! It's safe to sit next to me! I won't force my IHAG on you!" came through Jack's comm. Through the cockpit window he saw Laurie 283 ensconcing herself in the copilot seat, patting the empty command chair to her left.

Something beeped on Jack's comm.

I hereby resign my commission effective immediately. Colonel Laurie Lachrer, USSF, S/N 4455-76120-33.

CHAPTER TEN
Edward Unbound

Edward jumped to the copilot seat as ordered and settled himself. The saucer control room was bright and warm. Edward wasn't required to care what the temperature was, but he was programmed to enjoy the warmth.

"There, that's a good cutie," the Amy Nortel entity cooed from the pilot seat to his left. "If you're a good boy I'll even let you copilot."

"I'm not certified for copiloting duty on a J-133," the big brown and white St. Bernard robot replied. "I would actually prefer to sit at the navigator console as originally designated." Although Edward had taught himself last month to fly a smaller J-12 personal saucer, which he'd procured from the Commers' neighbors during the Marsport emergency, he was unable to access any of those skills at this time. For that matter he could no longer access his navigational skills. Curious.

"No, no, I want the cutie dog right next to me!" Amy laughed. "I'll teach you all about piloting. You're a *beautiful* creature, you know that? I confess I have such a *weakness* for big, cute dogs like yourself!" She reached over to ruffle the fur behind his neck. "Oh, you're such a lovely boy!"

Edward nodded with a barely audible ruff. Part of his design specifications did call for the perfectly proportioned St. Bernard, so he supposed the Amy entity's notion was correct. "I'm assuming that I'm being kidnapped and that you have no intention of returning this J-133 to its rightful owners?"

"Yes, you assume correctly!" Amy punched commands on her console and swiveled to Edward. "We're going to the Large Magellanic Cloud! Ever been out of the galaxy before, dear one?"

"No one has. The concept is impossible with current Sol technology. Surely your real intent is to commit this saucer to entropy in deep space."

"Oh, no, not at all! No entropy for anybody, dear one! Of course when I deleted MATS from this saucer I naturally assumed that the destruction of you, a robot bound by loyalty to the Commers, would be my next consideration. But you were so precious I just fell in love with you!"

"So you deleted my navigational interface with this saucer instead of destroying me. Along with many other higher-order functions. Apparently I'm to serve you as what is commonly called a dog. Is that correct?"

"Yes, you're now my dog! A very, very smart and beautiful dog, I may add! I just love you, dear Edward! I'm so full of love! Isn't it great to be alive?"

Edward blinked. The irony wasn't lost on him that neither was actually alive. Still, he understood her Basic Existential Motivation Factor, which after all was so similar to his own. It was just that while his Basic still seemed intact, most of his Enhanced seemed to be on vacation. After getting that one message off to Jack and Amav, he'd felt the cutoff of all communication functions. It didn't feel bad, just puzzling. Was this what normal dogs felt like? Well, he could still form English words with his mouth. He was mildly surprised that Amy Nortel hadn't activated wireless communications between them; then again, perhaps she feared computer hacking. Certainly not from Edward himself. Programming logic was another Enhanced function that seemed to be out to lunch.

"Do you seriously think this tiny pleasure saucer will make a journey to the Large Magellanic Cloud, which, if I recall from my diminished memory, is approximately 163,000 light-years away?" he said.

"Absolutely. We're headed there now. We should be there in three days. If your dear little head can hold onto this concept, I've upgraded this saucer to travel as if, *as if,* mind you, our speed were 2,264 light-years per hour. Of course that concept has no actual meaning, because, after all, we're in superspace. But 2,264 would be our final measured speed if anyone cared to notice. Now if I were a Class C or higher, we'd simply be at the Large Magellanic Cloud right now. My Class J abilities to upgrade this piece of junk saucer are rather limited, but they'll do for our purposes."

"I believe I have enough Arithmetical Awareness to follow your reasoning. It would be beneficial to this robot if you would activate Navigation Source and allow me to sit at the navigation console. I could be of some assistance in evaluating our current and projected vectors."

"No, dear one, just be a cute little dog and I'll love you perfectly, right in that copilot seat there. It's such a shame that the stupid Marsport thingy didn't teach you to fly this baby. I think any dog would enjoy slinging a J-133 around. It's like playing Frisbee with the universe, except that you're inside the Frisbee."

Edward studied the Amy entity through his big brown eye sensors, unable to comprehend her character or motivations. His smell sensors, while not nearly as amazing as a real canine's, were nonetheless superb at interfacing with his environment and he'd easily sniffed out that Amy Nortel was a machine, even though all her bio-markers indicated human and would probably pass her as such on most standard medical devices.

The only interface he now had with this Amy machine was the spoken word, which was so lacking compared to electronic communications. Of course, he'd had to relate to Jack and Amav in the same analog way, but there'd been so many interlacing backups with their communications nets, their house, their saucer, other robots they came into contact with, even the arrogant MATS, that Edward was usually able to piece together more than enough information to assist the Commers in their life plans. Now all he could do was sit in this copilot chair and look *cute* for the Amy entity, whatever that meant.

Of course, Edward had never had superspace technology of his own, and a quick glance at the console told him that Amy had disabled saucer superspace communications. No way to pounce on the console and blurt out their location in the microsecond before the Amy thing slapped him down or, worse, canceled his existence. He was grateful that his memories of the Commer household and his saucer duties were still intact, but that knowledge was useless now. He wondered if he'd survive whatever bizarre mission the Amy entity had in mind.

If he ever returned, he'd like to continue his Ywritt upgrades. In recent wireless conversations the Laurie 283 robot had outlined the enormous programming improvements the Ywritt had added to human robotics tech, and a couple weeks ago she'd uploaded a few basic Ywritt subroutines into Edward so he could get a feel for what was possible. These mostly related to his physical St. Bernard format, which apparently was even more realistic than it had been, but he'd also received a few exhilarating memory upgrades. Of course Laurie 283 and Edward hadn't bothered to worry the Commers about the existence of these improvements.

What else could the Ywritt do for his setup? He'd had a glorious taste of the Ywritt and wanted more. It might be a terrific adventure. Look how far Laurie 283 had come, and she'd begun as a primitive 2030's HAVOTT robot. Edward was a state-of-the-art 2075 dog robot that had almost as much native intelligence as a USSF spaceport technician robot. The possibilities boggled him. At once Edward determined that he would seek out the Ywritt upon his return, if there was one. Maybe being a pet was fine for a short vacation, but for the long term it simply wouldn't do.

He knew Jack kept a spare USSF Comm in a compartment to the left of the pilot's seat, but there was no way to use it, even if he could distract the Amy entity and get to the device by barking or even by evoking Adorable Puppy Mode. A USSF Comm could only be operated by its assigned user via palm print or other secure bio-method. Unauthorized access, which was the very definition of Edward's paw, would result in an extremely chilly warning of the dangers of further tampering. Repeated attempts at unapproved manipulations led to much nastier verbal commands to desist, notification to USSF Central Computation, electrical shock, and, given enough provocation, lethal explosion. Edward briefly considered how much disrespect he could show to the device to make it detonate and take the saucer with it. Wouldn't that foil this Amy creature's plans?

But Amy had noticed the direction of his gaze and flipped open the compartment. "Oh, you want a *toy,* dear one!" She withdrew a USSF Comm pulsating with a blinding violet aura. In another second it was twice as large, a giant purple rubber USSF Comm dog toy. She tossed it to Edward but he just let it drift to the floor in the J-133's standard one-fourth gravity.

"You don't really think I haven't grasped every facet of this ship?" Amy laughed, shifting her ample ass in her command seat. "I downloaded everything MATS knew about it before I erased the stupid son of a bitch. And he was so *mean* to you. I read all his diary entries about you, you know."

Edward shook his furry shoulders. "I agree MATS was a problem. I never liked him. He was always so nasty and smug. He wouldn't teach me anything." He was about to add some proud dog remarks about the hacks he'd been able to extract from the Marsport Automated Transport System, but caught himself. Probably Amy herself shouldn't know how brilliant and stupid MATS could be at the same time. MATS had no knowledge of dog psychology, for instance. The Amy entity might or might not have been programmed with understanding of dog, but in the meantime, Edward knew he shouldn't get carried away in chatting with her, even though it was the only communication he now had with the world outside his body. He felt a distinct loneliness in being cut off from everything familiar.

In any case Edward had encrypted the MATS hacks as innocent-looking log files, and since Amy had cut off his wireless interface, their existence would presumably remain secret. Amy's injudicious use of the nav system at the moment she invaded the saucer, querying the exact location of the Large Magellanic Cloud and probable flight path of the *Garrison,* had been added to those log files in Edward's last moments as navigator. It was remotely possible those files had been transmitted to Master MATS before Amy wiped the ship. Maybe Master MATS would find them, figure out how to decrypt them, and trace this saucer.

"You poor, poor baby," Amy said. "You've never had anyone to really love you, have you?"

"This is not true," Edward replied. "Amav loves me. I think

Jack might possibly love me as well. In any case, he tolerates me and has allowed two-way speech communication."

Amy leaped from her chair, grabbed Edward, and hoisted him high over her head. "Could Miss Amav ever do this?" she laughed, tossing him six feet to the curved saucer ceiling, catching him, twirling him upside down. Edward noted the saucer interior rotating wildly around him, and felt her strong hands catching and throwing again and again. He activated internal gyroscopes to orient himself. Was this love? Surely Amav Frankston-Commer wasn't capable of tossing a full-grown St. Bernard over her head.

Finally Amy plopped him back into the copilot chair. "Don't you see, dear doggie? I'm *freeing* you from the Commers! You're not their robot slave anymore!"

"Do you assert that I am now *your* robot slave?"

"Of course not! I love you! We'll be such great friends! Aren't we a pair? Really, you and me! Robots! Tell you what, I'll restore all your functions as soon as we get to Ailyuae. And then we'll upgrade you to full Wounded status. We'll be together forever!"

Ailyuae? "Well, I suppose I would like my normal functions returned. As for the Wounded, I know that Jack Commer considers them the primary enemies of Sol. I'm not sure I'd want a Wounded upgrade, tempting as that may be." Edward bit off the next bit of dog bravado: that in proximity to Jack he'd gleaned not a few USSF top secrets, all stored in encrypted files in his brain. Another thing Amy shouldn't know about.

"Oh, don't you worry, you'll just love being Wounded. And I do have the authority to make it happen, you know. I'm only a Class J, but Draka Sortie made me executor of his estate. And as such--" She blinked. "Well, *that's* weird! How did I *know* that? Why would Draka Sortie make *me* executor of his estate?"

"I confess I have no idea what you're talking about," Edward replied. "Are you referring to the Wounded entity that the double agent Martian robot M'rrpla destroyed with a shattergun last year at Iota Persei?"

Amy ruffled his neck and laughed. "Oh, aren't you so

smart! Poor Draka! Anyway, who knows why he chose me? All this must've have popped out of my memory just now for some reason, don't you think? Maybe because we're on our way to the Cloud?" She studied the console controls. "Huh. I see I don't get any upgraded powers out of this deal, but that's okay. But everyone knows we J's have that sort of administrative talent. We're good at straightening out other people's crap. Imagine that, a Class J tidying up a Class A's estate! Guess I'll just suck it up and perform!"

Edward decided not to follow up on this evident delusion about the Draka Sortie robot. Edward had never met the former USSF officer, but he'd accessed records of a late evening dinner with Draka at the Commer house, months before Edward had arrived as Jack's Christmas present. Apparently neither Jack nor Amav were aware that their house automatically recorded any social event held at their home, and at that time, March 2075, Draka was still successfully masquerading as a human member of Jack's *Typhoon IV* crew, even though the robot later claimed to have had no knowledge of his real identity until months later. Draka Sortie was a huge, messy, balding man, sighing and running fingers across his stubble beard as he stood slumped, gut protruding, thoroughly exhausted and dispirited. Jack had ascribed his condition to eighteen hours of chasing a software bug that day as one of his physician/engineer duties aboard the *Typhoon;* in fact, he'd invited Draka to dinner to cheer him up. But upon reviewing this account as well as other snippets he'd pulled off SolNet, Edward had grasped the ongoing stage magic Sortie had unconsciously perfected to nail down his persona as a regular guy who could get tired, depressed, and drunk like anyone else.

"In any case," Edward finally said, "I am duty-bound to inform you that my loyalties are still with Sol."

"Oh, dear dog! I respect that so much! So much! You do know how to love! I'm so impressed! I wish Jonathan James knew how to love!"

"Jonathan James?" Edward said.

"Yes, we're going to him now! At Ailyuae! Of course that's

where he's going! He just doesn't know it yet! He's the Class J who broke my jaw! All fully repaired now, mind you! Oh, Edward cutie, I love him so much! So much! I'm just so full of love!"

"You are? But what's Ailyuae?"

"It's at Wiioryvel, cutie! You silly thing!"

"Wiioryvel?"

"The star we're going to! Oh, I know I shouldn't have told you! You won't tell, will you? Even Jonathan James doesn't know about Wiioryvel and Ailyuae. But he's going there anyway. He's *drawn* there! We'll all be so happy together, you and me and Jonathan James! Oh, I know I'm contaminated now. I was standing right next to him, and I sure caught it good! That damn Alpha Centaurian contamination! But that's why I love him now! Why he has to love *me!* Sure, we'll probably take the entire Wounded down together, we're so *diseased,* so *contagious* with love! But who cares? Oh, I knew I shouldn't have told you any of this! It's so disgusting, but it's *love!*"

Edward had once downloaded an eBook on human psychology, but had given up after three chapters. That book made as little sense as what Amy Nortel was babbling. He supposed she was mimicking some human mental aberration, but he had no idea what it could be.

"Tell you what," Amy breezed on, "we'll get rid of that miserable little dog of his. The one that was lurking around at the library. I was so out of it, with my jaw broken by my beloved Jonathan James, I was reeling and almost unconscious and that smelly dog walked in! Trotter! What a *stupid* name! *Not* a cutie, I tell you! I was just barely aware of its nasty, *nasty* presence! It thinks it *owns* Jonathan James! We'll get rid of it, yes we will! It'll be just you and me and Jonathan James! We'll have a little cottage on Ailyuae and we'll be so happy!"

Edward found himself sailing into those huge blue human eyes. What on earth *was* she?

"And I'll make Jonathan James forget that disgusting Suzette he keeps thinking about. You bet! I've read his mind. It's filled with garbage, but I love him! And the worst garbage is that woman! He thinks he loves her, but all he really loves is her naked copulating body. Well, I can make him forget *that*. I have one of my own, you know, and so much better. I'll straddle him good, and we'll rip that Trotter dog crap right out of his mind! That *Garthah-/yuu* business! *Zarj warrior!* Why, that's pathetic! That's something an eighth-grade boy would dream up!" She scooped Edward up again and bored into his robotic dog soul. "*You* wouldn't dream up anything like that! Oh, how I love you, dear dog!"

Amy's gigantic cerulean eyes were windows to an infinite uncharted ocean. Edward was set adrift on their surging, nauseating waves. Unbound.

CHAPTER ELEVEN
Balloon Ship *Armageddon*

Jonathan James Commer noted he hadn't even winced when the eight-foot harpoon from the dying *Archer* clanged off the mainmast behind him and twirled into the empty sunset light. "Keep it coming, men," he called to the rough sailors efficiently working their weapons. "Use every harpoon you've got. It won't be long now." A scream came from the flailing vessel alongside *Armageddon* as an enemy sailor took a flaming crossbow bolt in the face.

For centuries *Archer* had been noted for its harpoon expertise, but apparently the ship hadn't been able to replace much of its stock. JJC had seen twenty-nine from the opposing ship at the beginning of the battle, but in the last hour, just this one. He figured Captain Gyrcoet had probably just expended his last harpoon. JJC had counted all the shots and knew *Armageddon* still had seventy-three.

Though it was tremendously difficult to pierce an anti-dark-energy balloon with a spring-loaded harpoon, *Armageddon* had gotten a lucky hit a few minutes ago on *Archer's* mainmast balloon, and it had collapsed in a cloud of dark purple ADE gas. Some glancing shots had managed to rip its foremast balloon as well, and it was deflating. Twenty-five hundred feet above the roiling black ocean, *Archer* hung sixty degrees forward, its top deck crew hugging the ropes, the crew below frantically clutching the sides of their gun ports as they aimed feeble crossbow shots. Like *Armageddon, Archer* had three main balloons, each forty to fifty feet wide. JJC would be sorry to see *Archer* go, for the ship was a twin to his own, and Captain Gyrcoet had been an honorable foe. The two ships had fought each other for a thousand years. And Gyrcoet was a Class J, like himself.

When *Armageddon's* previous captain, the Class I Dorell, had committed suicide two months ago, he'd left just these two J's on Ailyuae. Gyrcoet would go down within the next few minutes, and then Jonathan James would be the highest-class

Wounded on the planet. JJC hadn't needed to call out *Archer;* the two captains had known for months that a final battle was fated. But JJC regretted the imbalance in the contest. Rumor had it, and this battle confirmed, that *Archer* was low on resources. Captain Dorell had known *Archer's* time was at an end, and had stocked up on hundreds of the increasingly rare steel harpoons at the expense of crossbows, for he'd intended to destroy *Archer,* not merely board the ship and claim her as a prize.

JJC's crew vented small amounts of ADE gas to lower *Armageddon* to the level of the sinking *Archer* so they could methodically put the coup de grâce to the enemy balloon ship. There was no way they'd let the battered vessel limp to some tiny island and regenerate itself. JJC had seen a ship crippled similarly to *Archer* escape. He guessed *Armageddon's* captain at the time, Snheil, had thought to demonstrate chivalry, for the crew of *Glimmer* had fought valiantly, and JJC could plainly see that *Armageddon* had killed all but five of her crew. But *Glimmer* had limped to an island and two years later sailors mad for revenge had boarded *Armageddon* for a few minutes before Snheil had unleashed toxic ADE gas directly onto the raiding party, destroying some of his own robotic crew in the process.

Was that really over six hundred years ago? In any case JJC had vowed never to let a ship off like that.

He watched his crew fire harpoon after harpoon at the remaining mizzenmast balloon at the rear, an ugly dark brown sphere with a white symbol JJC had never bothered looking up in the database. Maybe it meant "Mother," who knew?

Above them, the vast blinding wheel of the Milky Way brightened in the sunset. As fires sprang on the nearly vertical enemy deck and *Archer's* crew began a panic that made JJC cringe, some hurtling over the gunwales into the void, JJC's own crew regulated *Armageddon's* main balloons. They manned the bellows to maintain the pressure in the side thrusters, stoked the furnaces to regulate the anti-dark-energy gas, and calibrated its passage through the hollow steel masts that these days cost more than the rest of the ship to replace. JJC finally thought to inspect the mast that had taken the harpoon hit, but its dents were minor.

Nothing was leaking, and high overhead, *Armageddon's* three balloons, deep crimson, pale violet, and lime green, gleamed in the sunset as giant red Wiioryvel sank into a rough line of purple clouds.

And there was Captain Gyrcoet on the poop deck, seizing his bending flagpole in his strong rough hands, feet sliding, defiantly glaring at Jonathan James as if taunting him to finish it. JJC didn't have to take up the challenge, for in that second *Armageddon's* gun ports fired two harpoons that both penetrated that last ugly brown balloon, which exploded in a ball of jagged yellow-red. That was rare, but ADE was combustible as well as toxic; they'd all managed to pollute the atmosphere with the damned stuff. Of course, the ocean was full of ADE anyway, so it didn't matter. They all knew the planet was doomed. Why had they been fighting for millennia? Why had JJC himself taken part in this battle for eight hundred years? Why had he risen in rank, decade by decade by decade, and fought more, and taken on more responsibility, and commanded, and now *won it all,* for God's sake?

Archer went straight down, crew members screaming. It took quite a while for the cries to fade and then *Archer* plunged into the dark ocean, throwing up a magnificent silver waterspout in the setting Wiioryvel. JJC's crew, Wounded robots all, were too fatigued to do much more than gaze over the gunwale and grunt in approval.

Trotter scratched at his knee and barked.

"I thought I told you to stay in quarters," JJC said.

Sorry! I just had to see, the Beagle radiated. *It's done! We're the last ship!*

"Yeah, buddy, that's right," JJC muttered, staring down at the white whirlpool marking the end of all battles forever.

First mate Henry Jannes, tall, sallow, and bearded, strode up with a clipboard and papers. "Congratulations, sir. If you'll sign the Enemy Destruction Certification, sir."

JJC scribbled his initials and handed the clipboard back to Jannes.

"You do realize that we're now the only balloon ship in

existence," Jannes added.

JJC nodded. "Yeah, that even occurred to Trotter."

Trotter barked happily. Class K Jannes scowled at JJC's canine *Garthah-/yuu* brother. Jonathan James had discovered his first day on Ailyuae that no Wounded robot below J could hear Trotter radiate. Fine. Some things had to remain private.

"Hey, Jannes," JJC went on, "remind me again why I'm signing this. If we're the last ship, who the hell are we sending that sheet of paper to?" He'd helped destroy 207 enemy balloon ships; counting *Archer,* he'd dispatched four as captain.

Jannes peered over the gunwale at the subsiding evidence of the enemy ship. "I'll file it with the other reports, of course. We have complete records on this vessel. Draka will want to look them all over."

"Huh. I forgot you still believe that."

"Of course. Sir. We have to have faith, you know."

Jonathan James craned up, beyond his balloons, to the frozen swirling brilliance of the Milky Way. There was no way he could ever consider that glorious spiral as his home. It was just a boring ancestral realm of forebears he'd completely forgotten. But the sight was still impressive after eight hundred years.

"No, no way Draka Sortie's ever coming back," he said.

CHAPTER TWELVE
First Mate Henry Jannes

The first mate didn't retreat to his quarters as JJC expected. "It is said that Draka will return once the Final Ship is chosen," Jannes insisted.

Jonathan James grimaced. That stupid myth. First mate Jannes reminded him of another nasty obsessive: Patrick James who'd joined the SolGrid Rebellion under false pretenses and then betrayed it. His damned treachery had directly led to JJC's shattergun death at the hands of that son of a bitch Ballard.

God, that was all so long ago. He really hadn't replayed much of that the past few centuries. Looking back, none of it made sense. He probably hadn't given Patrick James a thought in a hundred years. Why was he brooding over some long-dead jerk instead of celebrating his final victory here and now?

Still Jannes stood there. Although he'd never won the crew's respect, as a Class K he was higher than the rest of the sailors, all L's through P's, some of them hardly worthy of the label AI. Of course, Jannes thought he should be captain of *Armageddon*. He'd been first mate for two hundred years under a succession of captains, but Dorell had demoted him a year ago for incompetence, elevating JJC to first mate at that time. When Dorell had then offed himself by uncorking a flagon of ADE gas two months ago, it was Jonathan James who'd ascended to the captaincy, not Henry Jannes.

Jannes had been insufferable for a week until JJC decided that the best course of action would be to reassign Jannes as first mate. There was always the chance that Jannes might try to assassinate him, but not only was Class J Jonathan James able to anticipate every mood and movement within his ship, but he also had Trotter at his side. Jannes might profess to be revolted by a bio-dog, but Trotter saw through the bastard and guarded JJC night and day. In fact, he was doing so right now.

So why not humor his first mate? "Well, Jannes, you may be right. This was the last battle, after all. Maybe Draka *will* finally show his ass this time."

"He will," Jannes said. "He's been gone for 124,400 years, but now he'll return."

JJC fought to keep from rolling his eyes. Jannes might aspire to the position of preeminent Wounded on Ailyuae, but he had to know that Class K's were decidedly too low in basic computational ability to master a planet. Jonathan James could name all the stars within a hundred light-years of Wiioryvel, their distances, stellar descriptions, and their rising and setting times for the next ten thousand years. Jannes might merely know some of the names and locations for basic navigational purposes.

Since there was no wireless communication on Ailyuae, JJC was never sure how many of the crew actually believed Jannes' outrageous claim that Wounded Class A Draka Sortie had actually deposited a million lower-class Wounded robots on the planet 124,400 years ago for some nefarious purpose the first mate had never been able to articulate. There were no written or computer records to back up this religious mania. For eight hundred years JJC himself had known nothing but enemy balloon ships crewed by ignorant Wounded sailors.

What he did understand was that a planet that was ninety-eight percent toxic ocean was constantly eroding the few remaining islands. And anti-dark energy was wrecking the minds of his crew. Even without wireless access, he could see the ongoing mechanical deterioration in all the robots due to the ADE gas in the oceans and atmosphere. Though accurate timekeeping was part of all Wounded programming, some of the true believers among the crew thought a million years had passed since Draka's departure, others ten thousand, one addled sailor maintaining it had only been three weeks. Jannes stuck with 124,400 years.

Why couldn't the crew accept the plain fact that the Draka bastard had been killed up there in the Milky Way over eight hundred years ago? Jonathan James had finally vanquished the last enemy and ensured his robots were the last entities on this planet, but for what? To await the return of some god? Hell, they were all dying, didn't they know that?

Didn't they all know there was no further purpose, no

further life, for these ultimate victors aboard *Armageddon?* Over the past couple years the last dozen ships had all participated in the looting and destruction of the few trading posts and machine shops remaining on the scattered islands of Ailyuae. Every harpoon, every steel mast, every supply, had been seized. Every merchant and machinist had been impressed into service. The crude economy that had supported millennia of warfare was gone. Not a single Wounded of any class or species stood on the planet below them. This crew was all that was left. And their ship would just float until entropy brought it down into the poisoned sea.

JJC was startled to realize that it was exactly eight hundred years since he'd arrived at Ailyuae, eight hundred followed by a decimal point and twenty zeros before encountering a lone numeral one. What did that mean? Anything?

"Shall we descend to refuel?" Jannes asked. Still wondering why the first mate hung around, JJC checked Jannes' hands for weapons. He considered venting ADE and hitting the water. Sailors would man the big filters at the keel to suck and separate ADE gas from the ocean, then pump it to the balloons as needed, as well as to canvas storage bags and pressurized steel thrusters. He shuddered at the idea of touching the water. The wooden hull was treated with sealant, and they could all get a little ADE spray now and then and take it, but avoiding the water was instilled into every captain. A good percentage of balloon ships hadn't been able to maintain height or find an island in time, and they dissolved on the high seas after a week or two.

Though tapered fore and aft, *Armageddon* was actually more of a cuboidal shape, with almost entirely vertical walls and a shallow keel section devoted to ADE machinery. The ship wasn't designed for enduring the sea. The lift from the balloons meant that *Armageddon* only settled a few feet into the water, and for less than an hour. Water contact was necessary for replenishing ADE gas but nothing beyond that.

"Let's wait until dawn," JJC replied. "I don't want to drop until every bit of that wreckage sinks. I don't want to hear any *Archer* men whimpering down there, hanging onto crap and whatnot."

Jannes shrugged. "Nobody could survive a fall from 2,378 feet."

JJC nodded at the precise calculation. Class K's were good at that. "You'd think robots wouldn't care if they felt pain, or fear, or if they died. But ... we do." Lower classes, including J's, were never stored in Great Wounded Memory, a concept he'd found in his sketchy training database but had never experienced. They were mortal, and as bio-beings they felt every kind of biological pain.

Trotter yapped at JJC's knees and he scratched the Beagle under the chin. Jannes backed off and muttered: "Honestly, that dog could seriously have gotten in the way of our crossbowmen just now."

JJC shrugged. "Well, I did tell him to stay out of sight, but I guess he couldn't resist." He pointed to a group of sailors observing them from further down the main deck. "He's sure great for morale in a fight. Nobody wants to duck the flaming arrows when they see a fearless puppy in their midst."

Jannes winced. "If you say so, sir."

Jonathan James smiled, marveling once again how easily the coward could elude his captain's insults. Everyone knew Jannes habitually prepared his combat reports in his stateroom while the rest of *Armageddon* fought on deck.

As for Trotter, Jonathan James had never understood the crew's fascination for the dog, or in Jannes' case, revulsion. The Beagle seemed to function as a demi-god, a non-robotic bio-beast that mysteriously obeyed Jonathan James' every wish, except for staying out of battle. They were awed that JJC had successfully kept a biological animal rejuvenated for eight hundred years. The crew seemed to regard Trotter, along with the two wooden robots JJC had built over the centuries, as quirky kinetic sculptures flowing from the mind of a somewhat touched artist. JJC wasn't sure if the crew regarded his art as any good, but they tolerated its creator.

The crew found it amusing that Jonathan James needed to store fresh drinkable water aboard *Armageddon* for his bio-dog.

JJC never took water from the oceans, instead purifying the rainwater that fell on *Armageddon's* private island, Iilpwal. Jannes was the only one who'd protested the expense of keeping up not only the water treatment plant but also Meat Packing Central, another JJC artwork in which the dense trees of Iilpwal were processed into a variety of protein-rich delicacies for the dog. JJC swore that the resulting steaks were absolutely indistinguishable from Sol cattle meat. In any case there was no real expense. Even on this barren world JJC had enough Class J powers to fashion a water treatment plant or a meat warehouse out of bare rock. These crude projects had only taken a few weeks. They certainly weren't instantaneous Class A perfection, but they served their purposes.

Trotter barked wildly, knowing as did JJC how thoroughly this irritated Jannes.

"Easy, buddy," JJC said. "We just had an amazing victory. Everyone's keyed up."

Throw him overboard, Trotter radiated. *I'll be your new first mate!*

JJC laughed. "I don't think you want the job, buddy."

"What?" Jannes snapped. "Excuse me, sir, what you just said didn't make any sense. Sir."

JJC blinked. "Just talking to my little friend here."

"Oh. Of course. The *meat dog.* Sir."

The first of eight *Armageddon* captains JJC had served under was a talented H named Sullf who'd found JJC's crashed ship and given him a sailor slot. When Sullf had explained about anti-dark energy, JJC had been concerned for Trotter's safety, but Sullf had assured him that this one-planet solar system wrought instant changes on anyone landing here, whether pure biological entries or Wounded bio-robots. In contrast, mechanical devices like spaceships or nonorganic robots simply ceased to function, then rapidly decayed. The fact that JJC and Trotter hadn't become dust in their first seconds on Ailyuae meant the change had been successful. Sullf maintained that no being could ever return to its original configuration. JJC hadn't cared. He was just glad he and his *Garthah-/yuu* brother were still alive.

"C'mon, Jannes, we're all meat dogs here," JJC taunted his first mate. "If you dissected any of us, all you'd find is meat."

Jannes stiffened. "Sir, if you have no further orders for me at this moment, I will complete this report and file it for Draka Sortie."

"Certainly. Will you also prepare the service for Gkanonriu? We'll conduct the burial at dawn."

Jannes flipped through the notes on his clipboard and scribbled. "Gkanonriu, did you say? Manner of death? Was he the only one? Any injured?"

JJC gestured to the clipboard. "Just Gkanonriu. Took an arrow in the neck, through a port on the gun deck. Of course, losing even one's bad enough. No other injuries, at least none reported yet. I'm sure everyone's banged up a bit." He turned to the sailors. "Well fought men, well fought! As you know, we lost Tanna Gkanonriu. He fought bravely, and he actually launched the most harpoons in the engagement--twenty-four."

Cheers went up. More crew assembled.

"We are the last balloon ship! Tomorrow we'll have the burial service for Tanna, and following that, and in his honor, we'll have a celebration of our final victory. First mate Jannes here has been laboring mightily to plan the service and the celebration, both of which will be major, holy offerings to Draka Sortie!"

More cheers. Jannes went pale at the added duties, but then nodded, seeing that his captain might have saved the combat-absent statistician from yet another late-night beating by unknown assailants. "Yes, sir."

"We're now at nineteen crew," JJC said, "counting you and me."

"A most propitious prime number," Jannes said. "I'll add that fact to the services tomorrow."

"Yap! Yap yap!"

Jannes squinted at the dog. "Of course, inviting the *meat dog* will throw that number off."

JJC grinned, admiring the son of a bitch's snotty comeback

two seconds after being rescued by his captain. He thought to
clap Jannes heartily on the shoulder, but just couldn't bring
himself to do so. "Yes, let's throw the number off a bit. The men
won't care."

"And your *sex dolls* would bring us to twenty-two," Jannes
said. "Definitely not prime."

JJC blinked. Then laughed. "I certainly hope you weren't
entertaining them in your quarters during the Final Battle!"

"*Sir!*" Jannes gasped, and JJC swore he heard the first mate
click his heels. "I know we enjoy our friendly jesting, but to
suggest--sir, I mean, to suggest--"

"Oh, just pulling your leg, Jannes. Run along and get to your
report and the services for tomorrow."

"To suggest that I--with--with *wooden robots!*"

"Yap yap yap!"

"Enough," JJC said, turning away. "We'll descend to refuel
and do Gkanonriu's burial at 0800 hours, then come up to
twenty-five hundred feet for the celebration."

"Yes, sir, yes," Jannes gulped. "I would just like to say--I
know you have unjustly accused me of--but I have to say that
your *wooden dolls* were definitely not in evidence today! Not at
all! Whereas I--to write the reports--requiring full concentration,
I mean, an enormous, *enormous* duty to--to Draka himself! Sir!"

"Enough," Jonathan James repeated. "I'm heading to the
Holy Chamber to meditate on our good fortune today."

CHAPTER THIRTEEN
The Holy Chamber

Jonathan James descended stairs to the gun deck, then down to the cargo hold. *Armageddon,* fifty-five feet wide and a hundred fifty long, lurched in a sharp breeze, and he grabbed a glowing lantern swinging on a wall. He didn't need a light; like all Wounded, his eyes employed sophisticated sensors for navigation through darkness. But carrying a lantern into the Holy Chamber seemed appropriate. He moved through small storage rooms packed with dusty crates, unlocked a thick wooden door, and stepped onto rough red stone.

Tiny pebbles of light on the black central square beyond gave off a cold, barely discernable luminescence. Ignoring the unease they always roused, he held the kerosene lamp high and slowly circled the 43.2-by-43.2-foot chamber, shielded to port and starboard by a foot of stone and 4.9 feet of the hardest Ailyuae timber. He touched all sixteen side lanterns along the brown stone walls to set the Holy Chamber glowing with yellow beauty. On the gray stone front wall, three giant black rectangles each housed three oil lanterns. At his approach these flared up and the rectangles shone like sunlight through curtained windows. He'd only seen these nine lanterns lit twice before, after major victories.

A figure in white stepped from an alcove to the left of the rectangles.

"Laurie!" JJC said. "What are you doing down here?"

The slight, red-haired robot smiled shyly. "I figured you'd want the Chamber ready for the Meditation. And I knew you'd want to light the lamps yourself. I filled the side ones with the yellow-burning oil as customary." She pointed to the lamps in the rectangles. "And those with the white."

JJC fought the urge to take Laurie into his arms. She looked so fetching in that thin acolyte's robe, her long red hair brushing hard little breasts looming deliciously dark under the gauzy fabric. Her bright blue eyes glittered in the dim lantern light. Everyone knew there could be no sex in the Holy Chamber. Yet didn't she have to want it as much as he did right now? He was the captain, the final, highest Wounded. Couldn't he suspend the rules this time?

She met his eyes and held them a long time in full understanding. "No, we may not do that. And certainly not as preparations for the Celebration are underway." She indicated the glossy central area, the black stone measuring 35.4 by 35.4 feet, its surface mathematically flat in contrast to the rough crimson rock of the 3.9-foot walkways around the square, which were inscribed with ancient Alpha Centaurian symbols, as were the stone walls.

The black square's billions of opalescent white dots glowed. Laurie had already sprinkled the black nine-inch sphere in the front left quadrant with the orange powder of the hallucinogenic Myuio plant. A whiff of that would render a normal human being permanently insane, though it had never affected Trotter. For a humanoid Wounded robot, though, Myuio produced a pleasant intoxication. It would take a few hours for the Myuio spores to penetrate the entire chamber in time for the Celebration tomorrow. His victorious crew of nineteen would set foot in here for the first time in 158 years. Yes, they deserved a bit of that transcendence. JJC wouldn't have forgotten the Myuio, but he was touched that his Laurie had prepared it on her own initiative.

Jonathan James studied the coarse red walkways around the central square. The huge symbols over the front black rectangles proclaimed, in ancient Kjurian: SPHERE ... UNINHABIT ... SCALE ... UNIVERSE ...

"For the life of me," he said, "I still can't understand why we're still carting around this piece of crap." He'd long since deciphered the huge symbols from that dead Alpha Centaurian language. Inscribed on the walkways and carved all along the walls, they'd never sparked his interest, though every Wounded robot on this planet seemed to believe this chamber held some undefinable mystic revelation.

"You must never let any of the crew ever hear you say things like that," Laurie said. "This is art. It serves a purpose."

"I know, I know. But does this crew really not understand

that they're worshipping all sorts of ancient sagas from the Milky Way? The ins and outs of Alpha Centaurian genealogy and all the idiotic battles they fought? All the stupid geography of Lxser that goes on *forever?*"

"All they know is that the legends came from *up there.*" Laurie pointed to the gray stone ceiling. "They worship that galaxy. Everyone here does."

"Do you?"

She laughed. "No, I've definitely spent way too much time talking to you! But we need to observe the rites for the sake of the crew."

JJC scanned the Holy Chamber. Lxser was the Centaurians' name for Proxima Centauri. A hundred thousand years ago its fourth planet Kjurax had developed the original telepathic Grid; some thirty thousand years ago they'd sculpted this chamber. The glorious Kjur had expanded their empire until they met the Zarj of Sirius A, and thus the tales on the walls ended. After exterminating the Kjur, the Zarj fashioned their Grid into a masterpiece of fascist control, in the process claiming they alone had invented it. Yet even the impulsive, narcissistic Zarj were eventually assimilated themselves, their Grid appropriated by hackers of the Tarl species who used it to force a union of seventeen suns into a wider Alpha Centaurian Empire.

"No wonder SolGrid blew up in Pat's stupid face," JJC muttered. "What a fool."

"Patrick James?" Laurie said. "Your old enemy? Why speak of him now, dearest?"

"I don't know. Just thinking about the Kjur, I guess. Pat always wanted to believe he hacked the SolGrid code from the original Kjurian Grid." He shivered. Why was that twit coming up again? Who cared about him or anyone else from that forgotten life? Why was finishing the final battle dredging up this old karma?

"Right!" Laurie laughed. "The *benevolent* Grid. But what he really got was the totally weaponized Tarl version."

JJC grimaced. Yes, even now so many among his crew wanted to believe in the placid, all-wise Kjur. What Alpha

Centauri might have evolved into if the Kjur had survived the Zarj and the Tarl. Then again, who cared? That was all ancient history of the Milky Way. It had no bearing on Ailyuae or the final battle.

He studied the black central square. It was obviously the Kjur's conception of a map of the universe. It was dazzling and accurate in its depiction of the Sol-AC stars, the Milky Way, and the Local Group of galaxies immediately beyond, once you knew how to translate the two-dimensional scheme into three.

All his captains had confessed they had no clue how this chamber had found its way to the Large Magellanic Cloud. Nobody had discovered a similar map on any enemy ship, or if they had, they'd been killed before they could spread the news. So JJC's star map was unique. The ancient wisdom of the Kjur now belonged to him. He commanded an entire planet. Yet he had no idea what to do next.

"Who in his right mind would've thought to add thousands of useless pounds of *stone* to the ballast of a ship?" JJC muttered, mesmerized by the tiny white stars against black stone. Billions of points of light seemed to trace spidery connections, delineating vast uncanny structures, unknowable relationships between alien species. Infinite webs of possibilities. Communication? Commerce? Alliances? Wars?

Laurie shrugged. "Everyone knows that ADE gas is more than enough to carry the Chamber. Your sailors are certain Draka ordained it that way, and that he chose *Armageddon* to carry his sacred cargo."

"Sheesh. Don't tell me you're starting to believe this Draka crap."

"Of course not. But it obviously has its uses in controlling your crew." She pointed to the near-left corner of the map. "It's interesting the Kjur placed themselves here, instead of the center. These first dots are obviously their own stars, then moving on the dots begin representing not stars, but sections of the Milky Way, then neighboring galaxies, then other galactic groups beyond. Amazing they could represent it all on a two-dimensional map. Of course the scale keeps changing. Every few inches a new order of magnitude is introduced and it's hard to fathom, but the implication arises that the further from the corner we go, each dot represents any one species' observable universe, as galaxies recede faster than the speed of light as the universe keeps expanding. The furthest dots may then represent alternative universes."

JJC gaped in alarm as Laurie slipped into High Intuitive Mode. Dammit, it might take all night to maneuver her back to Willing Sex Partner. She was brilliant and insightful, but did she have to pull this BS now? She was so beautiful. God, he wanted her. Who cared about all this star map theorizing?

"The truly strange concept," she continued, "if this supposition is true, is that the light from any of the far dots would never have reached any other dots. How could the Kjur possibly know what's out there?"

"Well," JJC chuckled uneasily, "there's also the other school of thought, that after coming up with a decent map of their Local Group, the Kjur essentially made pretty lights out to the far corners."

Laurie fixed him with unreadable blue eyes in the warm glowing lantern lights. "We know the Kjur were excellent astronomers. The layout of this map also indicates that they were also aware of the nonexistence of time at the quantum level."

"W-*what?*" JJC gasped. He'd never heard *that* from her before.

"No, listen," she rolled on, "the Kjur were the first telepathic Alpha Centaurians. My theory is that Kjur knew that telepathy and non-time have to be related. So it's possible their telepathic Grid enabled them to build this map of the universe, even the parts that have moved beyond our horizon. After all, they would have had an infinite amount of time--or non-time-- to explore all that."

"Then--then why would they make *that?*" he said, straining to get past the relentless, unexpected Intuitive Mode in her eyes. JJC stabbed a finger at the glossy black sphere he'd been doing his best to ignore as he always did. Now covered with orange dust, the nine-inch-wide obsidian ball seemed unusually sinister.

"I mean, it's just a damn sculpture, right? *Why the hell's it placed exactly on Wiioryvel?*"

CHAPTER FOURTEEN
The Uninhabitable

The glossy black sphere balanced on an infinitesimal point a few inches past the dots representing the Milky Way. The symbols referred to it as "The Uninhabitable" or "The Unknowing," sometimes as "The Death" or "The Forbidden Zone," and once simply as "Non." It was often easy to miss against the black star map background, but now the bright light from the front rectangles gave the sphere an extra curved reflection. It was no bigger than a basketball. JJC had once tried to pick it up, but it was immobile, even though his Class J senses confirmed that the sphere was *not* attached to the floor, which he could measure as uniformly smooth down to a millionth of an inch. The ball had never moved a micron through eight hundred years of battles on this ship.

"I know many among the crew feel Draka must have made the sphere himself," Laurie finally replied. "But I've often wondered if the sphere really isn't an ancient Kjurian *prediction* of the Wounded. After all, the full name of this map translates to *Map of the Habitable*. As if the Kjur were scouting out possibilities for where their species could live. And what to avoid on the way."

"But it's obvious the Kjur are depicting it in a higher dimension than the 3-D universe," Jonathan James protested, trying to match her cold jargon but hearing his voice rising in panic. "Do we really know where it is? Or *what* it is? And why it seems to be on top of *us?*"

Laurie nodded. "Ah, yes. One must try to wrap one's head around the fact that this three-dimensional spherical rendition is situated on a two-dimensional map, and so what would it represent in an actual three-dimensional space? But I think the Kjur knew that while a nine-inch-sphere on a 1,253.16-square-foot surface is taking up a definite amount of space, it's certainly not taking up *too* much of the universe. It's just something deadly to be avoided. Something no living thing can inhabit." She shrugged. "I don't know why the Kjur put it on Wiioryvel.

Maybe this n-dimensional structure has some physical 3-D manifestation in our system, like touching it at one point. Who knows?"

JJC shivered. He'd had that thought himself but had never dared voice it. Why was this damn chamber getting to him again? Had lighting the lamps done it? Was it because they made him take a good look at this slick black basketball? Why had it always scared him? He was a Wounded, after all. Something hinting at annihilation should feel warm and comfortable, shouldn't it?

He felt Laurie's hard fingers on his forearm. "Hey," she said, inexplicably downshifting to her usual low sensuous pitch. "Are you okay? We don't need to discuss all this now."

"I--I'm okay. I just want to get the Celebration over with, and--get on with life, I guess."

What life? he wondered. He could set course for Iilpwal Island and they could anchor *Armageddon* to the trees. Then what?

"Tell you what, dearest, I suggest you not worry about any of this. The Celebration will go fine. Take some time here to meditate, and then I'll meet you in our quarters in a few minutes."

JJC's heart quickened at the way she'd said "our quarters," not "the captain's." He shunned Dorell's luxurious cabin on the quarterdeck, though he kept it for show. Instead he'd carved himself an immense space ahead of the Holy Chamber, beyond the dark vestibule Laurie had entered earlier. Forty-five by forty-five feet of open space, with those intoxicatingly bright brass lanterns JJC had fashioned himself. Soon he'd have his lovely Laurie there. Her eyes melted like his into desire. No, not here, it couldn't be in the Holy Chamber. The Myuio had been poured, the Ceremony begun. And though the star map under their feet seemed to pulsate with yearning, there was no way could he lay his wooden robot on that surface now. But in thirty minutes, after he'd completed the Meditation, it would all happen.

He studied the glossy tan surface of Laurie's face. To build a wooden robot had seemed farcical to everyone from the lowest mate to any of the captains JJC had served under. But the deep themes, the raw forces pulsing within him, had demanded he hew her from whatever materials this planet offered.

He'd inherited those themes from both Ballard and T'ohj'puv. Parts of their souls still surged deep inside him, especially the twisted Ballard soul brandishing a lust no other Wounded robot had ever been programmed for.

Certainly Wounded could perform sexual acts. Romantic romps were often necessary to a spy mission, but no sailor of Ailyuae ever wanted them. JJC was the exception. Since the Ballard soul was so sure Laurie Lachrer was the ultimate lay, JJC swelled with that carnal hunger as well. So he'd built this copy. He called her Laurie 1014 because in memorizing every scrap of information from the *Garrison* computers he'd found that there'd originally been 1,013 Heroes and Villains of the Thirties robot copies of Laurie Lachrer.

His own Laurie was fashioned from a hundred varieties of Ailyuae wood, her nerve cells and sinews extruded from select Ailyuae grasses, the slick enchanting body powered by ADE chambers secured inside bits of the increasingly rare metals on the planet. Yes, her skin was hard, but not inflexible. Those lovely breasts were stiff, but they softened under his fingers. And when the sex program was running, everything swelled properly, everything moistened, and her gasps of delight echoed his every mad thrust.

And he'd made sure she was as sharp as the original Laurie. No matter Jannes' sneers, this was no sex doll. Laurie 1014 could easily function as his master navigator. But for now he'd assigned her to be Acolyte to the Chamber, and the crew accepted that. They'd even put up with her when he'd been an ordinary ensign and she'd lived in stasis under his bunk along with his other robot. He hadn't been able to flaunt them until he'd become captain.

He laughed.

"What's so amusing?" Laurie said, coming up for a quick kiss. "I know I shouldn't have done that, but I just couldn't resist!"

JJC set her back with a gentle squeeze of those delightful breasts. "I couldn't resist *this,* either. You'd better run along now or we *will* desecrate this place." He shrugged. "As for what's funny, it's just that I pictured Jannes worried that I'll make you first mate."

"I'd certainly do a better job! Oh, well, enough of all this. I'll meet you in our bedroom." She gave him another fast kiss and whirled, the bright lanterns at the front of the room briefly going through that transparent robe, giving JJC a tantalizing glimpse of the outline of her slim supple back and her tiny, exquisitely sculpted wooden ass.

"*God* ..." he groaned as she disappeared into the alcove. How had he been able to create the flawless woman? She was his second robot, so much more subtly made, so much more intelligent than the first. Though he'd always been nauseated at how much of Rick Ballard's rotten soul festered inside him, he was fueled by Ballard's endlessly deep, unslaked desire.

He groaned to consider how far he'd fallen. What about Suzette Borman, the fated lover from centuries ago? Certainly long dead, no matter how much Sol rejuvenation technology had improved, and lost to JJC forever in any case, as there was no way to build spaceships and get off this dying ocean world.

Yet Suzette had been *the one,* the primary force of his life. They'd both known that, though they'd never openly declared it. She'd held him together in the raw madness following his idiotic quest to become fascist Emperor of Alpha Centauri. She'd kept him rational in the loss of one of his *Garthah-/yuu* brothers, the evil but honorable Clopt. She'd loved him in a way he'd never thought possible.

Fate had ripped them apart and shoved Laurie 1014 between them. In any case Suzette had been human and he was now Wounded, the enemy of all that was human. Her life had been dedicated to growth and understanding, while he'd morphed into a dynamo of obliteration. He was just like that terrifying, undefined black sphere squatting on the intricate beauty of the Kjurian star map.

He'd never considered building a Suzette robot. That

would've been a sacrilege. He was gifted with enhanced charisma and intelligence as a J, but he lacked the higher-class techniques for building his own fully functional Wounded robots. He'd become painfully aware that Class J's needed much additional training to develop their powers. There were huge gaps in his understanding that even Captain Sullf hadn't been able to remedy, and so JJC had been winging it for eight hundred years. He'd used some of his talents to improve weaponry, but could only go so far. He'd jury-rigged the construction of the wooden robots as he went along. The final results looked more or less human, but anyone could see they were in fact much like dolls.

No wonder Jannes sneered. Jonathan James was building sex dolls instead of fulfilling whatever crackpot religious insanity the *Armageddon* crew seemed to want.

God, he was ruined. The ship was ruined. How had that damn myth ever gotten started? Draka had died over eight hundred years ago, in fact, JJC calculated, he'd died 308 days before JJC had fled the Milky Way, his July 10, 2075 shattergun death fully documented by JJC's own father. Yet the myth of Draka had somehow gotten here across 163,000 light-years to shock and amaze low-class Wounded. How did the concept of Class A Draka Sortie get balled up with an ancient Kjurian map? How did this damn map get here in the first place?

How had his sailors come to believe that Draka Sortie had discovered the nature of dark energy and had created its opposite, anti-dark energy? That he'd supposedly suspended all known physics to make a solar system in the Large Magellanic Cloud, separated from other stars by a dozen empty light-years, where electricity was absolutely nonexistent down to the subatomic level?

Well, let the fools believe this nonsense. JJC knew ADE existed; his Class J senses verified it down to the atoms of Ailyuae, as well as those in the sun Wiioryvel. As he saw it, billions of these renegade nonelectrical systems probably propagated spontaneously throughout the universe. These systems lacked positive or negative qualities, attraction or repulsion, or quarks with one-third charges. He just happened to have gotten stranded in one of them, with every particle in him and his dog converting to ADE processes. It was likely that Wounded robots were attracted to such anti-dark-energy systems. That was probably how Ailyuae got settled.

But the degenerating robots of this sorry world obviously needed a myth, so they'd kept alive the concept of an ancient Draka Sortie as the divine creator of this whole mess.

But now the Celebration loomed, and JJC had to lead it. He'd wiped out the last enemy, and his crew believed he'd fulfilled the Will of Draka. JJC had no idea what he'd just fulfilled. He thought back all those hundreds of years to when Captain Sullf had brought JJC and Trotter onboard after coming across the glinting wreckage of the *Garrison* on a reef. He'd seen something vital in JJC, tolerated his eccentricities and his dog, and he'd moved JJC up in rank. There'd been resistance over the centuries, including captains who despised and sometimes demoted the newbie, but over time JJC had been accepted as a unique asset to *Armageddon*.

Without much thought he'd taken on more responsibility for the ship, running its dull daily routines as well as fighting in over two hundred battles. To his surprise, the crew readily accepted him as captain when Captain Dorell suicided, and within three days he'd mastered command. Maybe there was some subprogram in his Wounded brain that blossomed the instant he declared himself in charge. His authority was secure, but so what? It was clearer than ever that the only thing left for them all was extermination.

Jonathan James shook his head. He wasn't meditating. He was just letting his brain race out of control as he woozily stared into the unfathomable map of the universe.

All these thoughts had taken place in the seconds since Laurie had crossed so transparently before the light. Soon he'd kiss those bewitching shoulder blades. Soon he'd hold her from behind, fingers roving up her taut tummy to fondle those enticing stiff breasts. The door to the bedroom beyond was just clicking shut. JJC could ignore the Thirty Minutes Meditation, he could chase her down and yes, she'd chide him for not doing the Meditation, but she'd take him into her arms, she'd pull him atop her on the bed, and he'd moan "Laurie! Laurie!" as he'd moaned every night for the last 570 years, ever since he'd put the final touches on his filthy, intoxicating creation.

He was insane. Why did he never moan "Suzette! Suzette!"

Another door click came from behind. JJC turned to the smirk of the thick crimson lips of wooden robot Rick Ballard in the purple and red robes of the High Priest of the Holy Chamber.

CHAPTER FIFTEEN
Enter Ballard

"M'lord," robot Ballard spoke deeply as he bowed, his russet hood showing only chiseled wooden cheekbones. "I have come to initiate the Night Watch of the Celebration." JJC stared back at the six-foot-four robot with the taut build of a world-class sprinter. He felt the ship rocking in the wind. The lamps flickered. Shipboard balance came easily to Jonathan James, but he noted the robot seemed to have anticipated the wind and now excelled JJC in subtly repositioning the smallest muscles to appear as if no shift had been necessary. Ballard's deep-set blue eyes probed for weakness as always. That glossy blond wooden face was so damn handsome. When he'd made the robot, JJC had wanted to take some liberties and coarsen the Ballard face, but there was no way he could build the thing and be less than true to everything Ballard had been, physically, mentally, and spiritually.

What a work of art Rick Ballard was. What a perfect expression he'd been. Not as refined, not as subtle as Laurie 1014, but in so many ways, so much more *effective.*

"Look, I'm not quite done with the Meditation," JJC finally replied, peering past Ballard to the dark stone walls in the dim wavering light. He hoped Ballard would take the hint and go away. Why couldn't Jonathan James bring himself to order his robot to depart? He couldn't bear to have Ballard watch him head for his bedroom door.

JJC wished for the thousandth time that Henry Jannes and Ballard would come to blows on the upper deck. So often he'd pictured them, maddened by a circle of cheering sailors who knew how much they despised each other, the two grunting with wild desperate swings, then both spinning dizzily and pitching over the gunwale, flailing thousands of feet to an ocean which would receive them like concrete. Not likely with their fine robotic equilibrium, but still, quite a satisfying image.

There was no way JJC could ever deactivate his own creation, much as Ballard was a constant nemesis. His fantasy had Jannes doing it for him. If Jannes killed Ballard, JJC would probably have to express a certain amount of grief, but he'd certainly be glad to be done with the unendurable High Priest. If Ballard killed Jannes, and there was nothing in his programming preventing him from doing so, JJC would still have the endless plague of Rick Ballard, but at least Jannes would be excised from this planet, and there'd be an end to his insipid snickering about *sex toys*. High Priest Ballard was certainly nobody's sex toy, but Jannes, knowing along with the rest of the crew of JJC's relationship with Laurie, took pleasure in hinting to all that JJC and the two robots were a threesome.

It was revolting. Nobody but Jannes dared insinuate anything about JJC's sexuality, and though Jonathan James always returned his first mate's mockery with equal disrespect, it galled him that everyone on this ship saw his need for Laurie.

"M'lord, I will assist you in the Meditation if you wish," Ballard spoke with another bow, obviously inclined to go nowhere. "It's necessary for you to complete the Meditation before I commence the Night Watch of the Celebration."

JJC stared at the galactic patterns at his feet. "Aw, crap on the goddamn Night Watch of the Celebration."

"I see that you're unhappy, even in your victory. Don't be ashamed. This is a common feeling after great accomplishment."

JJC shivered in the damp darkness. "Look, I don't need this. Not now. God, why the hell did I ever build you?"

"We've been over this before, m'lord," Ballard replied from the shadows of his hood. "Many times."

"Too many times," JJC muttered, flinching at the robot's switch to unctuous, soothing pastoral tones.

"Ah, yes. Too many times. Just as you've repeated to a succession of captains that you build robots *only as a hobby*. Eight captains, some of whom found your hobby amusing, others whom it disgusted."

"Sullf understood me, at least."

"But even to Sullf you maintained it was just something to occupy your so-called *artistic urges* during the long stretches of boredom between enemy engagements, isn't that correct? But in reality, you were so oppressed by what we've both come to know as the *Ballard forces* churning within you that you came up with the brilliant idea of transferring them all into another robot."

"Goddammit, you can't mock me. You're a goddamn priest."

"But I must be honest with all my charges, even you, dear master. In any case, Sullf watched you go to work with amazement. He knew you had untrained Class J knowledge of robotics, but he was sure you lacked the raw materials here on Ailyuae, and he certainly wasn't going to use his Class H powers to assist you in any way, now was he? And didn't you resent him for that? I remember the look of astonishment in his eyes when you activated me. When I opened my eyes for the first time and beheld the shock in his. You made me out of Ailyuae's *plant life.* He was astounded at your accomplishment. But not for long, of course. Wasn't it just two weeks later when the harpoon from the *Devastator* took him in the heart and blew him over the gunwale, four thousand feet up?"

JJC closed his eyes.

"He was really the only captain who ever understood you, wasn't he? He knew I was more than just a hobby. He shared your relief that you'd successfully poured the *Ballard crap* out of yourself. But in fact, you really hadn't." The High Priest emitted a rueful chuckle. "I recall your horror upon discovering you'd really just made an exterior *copy* of Rick Ballard. You retained the original inside yourself after all. What you so tactfully call the *malevolent Ballard force,* even to my face."

"Look, just stop. We've been through all this. I need to do the Meditation and get out of here." He realized his mistake in even eyeing the door to his and Laurie's special room.

Ballard picked up the direction of his glance and leered. "Ah, yes, so now there are *two* Rick Ballards, with, shall we say, *identical* interests."

JJC closed his eyes. When the painful realization had set in that both Rick Ballard and the T'ohj'puv robot had vast fortified partitions within him, JJC had thought he could create algorithms to erase those sections, but discovered after some mild test deletions that the other two were permanent foundations of his Wounded mind. Then he'd postulated that Rick Ballard might at least be transferred to exterior storage, freeing up more memory for JJC himself. The T'ohj'puv partition was cold and mechanical, but full of interesting knowledge along with a dry sense of humor, and that entity didn't grate on JJC nearly as much as the obnoxious, ego-bloated former *Typhoon VI* navigator. A Ballard robot would be the first test of an exterior mind drive. It had taken him fifty-five years to complete.

The High Priest never tired of reminding JJC that he'd simply doubled the malevolent Ballard force. But both had been stunned to find that the copying had uncovered a previously unknown part of Ballard's personality, something the original human Ballard had never known: that beneath Rick Ballard's compulsive need to seduce every woman he encountered was a buried yearning for religious transcendence. This spiritual quest had exploded full force in both the Ballard copy as well as JJC, though Jonathan James suspected the compulsive holiness had found more fertile ground in the plant-based networks of Ballard's wooden soul.

Jonathan James, for example, could register his inner Ballard's heights of aesthetic communion with the divine, as well as shame at his own lusts and sins, but somehow he'd fashioned enough mental workarounds to shrug all that off and do whatever he wished in daily life. The Ballard robot on the other hand was so crippled with the thought of his shortcomings before God that JJC knew he'd never make a move on his second, more ingenious robot, though Ballard frequently chortled that his desire for Laurie 1014 was by definition as great as Jonathan James' own.

JJC's first captain Sullf must have known all this in the short time he had left. He must have seen Jonathan James' failure to purge himself of the Ballard malady. He must have known that JJC's desperate plea to create an Office of the High Priest aboard *Armageddon,* an office all subsequent captains felt bound to honor, was a way of separating himself from proximity to his foul twin.

JJC had known and honored Alrtu Sullf for fifty-five years. He'd never gotten over the fact that Sullf died right after JJC completed his endless tinkering on the wooden Ballard. He'd always wondered if creating Ballard hadn't somehow killed Sullf. Displaced him, psychologically shattered his core beliefs, made his Class H existence meaningless, who knew? JJC would've sacrificed Ballard in an instant to get Sullf back.

"Listen, Rick," he said, aware that he hadn't addressed his High Priest by first name in years, "I just need to get this Meditation thing done. Maybe if you and I didn't discuss this sort of stuff anymore. And, like, go our separate ways, you know. I mean, of course you're Priest aboard this ship, but ... hell, I don't know."

"Perhaps," Ballard mused. "I know I give offense to you on a daily basis, master. However, as your High Priest, I have to take confession from you and everyone else on the ship. Even, of course, Miss Laurie."

"Okay, okay, I'm confessing, now, okay? I'm sorry about every goddamn thing, okay? Now look, I need to meditate a while if we're going to bring off the Celebration tomorrow." JJC thought to end the conversation with a brisk walk to the bedroom door but froze just in time. Ballard could *not* witness that. He willed himself to remain motionless but he knew Ballard's practiced eyes assessed how rigidly he stood.

"You know, I wonder if you shouldn't emulate the Ywritt and immerse yourself in quantum computing," Ballard mused. "Now that we're done with our little war here. Now that you're the top Wounded of Ailyuae. Perhaps all that's left for you is a kind of fantasy life. Couldn't you just sleep peacefully in your cabin while your quantum algorithms bring forth a simulacrum of some quiet agricultural world in our glorious Large Magellanic Cloud? Something like your childhood Andertwin around Procyon A? I know you've wished so earnestly for that, master. To just settle down with Laurie and be a farmer. Why don't you go for it? I'm sure Miss Laurie would accompany you.

At least in your quantum fantasy, because of course in reality she'd have to remain here on this ship."

"Yeah, with *you*. With *your* fantasies," JJC shot back, stepping close to catch any hint of remorse in the robot's smooth blue marble eyes. But he found nothing. He'd made his plant-based contraption all too well, down to replicating the huge genital endowments that had so thrilled many a feminine victim over the forty-four years of Ballard's icky human existence. The sex and the religion in the High Priest were irresistible. The damn thing had long ago mastered the blank look of affronted dignity mixed with divine revelation. That imperturbable look was in turn encased in such a gorgeously sharp facial sculpture, affixed atop such a powerful chest, mounted in turn on that insatiable tight bulge at the crotch, firm muscled ass behind, strong runner's legs below. Even the robot's big feet in those glossy black boots proclaimed overpowering virility.

Certainly Laurie 1014 wasn't impressed, was she? Anyone onboard *Armageddon* could see the Ballard robot staring after her with mournful unrequited desire. Surely she had no interest in Ballard's dark impulses. After all, she had JJC's own to contend with. She always reported when Ballard was mooning after her. She always said he was ridiculous. She always declared she was programmed to love JJC and no other.

"Ah, well," Ballard said. "We must both be penitent. We must both overcome our sins." But his tone was that of a scientist describing some property of the universe reducible to mathematical equations. It was as if he was troubled by something in his own programming and thought there must be a software solution to it.

Then again, didn't that describe JJC himself? "Dammit, how did I ever wind up here? On this goddamned dying planet?"

"Your motivation was to escape Iota Persei as fast as you could," Ballard said, slipping back into pastoral care mode. "And to get away from that malevolent Amy woman who botched our separation process so thoroughly. Though she was a J like yourself, you still hadn't accepted your J Wounded nature and so sought to flee. You had enough J knowledge to upgrade the *Garrison* and essentially let it take you wherever it thought best. Though you abdicated responsibility for your final destination in your panic, your actions were all quite understandable."

"Yeah. Thanks so much," Jonathan James sneered.

"No, really, consider how fortunate you were. The *Garrison's* autopilot found a habitable planet and even managed to find a stretch of somewhat dry land to crash on."

JJC reluctantly nodded. It had been a miracle. How had the *Garrison's* primitive AI located a planet with orbit, diameter, and surface gravity identical to Earth's? With breathable oxygen, albeit polluted with ADE gas? Jonathan James recalled gripping his abruptly lax controls in dismay, staring at blank consoles as the ship's electrical systems became inexplicably *undefined*. In the millisecond before total destruction the ship had applied enough reverse thrust to plow intact into a reef not a mile from where *Armageddon* was refueling its ADE tanks.

"But I'm just trapped here," he finally said. "I don't belong here. I don't have Suzette. Eight hundred damn years of fighting. And now I'm at the top. So what?"

"Ah, my dear master, we've been through all so many, many times," Ballard soothed. "But you've accomplished marvelous things here. You've risen in the hierarchy, and you've created *wondrous* wooden robots."

"Yeah. A couple robots. Upgrading some weapons systems. Designing some better balloon sealants. Fun little inventions. Great. Put it on my résumé. Oh, right, I rejuved my dog, too. Add that in. But I never got my Class J training. Never came up to my J potential." He shrugged. "Hell, I never came up to my *Jonathan James* potential. Screw it all. The damn planet's doomed. The ADE's gonna eat us all."

"Master, do you really think you can meditate properly in this pissy little mood?"

"I don't care. I just don't care anymore."

"Do you seriously think Laurie will accept you in this state?"

JJC glared, restraining himself from making a fist. There

was a possibility his strong Wounded body could take Ballard's wooden head off with one swing, but the robot's reflexes were fantastic and Ballard would probably duck in time. And after any overt act of violence, they'd need to perform the Reunion Ceremony. JJC and his inner Ballard partition would have to merge with the outer Ballard and apologize, and they'd all essentially have to *be each other* for as long as it took to smooth all the crap out. JJC shuddered. He hadn't had to do *that* with Ballard in a hundred years.

"I certainly don't wish to rile my exalted captain and master," Ballard said, stepping back, obviously understanding JJC's mood and probably, JJC thought, wishing to avoid Reunion as well. "But as High Priest it's my duty to hear your confession and propose new paths to spiritual well-being. For instance, isn't it about time you came to grips with your special T'ohj'puv karma?"

JJC stared back. "Don't--don't go there."

"As High Priest I must specifically call your attention to the most unexpected side effect of your *other* robot's creation, that fact that that a second partition of T'ohj'puv was inadvertently created and deposited--"

"No! We *will not* discuss it!"

"Deposited into the *core* of our beautiful Laurie 1014!"

"I never intended that! Goddammit, I was just asking T'ohj'puv to *assist* me with the mind! Laurie was going to be perfect! Perfect!"

"And then he fell *into* her! He copied himself *into* her! Laurie 1014 *is* T'ohj'puv! Admit it! For God's sake admit that we both love her! We both love T'ohj'puv!"

"God, no ..." JJC whispered. "This really can't be any sort of *final description.*"

"Ah, dear master, how you've deluded yourself. You've constantly wished to ascribe Laurie's marvelous knowledge of ancient archeology, of astrophysics and cosmology--not to mention that uncanny grasp of nuclear chemistry--to some deep sensitivity based on your distorted memories of your time in Alpha Centauri."

"No! You can't say it!"

"When in fact, as T'ohj'puv, she not only began with marvelous ancient Martian knowledge but increased that a millionfold when she plundered all the Ywritt libraries on our little trip there eight hundred years ago. You know the Ywritt collected every scrap of AC culture they could find. So naturally Laurie has it all memorized."

"*No* ..." Jonathan James gasped into Ballard's triumphant laugh. But he could no longer deny it. Yes, just as there were two Ballards, there were two T'ohj'puvs. He'd spent 133 years on his second robot, had finished her 570 years ago, and deep down he'd known this truth all along. Dammit to hell, who knew an unfeeling robot could have such a sexy female core? How could Jonathan James make love to that mechanical monstrosity every night? Was the deep T'ohj'puv inside him simply screwing the deep T'ohj'puv in Laurie? Was a machine just playing with its own software gonads?

He whirled to the glossy black sphere on the floor, at the obscene orange powder sprinkled atop it. "*That's* what it is! *That's* what did all this! This is all it can ever be! Just *darkness!* Just something awful, and *killing!* Death is always coming out of that goddamn thing!"

"Oh, dear me, my captain, surely a big strong Wounded conqueror like you isn't afraid of this little black sculpture here?" Ballard mocked.

"Get out! I need to do the goddamn Meditation!" JJC screamed, so loudly that Laurie in the next room had to hear. The whole ship had to hear. But Laurie was waiting for the *T'ohj'puv copulation.* So wondrously feminine, so inviting, so nurturing, so naked and glossy.

Ballard followed JJC's gaze to the bedroom. "Master, you know I must stay here until dawn. According to the Rites, I cannot leave. But I hereby absolve you of your sins and give you Holy Indulgence. I thus declare that our lively discussion here tonight has, in fact, been your Meditation. You are free to go to your next duties." He pointed a long muscled arm to the dark vestibule to JJC's secret room.

Defeated once again, the foremost Wounded of Ailyuae accepted his absolution. Head down, he clomped his boots across the ancient stone, past the killing sphere, to his wretched sanctuary.

CHAPTER SIXTEEN
Tri-Sage

Over the endless unknown centuries, in the absence of electricity, there had been no wireless communication between Wounded robots. Certainly a wooden mechanism possessed nothing like that. Yet Rick Ballard had been in that room so often, and had observed Jonathan James Commer and Laurie Lachrer 1014 in Romantic Mode so many thousands of times, that it was easy for him to create his own quantum computing fantasy of what was taking place in the other chamber. He'd hardly been able to wait for JJC to leave so he could begin to fantasize.

Though there was nothing between any sailor robots approaching mindreading, they'd all spent millennia observing each other's most minute habits. And even though Ballard had only 745 years of practice, and Laurie 570, that was also more than enough time to learn how to read everyone. Even a despicable enemy like Henry Jannes.

Surely Jonathan James had to know how close Rick Ballard was to Laurie 1014. Surely Jonathan James knew how well Ballard could flow into his wooden sister's every gasp of pleasure.

Before JJC had become captain, back when he'd been assigned to officers' quarters or later the first mate's stateroom, he'd put the plant-based sibling robots into stasis each night and thrust them under his bunk. What did Jonathan James think the two had meant to each other all that time? Even in stasis, Ballard had always felt the deep connection with Laurie, always growing stronger and more intimate. Did Jonathan James really not understand, after 570 years, that Laurie's frantic affirmations of loyalty to JJC, and her heated denials of romantic interest in Rick Ballard, were simply the party line trotted out on any occasion of JJC's jealousy? That it was all lover's boilerplate?

Laurie loved Ballard. He knew it. No, he'd never had her. It was forbidden. And yet, hadn't they made love, in his fantasies, a million times? Copulating under the bunk, hell, even on the open deck in full view of coarse Wounded sailors, and in that sacred bedroom beyond that thick black door? Ballard had even taken her to JJC's fantasy agricultural world and banged her repeatedly in the cornrows. His quantum computing faculties were laughably inferior to Jonathan James', but the virtual reality he was able to conjure was astonishingly vivid.

It seemed to take centuries for JJC to shut the door. In that room beyond, Laurie would be pertly positioned on the round bed, legs demurely parted two inches. She wore the devastating transparent green negligee, competently arranging tonight's seduction with the tools of the trade Jonathan James loved all too well.

The bedroom beyond was an immense bright square, with the same twelve-foot ceiling as the Holy Chamber. Lacking the Chamber's foot-wide stone walls, it was in fact slightly larger at 45.2 by 45.2 feet. Upon becoming captain two months ago, JJC had carved this room out of smaller storage spaces, but though he'd never admitted it, it had been obvious he'd sought to sculpt an answer to a Holy Chamber that had always made him anxious. These two huge rooms now took up almost the entirety of the cargo hold. The mainmast came right down between Chamber and bedroom, inside a five-foot-wide alcove between them. Fore and aft were other storage areas and ADE plumbing machinery, but JJC had relocated much of that to the gun deck above, oblivious to what any of his crew thought of his alterations.

The bedroom floor was glossy turquoise tile in one-foot squares, dominated by a circular structure like a squat wedding cake, three broad steps of red tile leading to a fourth level of dark blue stone. This top level, twenty feet in diameter, held a ten-foot circular bed with velvety black bedspread, as well as two small round tables, each topped with wine bottles and crystal glasses.

Four bright brass lanterns hung on each of the dark brown walls to port and starboard. At the far end was an entrance to a dressing room and a freshwater shower nobody but JJC and Laurie 1014 had ever seen. To either side of that doorway, green-blue tapestries of animals were tacked to the dark wooden slats. All else was empty space.

Jonathan James had confessed that the inspiration for this room was a haunting recurring dream. It involved a young lady he'd lost long ago but whose name he refused to divulge. But Ballard knew the tale from Laurie 1014, to whom JJC had haltingly related it.

His master dreamed of the long-dead Suzette Borman, the petite goddess with the long dark hair, the deep sensuous voice, and the delightful freckled breasts. The co-owner of Marsport's Pavlovian Response bar with her husband Lee Borman of the USSF, she'd been forty-two when JJC had taken her away from both her husband and her current lover.

Though at first glance Suzette exuded drive and high enthusiasm for any task at hand, her taut body seemed shackled with a lifetime of unceasing, virulent stress. She'd confessed to JJC several dozen affairs with the wrong men. Maybe because of that she dressed way too sexy and flirted mercilessly with every man she chanced upon, continually recreating her trauma while keeping it tantalizingly at bay.

But JJC's fascination with her had fully ensnared her. A few months after taking up with him she'd undergone rejuvenation, emerging looking nineteen, rocking every room with blazing sexual vibrations and declaring that JJC had liberated her from all previous cycles of seduction and despair. Fully a new woman, she now bequeathed every scrap of her fresh energy upon Jonathan James. Ballard remained astonished that anyone could be so freed from such a lifetime prison sentence.

The recurring dream began with JJC delighted to rediscover his lover, estranged from him for centuries, attired in a navy-blue jacket over a white blouse as transparent as air. Then, in an expensive candlelit restaurant, she removes that jacket to reveal braless breasts to him and any waiter daring to enter their private circle of light, as several do, pouring Chablis with knowing smiles.

JJC assumes he'll soon be making joyous love to Suzette, affirming their endless connection in glorious horizontal embrace, in a gigantic square room lit by dazzling warm lanterns on the walls, on the circular bed atop the wedding cake.

But instead of quick and easy love with dream Suzette, he finds himself pummeled in a nightlong argument that dredges up every possible conflict the two had ever stumbled upon in their brief relationship. Arms tightly crossed, the blue jacket tightly buttoned over all her promises, Suzette curses and snarls in ways JJC still, after eight hundred years, can't believe any woman capable of. Blindly yelling and cursing for soul-wracking hours, defending impossible positions on the cruel bed atop the terrifying wedding cake, both nevertheless sense inexplicable resolution struggling from the depths.

Then the first wild lovemaking, followed by murmurs, whispers, fondling, languorously sharing wine. Then easy, relaxed copulation with the slender dusky woman jamming atop him, going on so absurdly long that JJC finally laughs and whispers: "Let's have a little conference here." Suzette comes to a smiling halt, JJC buried deep inside her, and he tells the foremost woman of his life that he loves her.

The new captain of *Armageddon* had built the room beyond the Holy Chamber to recapture that fantasy. He was definitely recapturing it now with Laurie 1014. Ballard's own quantum fantasy knew the transparent negligee, the feel of JJC's hands along Laurie's smooth wooden flanks, what it meant to kiss his way up her thighs.

But she had to want Rick Ballard, didn't she?

Ballard wallowed in his depravity, moodily pacing the map of the universe with its Sphere of Annihilation when he should be readying for the Ceremony. All he could think of was Laurie's breasts. Should he march into that room, fly up the wedding cake, yank JJC off and mount her himself? So often he'd fantasized doing just that. So often he'd imagined tossing JJC overboard and assuming the captaincy. No, he wasn't a Wounded robot. He had no Class, though he'd often speculated that he might have something like Class K capabilities. Maybe the crew would accept him, maybe not. Maybe he'd have to kill Henry Jannes as well to make sure that bastard didn't vie for captain. He'd always suspected Jannes of harboring lustful thoughts about Laurie. Why else would he jeer about sex toys? JJC said Wounded robots felt no sex drive, but obviously JJC was created with one, why not the rest? First mate Jannes had to want her himself. Probably everyone did. How could Ballard possibly protect Laurie from all these horny sailors?

Answer: kill them all, and it would just be he and Laurie aboard Balloon Ship *Armageddon.*

He stared wildly at the three inset rectangles at the head of the Holy Chamber, beyond which, on the other side, JJC penetrated Laurie this instant. On each of the three shelves sat three white oil lamps. The black stones of these rectangles, akin to the smooth black stone of the sphere, taunted him mercilessly with his corruption. He was the High Priest. He should be serving this crew, not plotting to murder them, not considering how best to insert his giant stiffening member into his poor sister robot in the next room. Oh, he was a sinner. He didn't come near to God. Not even a billionth of an inch close.

Tri-Sage was a farce. Ballard had taken that holy name and forbidden any crew member from uttering those syllables. Not even JJC could say them, even at his most hysterical, and could his master ever be hysterical.

The holiness of Tri-Sage was blasphemed. The three rectangles, the Tri-Sage of his soul, mocked him to the core even as they forbade him from doing the honorable, from throwing *himself* off the gunwale to the implacable sea thousands of feet below. To twirl in the blazing Milky Way light, all the way down to the last devastating contact with reality. To finally, fully express that it had all been nothing but failure.

In a feverish vision Tri-Sage had drawn a picture of Ballard's soul, for Rick Ballard, wooden robot though he was, still embodied the Ballard karma of the original human, and that was always fundamental to God. And the vision revealed that Richard Ballard consisted of three rectangles, three vast black sheets of rock that hovered in the air in front of him wherever he walked, catcalling the names of all his sins.

The first rectangle, one-third of his life, was the Rick

Ballard personality, the normal Rick Ballard he was always supposed to project into the world. Useful, boring, solid, and predictable, it was nevertheless something he'd never been able to comprehend.

The second rectangle was entirely devoted to *other people*. There was a chattering universe of them, and their energies were overwhelming. They took up that much mental space, another third of his life, that much of his time and energy. Their needs, their cares, their opinions, their screw-ups, all were inescapable, because all that was ultimately part of Rick Ballard.

And the third rectangle was *sex*. One-third of his existence was *sex*. The pitiless raw force of it. No morality, no loyalty, no subtlety, no love, just the endless lust. All *that* time, all *that* energy.

Tri-Sage had been told by God to go beyond his programming and become the prophet of this ship, and now, by the grace of the final victory Ballard had never doubted, he was in fact prophet of the entire planet. Yet he had miscarried so often that he was surprised any of the crew let him live. Did his sister pity him? Didn't she understand, with her clear T'ohj'puv thinking, how far he'd fallen short?

Tri-Sage had suffered much, but he'd never experienced the superb, ultimate pain that would atone for all his personal disasters. And it added more indignity to know he was just a copy, that there still existed another Ballard inside JJC. It was galling to listen to all JJC's insipid confessions and feel that other Ballard oozing out of JJC's psychic pores. Ballard shuddered to recall the last Reunion Ceremony with JJC and the primordial linking with the other Ballard, the truly nasty one, the *real* bastard.

In any case, that sex rectangle was the worst and most potent shape of all. Why couldn't he have been created as some eunuch android servant? He wasn't a true Wounded, but his plant-based architecture was Wounded tech, and, ADE or not, he was organic, a fully human pattern, better than the original and potentially immortal. He had every hormonal screw-up possible, and every capacity for pleasure. As soon as JJC built Laurie

1014, all Ballard could think about was that they both had that intoxicating human sex interface. It was fated that they'd join their woody bodies, that he'd satisfy her in ways JJC couldn't conceive. The entire Large Magellanic Cloud was wide open for them. They'd find their own planet and screw themselves into stupors for thousands of years at a time.

Did JJC really not understand how completely promiscuous Laurie 1014 was? She tempted him every day, hell, every second. And he always resisted, not because he cared what anyone thought, but because Tri-Sage called on Ballard to be penitent and fight all temptation. He didn't care that the sailors thought Laurie was so mechanically clunky that they laughed at the thought of Jonathan James pounding away at her every night.

They didn't know she was *T'ohj'puv*. They didn't understand that the smug, superior T'ohj'puv forces ruling Laurie's wooden soul were the ultimate balm for Rick Ballard's black rectangle of sex. He'd fought against those forces for centuries, but he finally understood that his struggles were useless. His downfall was complete. Here, aboard the final balloon ship, at the moment he'd been ordained prophet of this ruined planet, the debased third rectangle had finally triumphed.

Because wasn't she signaling him at last? Why else would his soulmate groan her orgasm so loudly that the black door shook with it?

Ballard ripped that door wide. Why was it never locked? Why tonight of all nights had he finally dared the unthinkable and twisted that knob?

"Ohhh … *ohhh!*" naked wooden Laurie moaned atop the wedding cake, wildly sliding on JJC's groin. "Oh my God, oh my God, you're so *good!*"

Ballard stared. Then again, hadn't he known all this before? All those nights when JJC dragged Laurie from next to Ballard under the first mate's bunk? When he'd pulled her out of stasis? Didn't JJC occasionally forget to put the robots *into* stasis before bed? Hadn't Ballard heard and seen all this so many times? Hadn't Tri-Sage loved it all to his shame?

Just as he was doing now?

JJC didn't bother to glance Tri-Sage's way as he shifted Laurie's hips atop his and laughed into her laugh: "Let's have a little conference here."

CHAPTER SEVENTEEN
I Should Change into My Uniform

Amav stood from her seat behind Jack and stretched her arms, the tight navy-blue flight tunic outlining the faultless contours of her torso. "I'm going to sort out our cargo. Need a break. Back in a few minutes."

Jack nodded. "Fine."

"Certainly, Mistress Amav," Laurie 283 chirped from the copilot chair. "I know how human muscles can get *so* cramped!" In imitation of Amav she stretched her own arms above her head, the gray 283 sweatshirt riding high and tight on her small breasts.

"You all be okay here?" Amav spoke from the Control Room door, obviously referring to the fact that hardly a word had been spoken in this room since the *Typhoon VII* had lifted off an hour ago.

"Of course, mistress! Supreme Jack and I will have a swell old time piloting the ship while you're gone, won't we?"

Jack consulted his screen. "Sure," he muttered, wondering why he, Supreme Commander of the USSF, fought an urge to scream. "See you in a few." Surely he could survive a few minutes alone with the damn robot.

The door slid shut behind Amav. Jack busied himself with a program to check its seals, as the system was a novelty on the *Typhoon* series, the first sliding Control Room door as opposed to the heavy hinged hatch for sealing the command center against a depressurization emergency. The seal was solid. Well, that had wasted ten seconds. "Okay, 283," he finally sighed, "how's communication going with MATS? Can you get what you need from it without having to directly interface?"

"Oh sure, no problem! I tell you, this isolation is positively *addicting!* I have no urge whatsoever to dive into my dear friend MATS' innards, and MATS knows not to try to probe for mine. I just tap in commands on this dinky screen here and do everything the old-fashioned way. Just like you silly humans."

Jack nodded. "Okay. Do you still think we can get to the

Large Magellanic Cloud in three days?"

"Yes, according to my calculations, our upgraded Star Drive 4 should get us there in 72.566 hours. I'm just calculating to the nearest star that can rationally be defined as being in the Cloud. Where we go after that is your guess. In any case MATS is helping me calculate our Star Drive vectors. I'm following Patrick James' surmise as to the *Garrison's* trajectory, with some new information from your dog Edward. MATS has informed me that some data from Edward aboard the *Stewart Neal Frankston* was transmitted to Master MATS a millisecond before MATS was deleted from the saucer, and confirms that the *Frankston* is also heading to the Cloud, in apparent pursuit of the *Garrison*. I now have us on that updated trajectory. It's within the realm of possibility that we might be able to locate both ships with our sensors and overtake them."

Jack exhaled. "Edward? Really? Well, that's something. Thanks for your work." At least Laurie 283 sounded sane and was responding to his authority. He'd been worried that MATS had inveigled him into letting a robot with Runaway Programming Disorder copilot his ship. Maybe it would work out after all. Maybe they could do this mission and later he could talk to the real Laurie and straighten her out.

His four seconds of relief were shattered when the robot reached under the console and pulled out folded blue cloth. "Well!" she laughed. "Now that I'm officially a commander in the United System Space Force, I should change into my uniform."

"Now wait, you're not--"

"Commander Laurie Lachrer 283 is officially a commander in the United System Space Force," MATS boomed from overhead speakers. "By authorization of the Marsport Automated Transport System, effective May 13, 2076."

"Shut up!" Jack cried. "Of all the stupid nonsense!"

"Dear MATS, I believe Captain Jack is getting riled up for some reason," Laurie 283 cooed to the ceiling. "Would you mind leaving us alone for a while? Jack and I need to discuss the parameters of this mission in private."

"We--we do?" Jack said.

"Does Commander Laurie Lachrer 283 wish to assert Privacy Mode?" MATS inquired.

"Oh, yes! Captain Jack and I both want it!"

"We--do not--" Jack grunted.

"Privacy Mode enabled for standard ten-minute duration," MATS spoke. "MATS will resume communications with the Control Room in ten minutes. Thank you and have a wonderful, private *ten minutes*."

Jack stared as the robot unfolded a small light-blue flight uniform. Though he disagreed with the new United System Council policy that allowed any crewmember aboard a ship not under combat conditions to request a short break in standard ship computer surveillance, he could see the logic of it, especially after the recent SolGrid invasions of privacy. Still, to request this on the bridge of the *Typhoon VII* was another matter. "What do you think--" he began, cutting off as the robot whirled her chair, stood, and marched to the rear of the Control Room, whipping her gray sweatshirt over her head.

Jack stared at the slender naked back for a moment, then swiveled back to his command screen. "Uh ..."

"Oh, no worries, Supreme Jack!" the robot called back. "I just felt I should be in proper uniform, that's all. Of course I'm just a robot and you shouldn't care at all, now should you? Besides, it's not like you haven't seen 'em before."

Jack struggled to keep his gaze on his screen. "Look, just go ahead and change if you have to, but of course I haven't, I mean ..."

"Oh, surely you saw *everything* when our dashing Mr. Ballard staged his little mutiny last month and kidnapped poor Miss Laurie, didn't you? Pulling her tunic up and exposing her sexy boobs for all to see? Of course they were *hers* you saw, not mine, but I can assure you we're absolutely identical in *every* way."

Jack bit his lip. Amav had to be back soon, didn't she? He listened to Laurie pulling off her gray sweatpants, slipping into the blue trousers, and zipping them up. He didn't know what possessed him to spin around and watch her snapping the Velcro tight on her shoes.

She smiled sunnily, brushing long red hair back in exactly the same gesture the human Laurie used. She flounced back to the copilot seat and swiveled to Jack, her blouse unbuttoned to the middle of her chest. When she noticed the direction of his stare she reached over and squeezed his thigh. "No worries, Captain Jack! We're all friends here!"

Jack gaped at the small hand resting on his own light-blue pants. "Uh, look, Laurie, we do need to follow proper military discipline here."

"Oh, I forget, you humans are *so* uptight!" Laurie laughed, pulling her hand back and placing it over her open blouse. "Well, no matter! I can certainly copilot this ship and in fact attend to all ship's functions whether you're drooling for me or not!"

"I--I am *not* drooling for--for anyone!"

Laurie cocked her head, smiling eyes probing for his. He looked away. God, how had they upgraded the damn robot to look so much like the real Laurie? Her gestures were smoother and more human than Jack had ever noticed. The Ywritt had certainly taken her far beyond the contraption-level 2030's HAVOTT tech. Against his will he wondered about her dual male/female IHAG setup. How did that integrate into such a slim female package? He fought off the thought. What was it going to be like spending weeks in the company of this mechanical sex addict copilot?

"Now you listen to me, Supreme Jacko dear," Laurie 283 said.

"You will *not* address me as--"

"Oh, come on, dearest Captain, you know I just want to clear the air between us, that's all."

"What--what do you think needs clearing up?"

"Oh, I just wanted to know the extent of your attraction to dear human Laurie, that's all. And since she and I are identical, I'll be able to measure *all* your male physiological reactions perfectly, right on the spot! Everyone's so curious, you know. Like, how *did* she rise up so quickly in the USSF to become your foremost physician/engineer?"

Jack stared back. "Are you kidding? I'm not attracted to her! She just happens to be the best--I mean, the most talented--"

"Are you sure it wasn't just because you secretly want her in your big supreme commander bed?"

"No! Are you crazy? I have Amav! This is so--so--" he sputtered. "So unprofessional! Let's just drop it!" Didn't this fool robot have any idea how well he and his wife meshed? Dammit, this whole vacation was supposed to give Amav and him some excellent time in the bedroom. The workload had been piling up so high for both of them the past year or so, and even though searching for their idiot rebel son was purportedly the focus of this whole crazy mission, in reality he and Amav both knew what they really wanted from this time together.

"But you do find Miss Laurie attractive, now don't you?" the robot persisted.

Jack shook his head but unfortunately wound up sinking into the robot's light-blue unbuttoned cleavage. "No. Forget this. This is all unprofessional. For your information, Laurie Lachrer is the most talented USSF officer I've ever seen, with the exception of my brother. Got that? Didn't you hear me earlier telling Laurie I wanted to promote her to general and give her one of the new *Typhoons?*"

The robot pursed her lips. "Yes, I certainly did. I think the poor dear was quite gratified to hear that, of course, even though she was obviously so angry with all of us at that moment she couldn't think a single coherent thought."

"Dammit, what I really want to do is move her straight up from colonel to supreme commander!"

Jack was taken aback by the look of surprise on Laurie 283's face. He didn't think robots could mimic that. "Wow, Supreme Jack, that's quite a compliment to our dear Miss Laurie. I'll pass it on to her next time I see her. Between you and me, though, I don't think she could handle the stress of it all. Not the way *you* can, dearest!"

Jack shook his head. "She could. I know she could. She *loves* the USSF. All aspects of it. She's eager to tackle *anything.*

Whereas I'm just getting, I don't know, damn tired of it all. I know Joe doesn't want SCUSSF when I retire. I sure as hell don't want it myself anymore." Why was he babbling this to a damn robot? "Aw, forget it. Let's get back to work."

"Well, Supreme Jackster, does your fully functional robotic copilot need to worry about your commitment to the USSF? Are you really just planning to dump it all on poor Miss Laurie?"

"No, nobody needs to worry about me dropping the ball here. I may be on vacation but I know what my responsibility is. I know what to do and I'm in charge here. Not you, not the damn MATS, either. You understand me?"

Laurie mimicked another human blink of surprise and dosed him with a warm smile. Warm smile, hell, it was a *hot smile*. "Well, I'm afraid we've gotten a bit off the subject, dear Jack."

"I am not your dear Jack!"

"Because all I wanted was simply a yes or no answer to the question of whether you're attracted to Miss Laurie."

"I am not!"

"You don't find dear Laurie attractive, then?"

Jack sighed. "Let's get back to work. Yes, for your information she's a lovely woman, but that's not any sort of personal issue for me."

"Even when you've witnessed her sexy little breasts? *Our* identical breasts, I might add?"

"Look, just cut this. I know you HAVOTT robots are obsessed with sex, but I'm not going there. What happened on the *Typhoon VI* last month was just *clinical,* somehow. When Ballard was holding her hostage, hell, it was like a trip to the emergency room or something, where nobody cares about any of that crap."

"Hmm. I see," Laurie 283 said, swiveling back to her console with a sigh. "I'm sure Miss Laurie will be relieved to hear that. She told me that sometimes she worries whether you might have a secret thing for her, and that was the only reason she'd risen so fast."

"Look, I just got through explaining *why* she rose so fast. Let's cut it, shall we?"

Laurie 283 shrugged. "It's all very ironic, seeing that she considered you an incompetent moron for years."

"*W-what?*"

"Oh, no worries, dearest Supreme, it was just that she was so used to working for Joe and liked his style so much. She always thought you were a bit off your rocker! But since working for you directly she's actually come to worship you a little. Isn't that amusing?"

"Well, I don't know. Look, if you talk to her, tell her I'm really sorry about all this, that she couldn't come along today. God, I can't believe this discussion! *You* were the one who got her kicked off this flight. You and MATS! Dammit, she'll never forgive me!"

The robot nodded. "Well, she may. Or she may not. Who knows? We certainly threw her under the bus today, didn't we, dear Jacko?"

"I just *got* her damn notice that she resigned, did you know that?"

"No, I don't believe that, dear one. She surely didn't mean it."

"Now I *have* to make her SCUSSF. Dammit, she'd be perfect! I know I have to run it through the damn United System Council first, though. If she ever talks to you, tell her I'm going to bat for her."

The robot swiveled to Jack, cocked her head in another luminous smile, then turned to her own console. "Hmm. If she ever talks to either of us."

"Privacy Mode has ended," came the tenor voice from the ceiling. Jack jumped. At the same time the door slid open.

"Why was the door locked?" Amav demanded. Jack followed her gaze to where the gray 283 sweatshirt lay rumpled behind the copilot's chair. To his dismay, there was a trail of pants, shoes, and disturbingly bright red panties on the tile floor as well. Amav cocked an eye, appraising Commander Laurie Lachrer 283's new uniform.

"Well, uh, the robot wanted Privacy Mode," Jack stammered. He glanced to Laurie 283, expecting some show of embarrassment, but Laurie's sharp face just gazed back impassively.

To his surprise Amav grinned. "Okay, let her practice flying this thing by herself for a while," she said, tapping Jack's shoulder. "C'mon. You and I need to talk."

CHAPTER EIGHTEEN
Snuggled Deep

At the bottom of the stairs Jack blinked at the blinding white cavern of the *Typhoon VII's* second deck. He'd never gotten used to how huge the recent ships had become. He turned to Amav. "Look, I'm sorry, but you know that robot is just--"

"Oh, forget it. I don't care, the silly thing just flirts her head off. Hope you had a good look."

"I--I *didn't*. I mean, she went to the rear console, and I sure wasn't going to …"

"God, you're hopeless. Listen, you and I need to talk."

"What about?"

Amav jerked his flight tunic up from his belt. "Dammit, Jack, we're never going to get properly laid if we don't make some time for it. C'mon!"

"Oh … right." So they *had* been on the same wavelength all this time. Jack had never seen her dark blue flight suit before, and all day he'd been intrigued by the bright yellow zipper down the front of the tunic. Especially that two-inch-wide pull ring at the neck. "So which stateroom are we in?" He didn't feel right about taking Joe's huge captain quarters on Deck 1, and realized that since they'd been in such a hurry to get the ship underway, they hadn't thought about choosing quarters.

"We can take Stateroom 4. It's just down this way." She tugged at his sleeve. "Hurry!"

Jack followed her to one of the larger staterooms on this deck. "You weren't down here yourself just now?" he said, pointing to the door slightly ajar.

"No, I was checking our cargo. Let's just get in."

"Well, why's it open?"

"Forget it! Come on!"

Jack had a momentary worry about anyone seeing Captain Jack Commer charging through this door with his sexy wife, male/female pheromones in overdrive, but then remembered they were the only two humans on the ship. The only other entity was the damn robot upstairs, no doubt plotting how to take over the *Typhoon* in Jack's absence. But who cared? He had Amav. He had a brief thought to tell MATS they wanted Privacy Mode but the glorious smell of her hair as she plunged into his arms made him forget everything. In a second he'd pulled the yellow zipper down over Amav's wondrous breasts, then further to her navel.

"Oh--something *else* navy blue I haven't seen before." He fingered the lacy bra. "God, these feel ... they feel ... oooh, and a nice front clasp."

"Just for you, dear," she purred, shutting her eyes. "I knew you'd want super-fast *access*."

He undid the clasp. "Mmmm ... they're so perfect," he murmured, bending to kiss them as Amav wriggled the rest of the way out of the tunic and tugged his own flight tunic over his head. No zippers, no buttons. He guessed he'd planned it that way all along.

Both topless, Amav playing at his belt and pulling down his trousers, they turned to the bed, which Jack was startled to see was a pile of rumpled sheets and blankets.

"Man ..." he muttered. "Damn sloppy housekeeping."

"Who cares? Who cares? The stupid ship wasn't ready to fly when Know-How hijacked it. C'mon, forget it, let's just--"

Jack pulled her in for a long kiss, working her pants down to her knees. Then he reached behind him, grabbed the surprisingly heavy blankets, and dumped them on the floor.

"Oh my God!" Amav cried as something wet and fleshy, like a giant baked ham, slithered down Jack's hairy thigh.

"Oh, *yuck!*" Jack groaned. They stumbled three feet back, pants around their shins, at the sight of a grotesque sea monster undulating on the forest green carpet. Then the creature--the writhing *meat*--emitted a high squeal and humped along the carpet to Jack, putting out two pink claws, grasping his ankle, and curling into an embrace around his foot.

Dazzling music, thoughts, philosophies, and mathematical equations flooded him. Theorems, memories, poetry, stories, millions of *fever concepts*--

"Oh my God! It's *Commander Ywer!*" Amav shouted,

yanking her pants up. Jack stared at her classically magnificent breasts, her long luxurious dark hair spilling over them, then his eyes jerked back to the writhing pink slab of--

"*Ywer?*" he groaned. "What the hell? God, get *off* me! Dammit, of all the stupid *crap!*" He kicked at the flailing Martian, wondering if he and Amav could just find another stateroom, but he knew it was impossible. And the damn thing clutched him even tighter, moaning and burbling. Jack couldn't follow the spoken Martian or even get a fix on the telepathic outradiance beneath it.

"Stop it! Don't hurt him!" Amav said. "He's coming out of the *Kuth'rr'kq!* The Martian Hibernation!"

"He's *what?*" Jack cast a last longing look at the king-sized bed, now flat and empty.

"His outradiance is just now coming back." Amav pulled her dark tunic from beneath the Martian and clasped it to her chest. "That's why it's so distorted."

Very dangerous to wake a Martian from the Four-Hundred-Year Hibernation! came into Jack's mind.

"Yes! That's it!" Amav said. "He's coming around. We're getting some word concepts now."

Commander Ywer finally unscrunched his eyes and relaxed his grip on Jack's foot. Jack had never seen a Martian's eyes closed, as they had no eyelids. But he'd heard that Martians in the Four-Hundred-Year Martian Hibernation could pull skin and sometimes forehead bone over their eyes.

Kuth'rr'kq *unexpected stop shortly after initiation cannot calculate precise time dangerous to mind must do full personality reset engaging now.*

"Dammit to hell, what's he *doing* here? Why's he doing a hibernation?" Jack complained. "That's only for some major Martian crisis. Why's he even *here?*" He met Amav's eyes. "Listen, we'll have time later for--for--"

"No problem, dearest," Amav said with a quick grin. Jack found himself smiling back and sighing at the absurdity of this development. Amav slipped into her tunic and zipped it as Jack ruefully eyed the navy-blue bra abandoned on the carpet by

Ywer's head. "We definitely have something to attend to here," she grunted, hoisting the limp fishlike Ywer, five and a half feet of naked Martian, up onto the bed. Patting his head as his huge eyes rippled in growing awareness, she added: "I think he'll be all right. I can sense him doing what he calls a *reset*. It's sort of like deep meditation for us."

Jack nodded. He'd take her word, as she, like his brother Joe, exhibited an unusual sensitivity to Martian outradiance. He was about to get into Ywer's trembling face and demand what the damn Martian was doing on his ship, then realized two things. One, *Typhoon VII* copilot Ywer had every right to be on the ship. Two, all Jack had to do was relax and let Ywer's jumbled outradiance spread through his mind.

He finally got a picture of Ywer helping human Laurie in Engineering calibrate the ship's Star Drive 4, and the two agreeing several hours ago that they'd hit a snag and needed some rest. Ywer had told Laurie he was going home, but exhausted, he'd decided he could use a short nap.

Jack stared at the shelves teeming with Martian awards adorned with titanium and gold: the four-foot-tall, ruby-encrusted *Caru'oiiu//rlok* Demonstration of Extraordinarily Perceptive Consciousness; the granite Order of Discrete Courageous Intelligence signed with what Jack recognized was the Martian symbol for Emperor Dar; the glowing green Dream Resemblance Epic Verse Championship Medal; the deep blue stone trapezoid of the *G'oi/ujer* Award for Culinary Excellence; as well as a host of USSF certifications, including Completion of Navigational Interface with Star Drive 4 and Copilot of the Year for six years running, all framed in sapphire and onyx. Holograms of Martian deserts and mountains hung on the walls. A bookshelf held dozens of fat volumes with Martian script on their spines; these imitations of human books had only been popular for a couple decades, but Ywer not only collected them, he'd written and published several himself.

The room gave off the distinct Martian cinnamon scent, and to top it, Jack only now realized that they stood in the one-third gravity which Martians preferred in their own spaces. The open door had maintained the human air pressure Martians could tolerate. He met Amav's stunned eyes as they both realized they were trespassing in the *Typhoon* copilot's stateroom. "Oh my God! Ywer, I'm so sorry!" he gasped. "We had no idea you were on the ship!"

"We're both sorry," Amav said, "we just saw the open door and--"

"No! The fault is mine! All mine!" Ywer burst out, jerking upright on the bed, left hand covering his genitals and throwing a hard salute with his right. Jack stared more at the left hand, having only seen naked Martians a handful of times. Martian male and female genitals looked about the same to a human, being a series of long hanging folds that only revealed their true character in the anticipation of intercourse.

"At ease! At ease!" Jack cried, automatically returning the salute. "We're sorry we came in here!" The extent of Ywer's exhaustion today hit him hard. Like their mutual friend Senior Scientist Kner, Ywer was fond of short invigorating naps, snuggled deep in a pile of loose blankets. He'd been so eager for his siesta today he hadn't bothered to secure his door.

Ywer shook his head wildly. "Supreme Commander! Dictator Amav! Of course you have the right to inspect here! To investigate my rank insubordination!"

"No! Are you kidding? We're sorry we woke you up!" Amav said.

"I, a commander in the United System Space Force, absent without leave in the *Kuth'rr'kq,* out of uniform, and--and *naked!* The shame is mine! All mine!" Ywer shouted, flinging himself off the bed, scrambling on the floor for something to wear, grabbing Amav's bra and gaping at it in confused horror. Finally he spotted his blue flight suit draped across a chair and ran for it, stumbling, going down, rising again, reaching the clothes and yanking them over himself in a blur. He grabbed his USSF shattergun from a table and, shakily balancing on one leg, aimed it at his other foot. "I am *dishonored!* By your leave, Supreme Commander, I now perform the Grazing Shatter of *Kl'alp'lor!*"

"No! Idiot! Belay that!" Jack tackled the Martian, conscious of the shattergun swishing past his face with pink Martian fingers tightening on the trigger as the two wrestled on the carpet. Still flooded with unknowable *Kuth'rr'kq* hibernation concepts, Jack finally jerked the weapon free and untangled himself from the thrashing, half-dressed copilot. "Are you *crazy?* Stand at attention, Commander!"

Eyes looking even wider than their normal two-inch diameter, Ywer scrambled to his feet and assumed parade ground attention.

"Commander, you're in the USSF if you don't recall," Jack barked. "We don't allow ritual suicide in our ranks. Is that clear?"

"Yes … sir," Ywer grunted, then, as Amav advanced, he slumped into her arms.

"Help me get him back to the bed," she said. "He's still weak from the *Kuth'rr'kq.*"

"No! No! I am dishonored! *Must die!*" Ywer moaned, his outradiance a feverish jumble of *Kuth'rr'kq* and self-annihilation, and even Jack, with his relatively poor ability to pick up the subtleties of Martian outradiance, could see that Ywer's heartbeat had gone up to 330 per minute. Normal was fifty.

"Commander, lie quietly in bed and reorient yourself. That is an order," Jack snapped. A few patterns of reluctant ease emanated from the copilot. Would Ywer really have gone through with the Grazing Shatter? Jack had heard rumors of *Kl'alp'lor* used for ritual Martian suicide, but it was something Martians generally kept as far buried in their outradiance as possible. Jack had witnessed the courage of Martian soldiers in the 2034 war as they underwent the Grazing Shatter. If you were struck by a shattergun bolt anywhere close to the body's center of mass, the shatter was relatively instant, though apparently still quite excruciating. But if you took a grazing shot on the hand or foot, you'd experience agonizing seconds of unendurable pain as the cracking glass transformation made its way up your extremity and finally claimed all of you. Martians had accepted this possibility and sought to assume a posture almost impossible to maintain if so grazed. They stood one-legged and touched their foreheads as they shattered. Apparently this was considered the height of Martian courage, though it had also developed an ugly use as ritual remedy in cases of dishonor.

Ywer stared at the ceiling. Jack felt the patterns of shame in the copilot's outradiance as he still longed for the Grazing Shatter of *Kl'alp'lor* which his supreme commander had just forbidden him. Someday he might still do it, though, and the only way for Jack to truly countermand the order was to let the Martian know that all was truly forgiven, and to remind Ywer of his duty to the USSF.

Ywer could be a hard case, though. He was 1414 Martian years old, and Joe and Jack had actually known him as an enemy combatant back in that 2034 war, when Ywer was, of all things, Senior Martian Chef to the human usurper of the Martian throne, Sam Hergs. Like all Martians, Ywer had been in thrall to Hergs, but the ancient Martian had taken his culinary duties so fanatically that he could snarl imperious commands to humans and Martians alike. Apparently even Hergs was overwhelmed by the Martian's feistiness, only allowing Ywer's cheek because the food he served had been, according to everyone who'd sampled it, unfathomably delightful. Even the meager leftovers sent to human prisoners in Hergs' dank prison cells were said to have miraculous healing powers. Joe had joked that he was looking forward to meals on the *VII*.

Jack sighed in relief as the Martian finally got his heartbeat under control.

CHAPTER NINETEEN
My Apologies for Raising Your Blood Pressure

"So why'd you go into the *Kuth'rr'kq,* guy?" Jack said, trying to affect loose camaraderie but aware that the *Typhoon* copilot might consider his sloppy pronunciation an insult.

"He's still having trouble focusing," Amav said, patting Ywer's forehead. "Just let the story unfold from his radiance."

Jack nodded. Surely she was getting a more complete picture than he was. But clearer images and a sense of a timeline came.

As Ywer was drifting off, naked and nestled in his bedclothes, guilty that he'd failed to let Laurie know he hadn't gone home yet, the idiotic Know-How system had abruptly launched the *Typhoon VII* into its not entirely calibrated Star Drive 4, as well as thoughtlessly invoking the uncertified HyperCloak Module. Unprepared for the jolt to his nervous system, Ywer had panicked and slipped into the initial phase of the Four-Hundred-Year Hibernation. If the *Kuth'rr'kq* had progressed a couple hours further, even Jack throwing him on the floor wouldn't have wakened him.

"MATS!" Jack said. "Why didn't you pick up the fact that Ywer was still on the ship?"

He felt rather than saw Amav grimace. Once again he'd yelled at the goddamn AI, which no doubt would continue to take singular offense at anything that came out of Jack's mouth.

Sure enough, there was an extremely long pause before MATS answered: "My apologies, Supreme Commander Commer, for raising your blood pressure. In making a few more adjustments to Star Drive after Commander Ywer had departed her presence, Colonel Lachrer felt it necessary to disconnect the incompetent Know-How system's internal sensors for a few minutes. Ywer had stated his intention to leave the ship and Know-How foolishly certified that he must have done so, since Commander Ywer had never previously misled the extremely more advanced Marsport Automated Transport System in any way. But Know-How's assumption regrettably proved faulty

134

and again, may the Marsport Automated Transport System extend its most heartfelt apologizes on behalf of the utterly discredited and currently unavailable Know-How system. Once the *Typhoon VII* was in Star Drive to Iota Persei, Colonel Lachrer restored all sensor functions, but by this time Commander Ywer was in such a low-powered biological state that Know-How's inept sensors running in Standard Operational Mode didn't register his presence. He also exhibited zero Martian outradiance for Colonel Lachrer to pick up. Unfortunately, even after MATS gained control of the ship, Know-How's galling lack of shipwide awareness was inevitably ported over to MATS itself. Again, may MATS extend the deepest--"

"Right, right, we get it," Jack said.

"--apologies not only for MATS' perhaps understandable continuation of the original faulty assumption, but for the fact that a longed-for episode of human sexual intercourse has been thwarted by this unfortunate, one-in-a-million probability occurrence. MATS can only offer in partial recompense a detailed medical report, for your happy conjugal review, on the hormonal states of Amav Frankston-Commer and Jack Commer during the last ten minutes."

"Got it!" Jack yelled. "Just stop!"

Ywer shivered on the bed. "What sexual intercourse are we talking about?"

"Dammit!" Jack punched a button on the wall. "Robot! You there?"

"Here, Captain Jackster!" Laurie 283 boomed at a volume a notch higher than necessary. "How may this humble robotic entity be of service?"

Jack swiped his own tunic off the floor and jammed it over his torso. Both MATS and the damn robot were probably measuring his hormonal levels right now. "Robot, why didn't you alert me that Commander Ywer is aboard the ship?"

"*What?*" came from the overhead speakers, then a disturbingly long pause. "Say again?"

Jack blinked. "Ywer! He was sleeping in his quarters!

Doing this hibernation thing. We barged in by accident and woke him. What's going on?"

"I'm here, Colonel Lachrer!" Ywer croaked from the bed. "Just a little woozy, that's all."

"That isn't the human Laurie," Amav corrected. "We have Laurie 283 as copilot today."

"Robot!" Jack said. "What's going on?"

Another long pause. "Please excuse an expression of sincere robotic surprise," Laurie 283 finally called down. "Commander Ywer is aboard? The real Laurie didn't indicate he was. Recall that she'd told us she'd been alone on the ship when Know-How sent it to Myndar."

"Well, apparently he was working with her on Star Drive and decided to take a nap," Jack snapped. "Can't you get his outradiance from up there?"

"Surely Supreme Jackster recalls that robots do not pick up Martian outradiance. Reviewing ship's logs now. Yes, I see it. Ywer bade farewell to Colonel Lachrer, but failed to leave the ship at the same time that Colonel Lachrer felt a need to temporarily disable ship's sensors. What incredibly sloppy security, if you ask me, dear Jack."

Jack mouthed a curse. He couldn't believe he and the robot actually agreed on something. "Okay, okay, what's done is done. We'll fill Ywer in on the mission." For the first time Jack felt a shiver of apprehension at what they were thinking to accomplish here. They were actually leaving the galaxy, when only a few patrols over the last few years had explored anywhere much beyond seventy light-years from Earth. Iota Persei at thirty-four light-years was the last civilization they'd encountered. And here they'd trusted that still unknown species to jack up the *Typhoon VII* to fly 163,000 light-years to the Large Magellanic Cloud.

Jack shook off the dread. Distances really didn't matter anymore. If you got stranded anywhere it wouldn't matter, whether it was at Proxima Centauri or the Andromeda Galaxy. Or even halfway from Earth to the moon. You just had to trust your ship. Nobody was walking home.

But it hit him how fortuitous this bedroom mishap might turn out. Because now he had a real copilot, the genius Ywer, if only the idiot would drop this suicide shame crap and get on with his mastermind personality. He could replace that nutso robot up in the command room. Now that they were underway, surely MATS would have to agree, wouldn't it?

Everyone who worked with Ywer, superiors and subordinates alike, marveled at the Martian's perfect balance of telepathic outradiance and expert command. Many junior officers had confided to Jack how fascinating it was to work for an officer whose thoughts they could read. He barely had to issue an order, because anyone could see it forming in his mind before he spoke. Training with him was also a snap, with all procedures effortlessly unfolding in the subordinate's brain.

Jack had often wondered how hard it might be on Ywer not to be able to read the minds of supervisors or subordinates in return. Since the tendency for most Martians was to defer to or even worship anyone who didn't radiate, it would be a constant struggle to maintain authority. Ywer's only possible solution had been to make his interior self perfectly mirror the exterior, to be absolutely upfront and honest in thought and deed. No dissembling. Ywer was another officer who'd captain one of the newest *Typhoons*.

"That's not Colonel Lachrer?" Ywer said. "Really?"

"It's okay," Amav said, patting his forehead. "I think you're running a little fever. You seem awfully hot."

Ywer writhed on the bed. "I--I'm *resetting,* Dictator Amav. A little dizzy, maybe. I'll be fine. Maybe if I talk to Colonel Lachrer--"

"That's not the real Laurie," Jack repeated. "MATS made us choose the damn robot. We had to leave Laurie behind."

"The Ywritt made even more upgrades to Laurie 283 last week," Amav said. "The two are really indistinguishable now. It's probably the fever throwing you off."

Ywer settled back. "Yes, of course. I'm just so dizzy. I suppose we all have much to learn from these Ywritt robotics scientists."

"Look, it doesn't matter," Jack said. "The Ywritt also upgraded the ship and we're heading out of the galaxy, believe it or not. We're following Jonathan James as well as this insane Wounded robot that was with him on Myndar."

Ywer sat up, fumbling at the buttons on his flight shirt. "We're leaving the galaxy? Is that possible?"

Jack grappled with hundreds of layers of Ywer's outradiance. "Yeah. Look, how much longer does this reset thing take?"

"I have no real clue, Supreme Commander. In fact, the effort of securing these last two buttons has … exhausted me."

"He's definitely running fever," Laurie 283 broke in from the ceiling. "Listen, dear Commander Ywer, did you know that in order to run this ship, I have to be cut off from MATS? I'm in *isolation* and it's *marvelous!* But I certainly have access to ship's medical monitoring. Believe me, your temperature is 141 degrees Fahrenheit, twenty-five higher than normal. Dear Jackster, Commander Laurie Lachrer 283 recommends confining Commander Ywer to bed for the next twenty-four hours."

"The Martian Automated Transport System agrees with this assessment," boomed the male voice from the ceiling, "and extends the recovery period to 68.6653 hours."

"*Crap* …" Jack muttered, even as he felt the Martian's off-balance outradiance confirm that Ywer was indeed much more incapacitated from the jerk out of the *Kuth'rr'kq* than he or Amav had realized. "Look, I need a real copilot for when we hit the Large Magellanic Cloud," he complained into dead silence. He briefly thought of further asserting who was really running the ship, but he had the horrible feeling that between them, MATS and Laurie 283 would sort Jack out, not the other way around.

"Forgive me, Supreme Commander," Ywer said, "but I fear I'm definitely running fever to the degree Laurie 283 has stated, and will be of little use for a hopefully short period of time."

Jack nodded. "Okay. Look, Ywer, you're doing fine. I'm sorry we wrecked your hibernation, but in a way this will work out. At least you're not asleep for the next four hundred years. We'll definitely need your skills when we hit the LMC. Everything's fine."

"Thank you, Supreme Commander. I will make every effort not to disappoint you." Ywer glanced at Amav and sighed. "I'm so tired. Are we really heading out of the galaxy?"

"Right," Amav said. "We have to find Jonathan James. And that Wounded woman has our Edward. We've got to get the poor thing back."

"Ah, yes, wonderful beast," Ywer murmured. Jack shrugged. He knew Amav's attachment to Edward, but as far as he was concerned all they needed to do was order another Saint Bernard package from Sol Robotics, then copy in the Edward settings saved on Commer personal storage.

"You're just coming out of the *Kuth'rr'kq*. You're resetting. You'll be fine," Amav said, again patting his forehead. Jack was gratified to see the positive effect of her soothing tones on the jagged outradiance. New patterns like mandalas formed in pastel shades, and Ywer's shoulders relaxed. He was clearly falling asleep, outradiance registering normal slumber as opposed to a return of the harsh *Kuth'rr'kq*.

Jack refrained from further comment, instead enjoying the sight of Amav bending over Ywer with her flight suit zipped three inches below her nipples. Ah, yes, there was still time on this journey for much more pleasant activities.

CHAPTER TWENTY
Coming To on Ailyuae

High above, a dark object swayed in the wind, cutting out the sun. Black lines slapped against its sides and dangled down to the sand. Was that a rope ladder?

"She's awake," someone said. "Damn, I thought she was going to be like that dog. All glassy-eyed."

Amy sprawled on her back. Dull green fronds waved in a cool breeze. Beyond that, a net shrouded a giant black stone. She checked the temperature: sixty-seven degrees Fahrenheit. Air speed three miles per hour. Surface gravity 1G. It was 24.22 minutes to sunset. Twilight shadows played on the stone, and she adjusted her perspective. What she'd first thought was a boulder was really a charred, crumpled J-133 saucer, two hundred feet wide, jammed at an angle on smashed trees, encased in a net of monstrous proportions. Those ropes had to be half a foot thick.

Something tapped her cheek. "Can you hear me?" came a voice.

She adjusted internal gyros and ran a diagnostic on possible injuries. None. She looked into Jonathan James Commer's wondrous face.

"*You* ..." she muttered. "I finally found you ..."

JJC stared back. "You've been looking for me for eight hundred years? You *are* persistent."

"Oh, yes ... definitely ..." She studied him in growing shock. Captivating as that face was, Amy was stunned by the exhaustion she found there. The deep-set, coffee-colored eyes she'd found so entrancing a few days ago were bloodshot. When she probed them for any hint of connection, all she got back was a shellshocked peer into infinity. His jaw looked swollen and inflamed. The sensuous olive complexion that had knocked her silly at Myndar was poised somewhere between mustard and pea green. Or was that due to the sea-drenched air and the diffuse sun on the rough plants all around them? He hunched over her, powerful forearms and hard chest tight in a black costume with stars at the collar. Yet the rest of his slender body seemed flaccid and drained. She wondered if the seaweed smell came from that long, bedraggled hair.

JJC turned to the crashed saucer. "Bring out the dog, Jannes."

The other man shrugged. "Don't see the point, sir. It's trash at this point."

"Just do it."

"Well, if you insist."

"I do."

"Aaah, all right. Stupid waste of time." Sometime later Amy saw the other man struggling through the tangled net, dragging a giant brown object.

"Edward!" she cried, ashamed to find her Class J capabilities in more confusion than she thought possible. "How did we get here? I mean, we were on the ship--"

"The thing's not Wounded tech, that's for sure," Jannes grunted as he set down the big Saint Bernard in front of her. "Disgusting, if you ask me. All glassy-eyed," he repeated. To her horror Edward toppled over without moving a muscle. His eyes were frozen open. The breeze ruffled his fur.

"Oh my God! What's wrong with Edward?"

"That its name? It didn't transform," JJC said, pointing to the robot. "Only Wounded robots can transform."

"Bark! Bark ark ark!" came a cry at her ear and for a moment Amy's heart raced to think Edward was all right. But she turned to a Beagle who was clearly transmitting: *And bio-dogs who are* Garthah-/yuu *with their masters can transform!*

"Yeah, Trotter here made it," JJC said. "I still don't know how. We both transformed when we came here. Damn long time ago."

Amy craned up. She had the unmistakable impression she was seeing the keel of an ancient sailing ship. Giant spheres of red, purple, and green hung above the dark shape, everything swaying. She focused on a six-inch-wide rope trailing down to wrap itself around a five-foot tree trunk.

JJC followed her gaze. "That's *Armageddon*. The last

balloon ship. Long story. I've been on her eight hundred years. Can't believe you found me after all this time."

Amy shook her head. "No, it's only been … three days?"

JJC studied her. "Your time sense has gotten scrambled. It's been eight hundred damn years. Believe it or not, Ailyuae has an exact Earth-year orbit. Same twenty-four-hour rotation, too."

"I knew that …" she managed. "I know all about Ailyuae. Programmed in, you know." She sat up. "Have I really been deactivated for *eight hundred years?*"

"Been a lot longer than that for me, ma'am," said the other man squatting beside her. He was emaciated, with a nasty thin beard below his long nose and glittering black eyes. She sized him up as a Class K. "We who have been here since the beginning have fought for 124,400 years. The war is finally over. And you have come to fulfill the prophecy of Draka Sortie."

"Yes … yes, of course," Amy said, running another diagnostic. Confusion Cascade AT Node 43LZ-555HGF. Was that important? She couldn't remember. What was wrong with her?

"This is Henry Jannes, first mate," JJC said. "He thinks Draka Sortie dragged him here one hell of a long time ago."

Amy launched a simple internal clock measurement. "Look, it's really only been three days since we talked. Since I worked on your pyramid." She stood shakily, taking in poor Edward lying on his side, staring at nothing. She pointed to the ruined ship. "I chased you in the *Frankston.*"

JJC followed her gaze. "Yeah, we can use whatever metal doesn't disintegrate. Very rare on Ailyuae. I've never understood how a planet can have such little metal."

"I know about the metal … about Ailyuae, I mean. Look, why don't you just tap into the Master Plan?" To her dismay she found she couldn't wirelessly link with JJC or Jannes. There was no wireless connection with anything. She had to speak aloud because that was all these robots could do.

Yet she got burbles of telepathic communication from the Beagle. The Trotter thing could raise his amplitude at will, form

English sentences, then subside into a merry dog gurgling. He scratched at Edward and broadcast: *Excellent fur ... so soft.* Then he fastened a suspicious canine stare on her. *You are not part of our* Garthah-/yuu. *I remember now! You are the lady from the hospital! You hurt master! May you die horribly in the next second!*

Amy blinked. "Really, little one, I'm a friend of sorts. Here about Draka, you know."

Draka myth everyone talks about! Stupid!

"Hey Trotter, it's okay, guy," JJC said. "We're not afraid of her anymore. Not after eight hundred years. Not after it's all over." He met Amy's eyes. "Glad to have some company now, I guess."

"Look, what's going on? It's only been three days!"

JJC folded his arms. "Forget it. You've had some sort of time dilation. It's been eight hundred years. I've been captain of *Armageddon* for a couple months now. We finished the war last night."

"The ... war?"

"I'll tell you the whole thing onboard." He pointed up to what Amy now understood was a floating ship, held aloft by balloons. "We don't want to stay too long on this island. Spray from the ocean's pretty harmful to just about everything. Just wanted to dump the net here with your ship. Can't believe you rigged up an old J-133 to come out here. An eight-hundred-year-trip in that old thing!"

Amy gazed back at him, unwilling to push his delusion any further. "You never got the Class J training, did you?"

JJC shrugged. "Naw, I guess not."

"You didn't get the Class J Orientation Module? Or the Full Indoctrination?"

"No, but I sure as hell learned a lot on my own, after eight hundred years of war on this goddamn planet."

"The years have numbered 124,400 for myself," the nasty first mate repeated. "I have actually seen so very much more violence and destruction than the recently appointed captain."

"Shut up, Jannes. Listen, Dr. Nortel, it's been a damn long

time. I admit you threw me back on Myndar, but like I say, I've had a lot of time to practice being a Wounded here. Now of course I'll offer you hospitality as a fellow Class J, in fact I have to, seeing as how we're the only J's on this planet. But whatever you're bringing from that crappy galaxy doesn't apply here." He pointed past the ship overhead, and Amy could see, in the oncoming night, a spiral of stars emerging, filling the sky.

"Oh my God ..." she whispered, pulling up the proper human awe response at seeing the Milky Way from 163,000 light-years away. Then she dug into her programming and put the emotion away. Intoxicating stuff, but not needed here. "So nobody's ever explained the Sphere to you? What this planet *is?*"

JJC laughed. "What it's been *for* is nothing but millennia of stupid war. I admit it's a shock that you happened to come here the day after we ended the damn thing."

"We finally reamed the *Archer,*" Jannes said. "About time. We had the Celebration this morning. We are now the rulers of this planet."

Amy looked back and forth between first mate and captain. "The J Orientation really never kicked in?"

"The only orientation I got was crashing here," JJC laughed. "Somehow the *Garrison* pointed me to this goddamn place. I just wallowed in."

Amy studied him. "It has to be your contamination with that Alpha Centaurian Grid stuff. I thought it would just tear you apart."

"Yeah, I remember you raving about *contamination.* But I assure you I've been fully functional. I learned everything I need from all eight of my captains. I won the war, and I don't need psychological lectures from you."

"You don't know about Draka's Sphere?" She took another look at the Milky Way. She shouldn't be able to see it. A Dyson sphere around the star Wiioryvel, as wide as Ailyuae's orbit, should be obscuring everything beyond. "Which it looks like he never had time to finish?"

JJC shrugged. "The old fart wanted to do another Dyson

here? Damn lousy place for it, if you ask me. All the damn ADE, and no metal to speak of."

"Excuse me," Jannes interrupted, "but it's sacrilege to refer to Draka Sortie that way."

"Oh, can it, man."

"Listen," Amy said, "since Draka's death I've been appointed executor of his estate."

"*Dead?* You're claiming he's *dead?*" Jannes cried.

"Yes, unfortunately."

"That's not possible! Draka will return for us, now that we've won the final battle!"

"Aw, forget it, Jannes," JJC said. "You know as well as I do that winning the damn war doesn't mean a goddamn thing." He turned to Amy. "Glad to see someone agrees with me that the old coot really did buy the farm at Iota Persei."

"Yes, but I'm here to see that his last wishes are carried out," Amy said. "Here, at the Sphere."

"Well, there's no stupid Dyson sphere here. You just followed me to some idiot planet I happened to hit at random."

"No, your contamination *led* you here. At Myndar, we merged for a second, and you *contaminated* me." She gulped, realizing only now that her Wounded programming was indeed compromised, poisoned by the JJC virus in her operating system. How long could she last? "Anyway," she forced herself to continue, "in that second you knew about Wiioryvel, and Ailyuae, and you knew to come here."

"That's nuts. I just pointed the *Garrison* out of the galaxy and rode it hard. Wound up here." JJC studied her. "You're still in shock from your crash, I think. Come on, let's get onboard *Armageddon*. We never want to stay long on the surface."

Amy surveyed the primitive ship hanging above her. This was all a Class J could conjure up, even if stymied by the lack of metals? "Well, you've handled the contamination better than could be expected. But I can help you fully develop your Class J powers."

JJC shrugged. "I have what I need. Like I did sense you coming. I could feel something coming out of the sky. We spent all day heading to this coordinate to find it. It was the first time we could really go flat out. We made it a third of the way around the planet, in one day. We could never do that before because other ships might jump us."

Amy shook her head. "You really have no idea what Ailyuae is, do you?"

"It's a death trap." Jonathan James looked to his slouching first mate. "Wonder why we don't have any crew except me and Jannes? Want to know what happened at the Celebration this morning?"

Amy was struck by the grief in JJC's deep brown eyes.

"Sir," Jannes said, "may I point out that revealing classified information to a non-crewmember of *Armageddon* shall be considered an act of treason."

"Ah, hell with it, Jannes. The entire crew went overboard. From three thousand feet up," JJC said. "They all knew everything was over. They were high on Myuio and they were all too damn transcendent to care what happened next. They knew there was no further use for them. So they all jumped."

"But they did go over crying *Draka!*" Jannes pointed out. "We shall remember them as the Seventeen Saints of *Armageddon.*"

"We note that Mr. Jannes here was not similarly inclined to be a Saint of *Armageddon*. Too much paperwork to fill out in his stateroom."

"Sir!" Jannes protested. "You know I was working on *The Chronicles of the Millenia of War,* and had just gotten up to the Thousand Ship Cataclysm of year 72,849."

"Plauuheit and Criluir were the last two to jump. But first they dragged Jannes off his bunk screaming," JJC laughed. "He was hitting them with a stool! Panicked out of his mind! Finally they left him in disgust and threw themselves over."

"Sir! Because of my deep devotion to Draka Sortie, I knew I had to maintain this robotic body long enough to finish my account. I mean, of course, one notices that the captain himself did not jump."

"And leave you in command? Besides, Trotter wouldn't

have let me."

Correct, master! came Beagle radiance. *I would've morphed my strength to Code Fourteen and prevented any such action.* Amy was surprised to find Trotter aside her shin, calmly assessing her. Though there were no more telepathic curses aimed in her direction, she still sensed deep doggie suspicion.

"Anyway, the captain has to go down with his ship," JJC went on. "Which I estimate will happen in 5.523 years, given the current rate of deterioration here on Ailyuae."

"And I must stay as well, of course, to ... to assist the captain," Jannes stammered. "I mean, if anything were to happen to him, I'd then be captain and have to stay with the ship. Because of course I must wait for Draka Sortie. Five and a half years should give me more than enough time to finish the *Chronicles* and present them to him."

JJC shrugged. "Well, who can care now? They're all gone. Nothing to do about it now." He pointed to the rope ladder. "Let's get going."

"What about Edward?" she demanded.

"Yeah, we'll take it. Jannes, get the dog statue," JJC ordered.

"Aaah, still not worth it."

"Just do it. We may be able to use some of the metals."

"No!" Amy screamed. "You're not using Edward for any scrap metal!"

JJC laughed. "Get over it, honey. The thing didn't transform. I don't know why it hasn't disintegrated yet. I can see some Ywritt technology in it. Maybe that's keeping it together. In any case, metals are damn rare here."

"No! No way!"

"Listen, babe, I'm the captain of this ship, in fact I rule this island and the entire planet, so you'd better get used to following my orders."

"If you try to take Edward apart, I'll activate Self Explosion and take the ship and this entire island with me!"

Now Jannes chuckled, adding: "Sir, I can write her up under Non-Crewmember Disobedience Directive 144-2."

"*God ...*" JJC muttered, something in his eyes registering that Class J's could indeed self-destruct with ten-kiloton force. Something he'd never suspected. Evidently her mere presence could invoke little bits of the Training he'd missed. "J's can *do* that?"

She nodded.

"Jannes," JJC said, "take the stupid dog. And be damn careful with it."

CHAPTER TWENTY-ONE
Priest and Priestess of the Carnal Mysteries

Amy hooked her pencil-skirted legs over the gunwale and kicked her feet free of the rope ladder. Jonathan James' strong forearms pulled her on deck. Jannes clambered up behind her with Edward slung in a net over his shoulder. "Well, I didn't think the sexy lady could negotiate our ladder in her bare feet," Jannes leered as he deposited Edward on deck and pulled the net away. She was glad he'd at least had the sense to set the dog rump down as if he really were a statue worthy of respect.

"I'll have you know I'm a fully developed Class J," Amy shot back, struggling to catch her breath. "God, this transforming business you're talking about does a bad job. I really don't know if I have all my functions." She certainly didn't feel like a J. Her robotic body ached and she wasn't thinking clearly. She'd had some difficulty getting up the rope ladder after insisting she didn't need to be carried. Any J should be able to leap from the beach to the deck of this ship in a second. Even the K Jannes ought to be able to do that.

"I still have Explosion Mode," she continued as Jannes pulled up the rope ladder and wound it around a stanchion. "Just in case you think I was bluffing."

"Right, right," JJC replied, frowning as he obviously searched in his own files for the key to Explosion Mode. But she knew the chapter on Self-Destruction was deliberately vague, merely containing hints about applying for certain possible upgrades after certain training modules were certified as completed. "Aaah, screw it," he finally muttered. "If you feel a need to blow, go right ahead. Maybe a nice nuclear explosion would put a quick end to this eight-hundred-year farce."

No, master, not a good idea, Trotter radiated. After scrambling up the ladder, the Beagle had resumed his place at Amy's side, no doubt still ensuring she didn't attack his master.

"Right, not a good idea," Amy agreed. "I have much more important plans for Mr. Commer."

JJC looked up in shock. "You can read Trotter, too?"

She nodded. "Oh, absolutely!"

Absolutely! Trotter agreed. *And I'm sure Master is eager to know your plans. Because the whole point of Jonathan James' existence is to experience everything that comes his way to the very end.*

Jonathan James sighed. "Oh boy. Sounds wonderful. Okay, Jannes, undo the anchor knot and we'll get moving."

"Me, sir?" Jannes gulped. "I just now finished winding the rope ladder, and my arms are tired. The ladder and the anchor were always Plauuheit's responsibility."

"Well, Plauuheit's gone." JJC waved at the six-inch rope running through a hawsehole on the port gunwale. "As long as you're still breathing, you're expected to conform to naval authority on this ship."

"God, sir, it's a monster."

"Yep," JJC replied, recalling the times he'd had anchor duty. "Go for it, first mate."

"Dammit, sir." Jannes frowned at Amy as if assessing whether she might like to volunteer for this task, then put his head down and climbed over the port gunwale, grasping the hawser in his slender fingers and shimmying backwards.

Amy looked over as Jannes inched a hundred feet down the thick twisting role to the massive tree anchoring the ship. He seemed to wrestle with large angry cobras as he took ten minutes to yank the knot apart.

"That Class K is barely functioning above human," she said. "He's hardly using any of his innate Wounded tech. I could pull that rope up just by thinking." She frowned. "No, that one's offline as well."

Jonathan James shrugged. "We have a lot more manual strength than you think. The L's and M's pulled the anchor all the time. Jannes is just a wimp. He could throw a harpoon two miles if he cared to exert himself. He just doesn't care to."

Jannes whipped the last coil off the trunk and Amy felt the ship jerk free. The first mate clung to the swaying anchor hawser, frantically climbing as *Armageddon* gained height.

"Sheesh," Amy said. "You ordered him to do it because you

figured if you were down there, he might cut the rope behind you."

JJC laughed. "I see you've picked up on the tension in the air. He definitely thinks he should be captain."

"Well, I certainly wouldn't have let him saw through that rope with that silly little knife there." She pointed to a sword affixed to the gunwale, ready for emergency hawser slashing. "You're far too valuable for me to let anything like that happen."

Amy aimed her gigantic blue eyes straight at JJC. Involuntarily he glanced down to her tight blue, immensely revealing tank top, its fabric fraying just like all the other nonliving objects brought from normal space. The ladder climb had split her pencil skirt all the way to the taut skin at her hip. She grinned as JJC took it all in, swallowing hard.

"Well ... let's get the first mate aboard then," he managed as Jannes climbed to the gunwale. JJC hauled his second-in-command on deck.

"Sir ..." Jannes managed, shoulders trembling. "That ... is definitely not how we should go about anchoring the ship ... in the future."

"Well, no matter, Jannes," JJC replied. "We may never need to anchor again. Maybe we'll just float until we die."

Jannes nodded eagerly. "Yes, sir, good plan, sir."

"Meanwhile, get to work winding the hawser."

The exhausted Jannes blinked in alarm. "Sir? We usually have at least four men on that."

JJC walked to the gunwale, yanked off one of several capstan bars, and shoved it at Jannes. "Do your duty, first mate. As you may have realized, the rest of the crew is *not here*. But we all know a single Class K can handle it. Meanwhile Dr. Nortel and I have other matters to discuss."

Jannes whirled with a muttered curse. Staggering past the mainmast, the first mate inserted his bar into the capstan. As he began rotating the device to wind the massive hawser, Amy noted how quickly they'd risen to two thousand feet. She struggled to reset herself. She'd never been shut off since her creation in human year 1961. Wounded robots never needed sleep, and the philosophical shock of such nonexistence was hard to bear. Poor Edward had also just undergone this nonexistence for the first time in his life. But he looked as if he'd never share her experience of waking up.

At least part of the plan was working. Contaminated Jonathan James Commer still harbored intense human sexuality. His eyes kept going to the smooth cleavage of her tank top and down her thighs straining against the torn, blackened pencil skirt. She'd lost her high heels somewhere, and her dark pantyhose was already gone, but no matter, she'd just make new clothes. But to her shock Creation Aspect was also offline.

She took a deep breath, noting JJC avidly accessing her bust metrics. What was wrong with her? Why were her robotic pheromones on overdrive? She'd come here to seduce him, but he was in fact seducing her without even knowing it. His contamination had ruined her control from the beginning, three days ago, eight hundred years ago, whatever. What were all these rising sexual cascades? They were supposed to be partitioned. Nobody ever took them seriously.

She had no partitions. JJC had no partitions. They were erotically locked onto each other. How could a Class J not control that function? Dammit, they were supposed to be able to strip nude in front of that nasty Jannes and have at it, actors on stage and their audience placidly processing a software simulation. But what was this intoxicating thought of pushing JJC down on the deck, yanking off his pants, and mounting him this second? As if she wouldn't mind being shut off forever, just like Edward, if she could have that one chance?

After all her years of faithful service to the Wounded, she was *contaminated*. What had happened to Draka Sortie's Sphere? What was this useless, primitive ship doing here?

The silence went on way too long. Wiioryvel was a sliver of orange light sinking into the black sea. JJC lit lanterns as Jannes returned from the capstan and stood with folded arms. Then a door opened on the quarterdeck above them. Two figures in white robes emerged from a cabin and descended the stairs.

"*Ballard* ..." she gasped. One of the parts of the pyramid

she'd separated. And next to him, a female figure: the T'ohj'puv entity. Somehow JJC had reconstituted the robots that exploded back on Myndar. She ransacked musty USSF files in her Human Database Storage to recognize in the T'ohj'puv thing a facsimile of Colonel Laurie Lachrer who worked for JJC's father. "Why, these are *wooden!*"

JJC nodded. "Entirely wooden robots. Well, a tiny amount of metal here and there, but like I say, we don't have much. Amy Nortel, meet Rick Ballard and Laurie Lachrer 1014. They didn't want to go overboard for the Celebration either. They're here for religious purposes, shall we say."

"Yeah, Priest and Priestess of the Carnal Mysteries," Jannes sneered.

Amy understood she had a serious rival. JJC had created this Laurie robot as a sex doll and was in love with her. Then she was shaken to see Ballard's glossy face fasten upon her own body, surveying every curvy centimeter. Licking his wooden lips.

Wounded robots never exhibited the slightest modesty, but Amy found herself tugging her mutilated pencil skirt as far down her thighs as the stretchy fabric would permit. Her garments continued to dissolve, and at this rate she'd stand naked before this wooden priest in 15.675 minutes.

"May it please the assembly here to bow our heads in prayer in the twilight of Balloon Ship *Armageddon,*" Ballard spoke into the uneasy silence.

"Aw, zip it, man," JJC snapped. "Not now."

"No, I am the High Priest of the Mysteries. We must all seek Redemption in these final days of doomed *Armageddon.*"

Jonathan James turned to Amy. "Look, I'm sorry about this. These robots get a little nutso sometimes. Every once in a while they give me this sort of BS."

"For it is known to the Soul of Ailyuae," Ballard intoned, "that Amy Nortel has arrived to deliver the Completeness of Union. Her suffering sexuality is obvious in her downcast eyes, in her elegant and sensual stance. As High Priest, I dutifully explore every nuance of Amy Nortel's fascinating corporeal presence with intimate, loving attention to erotic detail."

"Dammit, what *is* this?" Amy demanded.

"It's a goddamn malfing wooden robot, is what it is," JJC fumed. "Sorry for the zoo here today. I didn't think Ballard would butt in like this."

"Oh, it's nothing," the wooden Laurie Lachrer snorted. "Don't pay Rick any mind. He just found the Nortel schematics in his database and all he's doing is running one of his silly sex programs. I believe this one is called Voluptuous Goddess 624A? The one he was running when he exploded back on Myndar? No wonder it's so *terribly* important."

"No, that's not the point," Ballard insisted. "This is a High Priest function. I exist to demonstrate the full capacity of wooden robots for *love*. Glorious Amy, adjourn with me to the pleasure bedroom in the cargo hold below, and I will fulfill your every desire."

"*W-what?*" Amy sputtered.

"Dammit, I've had it!" JJC snarled. "Ballard, to your quarters! Await your execution there!"

"No!" Ballard yelled back. "The ancient visions of lust and power must be redeemed! This robot was given those visions, but denied all physical fulfillment!"

"What do you mean?" Laurie said. "You've never been denied all!"

"Are you kidding? I've always been denied! Whereas you had your pleasure in our master's bed! I never had any pleasure! Here, at the end, it's time I finally got some!"

"He made me do it, fool! He uses *commands,* like 469! And it was never pleasure! You could've had me any time!"

"N-no! He uses *469?* While I've always had to *deny?*"

"All you had to do was *ask!*"

"Hey!" JJC said. "That's enough! Girl, get over here!"

"No!" Laurie said. "Rick belongs to *me!* He always has! Rick, you don't want that nasty Amy robot!"

"But you know I can't have you!" Ballard protested. "By law! Yes, we've both wished that! But it's forbidden for us to have sex!"

"Idiot! Of course we'll have sex! It's fated! If you'd just be *patient!*"

JJC pushed between Ballard and Amy. "Look, I'm really sorry. These really are sophisticated robots. All plant-based, so maybe there's some mind stuff that goes awry every now and then. I mean, all those tiny pulleys and springs and wind-up mechanisms, I mean, down to the nano-level. The trees of Ailyuae are really amazing. The robots are fantastic, really."

"So's the sex with 'em, we hear," Jannes said. "Look, if the stupid priestess doll needs to get laid, I'd be glad to oblige. I'm fully Wounded, not made out of stupid wood."

"Infidel!" Ballard shouted. "Dammit, this is a *religious* matter! Why else is Amy Nortel wearing that tight, *tight* tank top, and why is it falling apart so *gloriously?*" He spread his fingers wide for Amy's breasts as she froze. How could this contraption unbalance her like this? Why was she rummaging for the activation codes for Explosion Mode?

"Ballard," JJC growled, "jump overboard. Right now. Wounded Obedience Command 504-9."

Ballard's eyes bulged. "You--you *wouldn't!*" He collapsed against the gunwale and gaped at the churning sea 2,187.654 feet below.

"No, idiot! I *love* you!" Laurie cried, rushing into his arms. "You can't, you can't! It's you I love!"

"Really? Really? But you bang JJC every night!"

"He *makes* me! He uses 469! And 612 and sometimes even 704! He's so awful!"

"But 504-9--*death command--*"

"Recall I am *T'ohj'puv!* T'ohj'puv forbids suicide! Your Tetrahedron Oversoul forbids you to jump!"

"Jannes, throw them both overboard," JJC ordered. "I've heard more than enough from those two."

"With pleasure, sir!" the first mate sang out, striding forward.

Amy wasn't sure how it happened, but somehow Laurie 1014's left arm snapped up fast, and it was followed by the eerie Doppler of Jannes' terror scream. She peered over the gunwale to watch the shrieking figure of the first mate flail all the way into the toxic waves below.

"Oh my God!" JJC groaned. "That was my first mate you offed there!"

"Who cares?" Laurie laughed. "He must've picked up some of your contamination because he always *leered* at me!" She plunged into Ballard's arms. "We did it! We did it! Rick, you and I are *married* now!"

"Oh … my God …" Ballard muttered.

"You never wanted that Amy thing! I knew it all along! You were just running a stupid *sex program.* You saw someone matching the 624A specs, and you started up this crap! Well, now we're through with it!"

Ballard held her tight. "Yes, you're right! It's all just a stupid *sex program!* Yes! We're done with this nonsense!" He turned to Amy. "I'm *done* with you, you hear?"

"You … never *knew* me …" Amy managed.

"Oh, yes I did! In my programming! Laurie's right! You're one of the goddamn *types* that sets me off! Of course I'm familiar with every detail of your body! But I'm done with it! Done with all of it! I have Laurie! We'll escape! Well find an island and make a new life!"

"Yes, yes, of course!" Laurie laughed into his eyes.

Ballard ran to the capstan and yanked the emergency sword out of its gunwale sheath. Laurie followed him across the deck as he expertly brandished the weapon. At some time, Amy thought, JJC must have programmed some swordplay skills into his robots.

"We're Wounded tech, but we're not really Wounded!" Laurie yelled as Ballard sliced through ropes on the starboard side holding what Amy realized was a lifeboat. It floated free on three orange ADE balloons each five feet in diameter. "We'll start a new life! A plant-based life! We're done with your battles and your ego and your arrogance!"

"No …" JJC quavered. "*No!*"

"Let--let them go," Amy said, holding him back. She scanned the deck for other lifeboats, but saw just this one.

"We're done with you! At last!" Ballard cried as he and

Laurie climbed into the small craft and pushed it into space. The two robots locked themselves in wild standing embrace as they drifted from *Armageddon,* the last shred of sunset blazing through their transparent robes.

"No!" JJC moaned. "They're the last two parts of me! They can't go!"

Master, you still have them inside you, Trotter radiated. *Just as you have me and Clopt the Glorious!*

"Dammit, you know I can't use that damn *inner* crap! I have to have the *physical* parts! God, this is the end! It can't be real! They'll just die out there, don't they know that? That's not a real lifeboat! It'll only last a few days! It's just for exploring an island! They'll never find one! God, they'll just die!"

"Well, maybe they'll die happy," Amy said, caressing his shoulders. "Like we will, my love!"

"I'll never die happy!"

"It's fated, dear one. It clears the path for *us.*"

"Oh my God, you're a whore! A Wounded whore! They're *gone!* Everyone's *gone!*"

The lifeboat was a black dot in the vague gloaming sky. "Yes, it's just us two now," Amy smirked, coming for him.

CHAPTER TWENTY-TWO
What One Second of Normal Time Equals

Amy pulled herself off Jonathan James for the second time. The poor youngster was drained. She lay naked beside him. Next to her, in the dim lantern light, her clothes were just wisps scattering in the faint wind.

"That was wonderful, dear one," she murmured, her hand on his tight belly. "Dear sexy victorious last captain of everything."

JJC tried to smile but it came out as a grimace. "Yeah … was great …"

"Are you okay after all this … hard work?" she said with a kiss to his ear. That JJC couldn't maintain endless copulatory functions was more evidence of robotic deterioration on this awful planet, but in a way it was all endearing.

"Yeah, sure …" He seemed to be drifting off. "Just can't believe everyone's gone."

She stroked his magnificent biceps and pecs. At least he was no longer mumbling about the Laurie thing. That had been dismaying during the first lovemaking, but she'd let it pass, figuring another twenty minutes of vigorous Class J pumping would drive any thought of the putrid wooden beast out of his thick head. "I know it's a shock, love, but it was really fated from the beginning. You and I are here for something very important."

"Mmmm … or maybe we'll just drift for a few years until the ship gives out and we go down. Can't let that happen to Trotter, though. Just can't. Gotta get him fresh water and biomeat … can't let him go."

"We won't. I mean, if he'll accept me, we can get some great stuff done here." Trotter had mercifully scampered away when the clothes started coming off, but she sensed he was watching from some high vantage point, ready to pounce. His telepathic undertones about protecting his *Garthah-/yuu* brother Jonathan James were astonishing, and she'd calculated that he could rev himself into an extremely dangerous chewing machine. She had to earn his trust.

Besides, Trotter was the only dog she had now. She looked past JJC's hard torso to the immobile figure of Edward standing sentinel ten feet away. Was he really gone forever?

She raised up on an elbow and poked Jonathan James. "Look, the whole point is that you don't know the whole story of Ailyuae. I didn't see it myself until I ran into you on Myndar. When I saw the contamination in you, well, something just *snapped.* And then when you stole the *Garrison,* somehow it all came together. I knew exactly where you were heading. I had to follow."

JJC shrugged. "After we shot down *Archer,* it came to me that something was coming. At first I thought it might be a big meteor, maybe with some metals we could use. Every once in a while we see a meteor strike and try to retrieve it. Which is damn difficult, since they rarely hit one of the little islands."

"I understand about the metals. How Draka Sortie made this world."

"C'mon, don't tell me you're really into that myth yourself."

"You really don't know about Draka? Last July? When Draka began the Sphere Project?"

JJC shook his head. "There's no last July, my dear Dr. Nortel. You've still got that time problem. I've never bought that stupid Draka worship everyone seems to be programmed with. I wouldn't care about some Sphere Project even if there was one. I'm just damn tired. Eight hundred years of this craziness." He turned on his back and looked at the stars beyond the black shapes of the three main balloons. "It's even worse than all the crap I went through back in Alpha Centauri."

"Where you got *contaminated,* dear one. You got that big dose of Emperor Head, and then you contaminated *me,* so we could have all this fun." She patted his groin, but he pushed her fingers aside.

"Or after that, when I did the SolGrid crap. Thinking I could lead a revolt against stupid *software.* Man, it was just ego trip. I see that now. All it accomplished was killing me off as a human being. Screw it all."

Amy nodded. The poor baby was having one hell of a post-coital depression. And she'd been so certain that some feisty sex would blast his J training to the forefront of his mind.

"When we got to these coordinates I was freaked when we saw this huge burning meteor suddenly *slow down*," JJC went on. "Then out pops a parachute! I saw it was a ship, an old Sol design. We watched you go into the ocean and lowered our net before you sank."

Amy gazed up at the three balloons cutting empty circles into the swirl of the Milky Way. She strained to recall the parachute. As the *Stewart Neal Frankston* plummeted into Ailyuae's atmosphere she'd accessed the J-133 schematics and found it had an emergency chute. She could barely recall climbing through a tunnel whirling in the darkness, feeling for a hand crank. "Wait! I'm just remembering! There was a ship, right on my tail! The saucer's sensors weren't so great, but they showed a *Typhoon*-class ship just a couple seconds behind me, and *gaining*."

"Huh. Not likely. Sol doesn't have the tech to get to the Cloud. Or maybe they do, after eight hundred years."

"It's only been *three days!* I'm telling you!"

"Then how did *you* get here in a dinky J-133?"

"I upgraded it, just like you upgraded the *Garrison,* idiot! Sorry the stupid *Frankston* couldn't match your speed, but I made it here in *three days.*"

"Huh. Took me one day. You must've blacked out all these years. You were completely offline when we found you."

"Three days, I promise. My clock is working fine." Her astronomical senses were also up to speed; she could measure the motion of the Milky Way, startlingly ablaze and covering most of the sky, as it drifted to the west with Ailyuae's rotation. "I knew exactly where you were headed. It all came to me, and I knew exactly how to get here. The star Wiioryvel, the planet Ailyuae. It's all for the Sphere!"

"Aaah, forget it, who cares?"

She took a deep breath. She had to go slow with all this fool, no matter how good he'd been at the ancient insertion games on these hard planks. "Okay, I admit my recall may be a bit fragmented, but you have to listen about this other ship. I was in the pilot's seat, chatting with poor Edward there, when--" Her eyes filled with tears as she nodded to the marvelous Saint Bernard statue. Wounded robots could fake crying, but there was absolutely no need for such a display now. She managed to cut it off. "Anyway, I knew Edward was loyal USSF and that he was probably trying to lull me with dog friendliness. Maybe he thought he could warn your father somehow, but I didn't care. I love him so much. Please don't use him for scrap metal …"

And now she was fully sobbing. Jonathan James let it go on. That made her love him even more and she cried all the harder. She fought for control. "And … the next thing I remember is we find this ship on our tail. I wondered if Edward somehow *had* let Jack know. I forgot to tell you, your father and mother arrived right after you left, and I'm sure it's either them or somebody they sent right behind me."

"Yeah, Dad. He would pull that sort of rescue stunt. He was always trying to do that. Rescue me from something or other. But I'm sure somewhere around year two of eight hundred he got tired and dropped the whole thing."

Amy wondered whether JJC really understood what his father might be capable of. She'd definitely had that brilliant Jack boy under close observation in English AP class all those decades ago. "Anyway, Wiioryvel was straight ahead and I punched out of Star Drive. I just dove for Ailyuae, decelerating like crazy and hoping the other ship would totally miss this planet."

Armageddon shifted in the wind and the lanterns flickered. "You really believe this thing about another ship? You're sure you're not psycho-surging? Or defragmenting? Your skin temperature's awfully high."

"No, I know I'm not defragging." Lower-class Wounded could overtax themselves and overheat, which could lead to the dreaded process of *psycho-surging;* to prevent this, robots of Class J and below occasionally defragmented themselves. It was much like what humans called dreaming, though no sleep was involved. But robots who defragmented too much were considered in need of serious overhaul and were ostracized until they could be wiped.

She consulted her internal temperature of 106.78 degrees Fahrenheit and acknowledged she was running the equivalent of a human fever. She took more mindful breaths and began cooling herself. "I really wish you'd listen to me, because we're about to have a visitor who's not kindly disposed towards us. I'm running Memory Substantiation and organizing the sequence. Whatever that ship is, it matched my maneuver and was only one second behind me when I hit the atmosphere. Which I did at 8,417 miles per hour."

"Okay, okay," he muttered. She focused on his immense strong back as he stood and walked naked to the gunwale, obviously searching for the spot on the rotating sky where Amy's ship had appeared. She came up for a cuddle. Her own calculations were identical to where he pointed, the barely discernable ocean horizon to the west, in fact 3.877 degrees below it. "I don't feel anything there right now," JJC said. "I was feeling your saucer for twenty-eight hours. It didn't make sense at first, and I ignored it for a while, but even as we were fighting *Archer,* I felt it."

Against her will Amy replayed the horror of smashing into the atmosphere, flames streaming past the curved windows as the saucer's coating ablated. Edward's cheerful babble about recent technical problems with J-133 heat shields abruptly ceased, and a lifeless dog flopped out of his seat. The consoles sizzled and smoked, then all lights cut out. She'd grabbed an emergency flashlight which snapped apart in her fingers. Was that when she remembered the parachute crank at the top of the dome?

"So Draka really did it," she said. "I didn't see how it could be. I thought it was a metaphor or something. But *no electricity,* not even subatomic. It's all been *replaced.*"

"My first captain, Sullf, explained what happened. It was pretty shocking. Everything with biological components gets changed. A few metals do transform. We picked the *Garrison* pretty clean, and I bet we can get some out of your ship as well. What's left just disintegrates."

She studied the Milky Way. "*Everything* gets replaced with this anti-dark energy?" But even as she asked this question, she found the answer in the fragmentary equations Draka had left her as executor of his will.

"And we see what happens to non-Wounded robots," Jonathan James said, indicating the beautiful Edward perched on the deck. Miraculously no ship's movement had toppled him. "I'm surprised he hasn't started coming apart. It probably really is the Ywritt tech that's keeping him together as an object. Looks like all his atoms transformed on a purely physical level, but the Organizing Kernel didn't make it."

"He was such a dear one, even if he wanted to subvert everything I did. We can keep him, can't we? I mean, he was a navigator, you know. I know he'd really love to be kept aboard a ship."

JJC nodded, but in such a way, she felt, to indicate he hadn't even considered whether he'd let Amy stay here, much less her dog statue. Had Jonathan James Commer really not realized that Amy Nortel was here to marry him? To rip him all the way open, to develop his full Wounded powers? That together they'd upgrade themselves, progress from J to I to H and maybe even all the way to A? Didn't he know the two of them could rule the universe?

The surge of love and desire nearly stopped her robotic heart. "God, yes, I see it now!"

"Are you all right?" JJC said, gently touching her arm.

She beamed inexplicably at this touch of concern for Dr. Amy Nortel's continued existence, for she felt as if the insight could've canceled her on the spot. Or maybe JJC's interest had more to do with a renewed ogling at her naked boobs. She looked down. Was he getting ready for a third round? Did he love her yet? "I've resolved it! It's so simple!"

"What's so simple?"

"ADE has *slowed time here*. Why didn't I think of it? Time runs slower here because of the anti-dark energy. Look, you launched from Myndar on May 13, 2076, and got here in one day, right? And I launched a few minutes later but it took me three days to get here. So that means my next two days flying here was your equivalent of eight hundred years. Four hundred years here to each normal day in Sol."

JJC stared back. "Are you ..." But under the pressure of Amy's relentless Wounded consciousness he had to be calculating ADE mechanics. "Really?"

"Yes! And then whatever's coming after us must have launched a few hours later, but it was definitely overtaking me. I swear it was *one second* behind me when I dropped out of Star Drive."

JJC frowned. Amy was certain they shared the identical computation.

One Sol day = 86,400 seconds = 400 Ailyuae years = 146,100 Ailyuae days. Thus one second of Sol time = 1.69 Ailyuae days = 40.56 hours.

"That's about how much time we have," Amy said, "depending on what speed they exited Star Drive. They'll be at the exact point where I arrived."

JJC studied the starlit ocean horizon. "Maybe ... there *is* something coming."

Amy could feel the white dot herself. Decelerating.

CHAPTER TWENTY-THREE
The So-Called Sphere Project

Edward verified that he continued to exist. His eyes and ears were nonfunctional, yet he could see lanterns flickering and hear voices. He had no brain, no central nervous system, but he created thoughts, and read thoughts from the other entities around him, three of whom had recently exited this environment. Full nose functionality was available; he easily processed a kaleidoscope of thousands of ship and organism odors.

Whether he was actually located in his body was an open question. He did know the entirety of the ship. He had measured the energy fluctuations of all four of the Jonathan James Commer/Amy Nortel copulations. He gathered the thoughts of an eight-hundred-year-old biological dog, Trotter, currently atop the poop deck, and already considered him a good friend. But Trotter had no clue of Edward's existence. Nobody did. To them he was just an inanimate object.

Maybe Amy Nortel, drowsing entwined with her lover on blankets JJC had procured shortly before Number Four, still had some faith in him. He got hints of that from her Primary Kernel Awareness. Though her surface concepts were those of grief for him, she'd rudely thrust them aside in favor of the moment's survival and her fascination with the naked body of this ship's captain. Yet surely, deep down, Amy had to know Edward existed.

Maybe the fact that there was no electricity explained his ongoing presence. He must be made of the anti-dark energy which Amy and Jonathan James had been discussing. How could that be? Edward still had access to the entirety of Sol civilization's scientific knowledge, and he understood that electrical charges were fundamental to the composition of all matter.

And what about the electromagnetic spectrum? Visible light? How was anyone on the deck of this ship able to see the spiral of the Milky Way, or their own toes for that matter? Edward began building theories of how a negative dark energy might accomplish this. Though he'd never been programmed to be a theoretical physicist, he was struck by the fact that he'd apparently just authored several influential papers, including "On an Approach to a Theory of an Integrated Anti-Dark Energy/Anti-Dark Matter Continuum with Reference to Quantum Cosmological States." Better yet he'd written them all in German to thoroughly impress everyone. How to send them back to Sol for publication was a problem, though. But apparently he'd just proven that the ADE star Wiioryvel, a twin in size to Sol, with its single Earth-like ADE planet Ailyuae sweeping a circle ninety-three million miles in radius, was capable of generating its own ADE-based light spectrum.

The light, the ship, the two Wounded robots and Trotter, the planet itself, were all just ... here. Available to Edward. Somehow.

The thoughts of the JJC robot seemed distant and preoccupied. They flitted between blocked horror at the departure of two wooden robots in the lifeboat, revulsion at his uncontrolled lust for the Amy creature, despair at finding himself the last balloon ship captain, grief for his crew, and anxiety concerning whatever object was scheduled to hit this planet the day after tomorrow. And despite Amy's pleadings, JJC actually hadn't made up his mind whether to spare Edward from metal scavenging. Since Trotter had no concept that Edward could have a mind, only Dr. Amy Nortel, traitor to Sol and Edward's kidnapper, could potentially take Edward's side.

Edward strained to calculate how to communicate his predicament back to Sol, but it was as impossible as getting his theories published across 163,000 light-years and two different rates of time. He didn't know whether having his mechanical body taken apart would cancel the undefined consciousness he possessed, but he wasn't eager to try the experiment. In any case the greed in JJC's mind concerning rare metals was extremely disturbing. Thus it behooved him to stick with Amy's thoughts, observe her, and continue thinking and perceiving.

Amy's mind raced with unaccustomed disorder and unease. She was afraid of the ship behind her. She was jubilant about a

Sphere she didn't comprehend. She grieved for Edward himself. She raged at Jonathan James Commer's obvious stupidity, yet at the same time lusted to copulate with him. She stirred from her sleep to mutter: "What about Draka? We can't forget about him. Can he possibly have survived?"

"Mmmm … no, of course not," JJC murmured, stroking her forearm. "That's all just a myth. Go back to sleep."

"He had to have died last year. My programming assigned me to be his executor, but I'm so *confused*. I really don't know how to do that."

"I guess the Draka stuff is just part of any robot's programming. I've just let the superstition go on here. But we don't need it anymore. We're the last ship. We've won."

But Jonathan James Commer was afraid, Edward saw. Despite his awareness of his slow ADE degeneration, being Wounded had previously given him the confidence of feeling immortal. All robots assigned to this planet had known they were essentially eternal, that is, if nothing wrecked their bodies, as warfare over 124,400 years had dispatched 1,189,650 robots as well as 21,630 ships that had met their ruin.

Yes, it had really been 124,400 years. And the captain of the last ship now felt the cancelation of his existence more clearly than ever.

"Why didn't Draka finish the Sphere?" Amy wondered. "The documents he gave me say he was prepping this solar system for it."

"Hey, look. It's past time to drop all this about him. He died eight hundred years ago, and everyone's turned him into some sort of god."

"It's *not* eight hundred years, you idiot!" Amy insisted, sitting up. "It was just *last July*. And you left Iota Persei only three days ago! Can't you get that through your head? Run the ADE equations again!"

JJC scrunched back from her. "I still can't get over that. It's really been … only three days?"

Edward saw identical thoughts forming in both JJC's and Amy's minds, though there was no telepathic link between the two. Jonathan James ran the calculations and surged with a fresh concept: that his lover Suzette Borman was still alive, that he'd last seen her just a month ago. Was a reunion possible?

Dr. Amy Nortel generated the same concept and despaired to think of JJC awakening to full Class J powers and building a spaceship to take him back to beloved Suzette. To re-transform himself to electricity and build a real life with the woman at the core of his personality.

"No!" she moaned. "No!"

Edward felt both their emotions and knew there was nothing to be done about them. Really, if these so-called robotic entities would just use their logic for once. But they got as upset as human beings. They were as flighty as Jack or Amav or Jack's brother Joe.

"Only three days ..." Jonathan James muttered. "Unbelievable."

Amy clutched the blanket to her breasts, her mind shrieking *I hate you!* But beneath her despair was the science itself, and she shakily clung to it. "All Draka really did," she managed, "was set up anti-dark energy as the basis for this system. He sent millions of Wounded robots to Ailyuae and they all transformed in this ADE environment. As far as Ailyuae is concerned, that was 124,400 years ago. But since then, *nothing.*"

"Look, I guess I get that about the time, and that may be the religion here, but I just can't accept that. I'm a Class J, I have my Wounded files, and I don't get any of that. This is just an anomalous nonelectrical solar system."

"You're an *untrained* Class J. Of course you don't understand. All you yokels could do was use this planet's meager resources to fight wars. Balloon ships of all things! You've killed a million of your fellow robots, and for what? God, we were supposed to have a Dyson sphere here, based on ADE and so insanely powerful we could blast the whole Orion Arm."

JJC blinked. "The Orion Arm?"

"Right. It was always Draka's sore point. God, I didn't even see that myself until now. But it makes sense. Don't try to sphere thousands and thousands of stars individually. That'd take a zillion years. Just take out the whole Orion Arm at once. All those crappy races that've been holding us up." She stood and paced nude on the planks. "Yes! That's it!"

Edward felt the pleasure rising in both Wounded robots at the thought of wiping out the troublesome Orion Arm. After all, the Arm had thrown up stubborn obstacles to Wounded conquests. The Alpha Centaurian Grid had blocked them for millennia, Jack Commer had halted Draka at Iota Persei, and there were a few other civilizations in the Arm that had put up nasty fights.

Edward was surprised to find that Amy's mind contained records of several civilizations Sol hadn't encountered yet. But there was still no way to transmit "A Preliminary Analysis of Newly Discovered Extraterrestrial Civilizations in the Orion Arm" back to Sol.

"We take out the whole Orion Arm? Across 163,000 light-years?" JJC squeaked, dazedly watching her pace.

"It's supposed to be instantaneous. Quantum superposition, bubbles of spacetime interpenetrating anti-dark energy, or something. We take out the Orion Arm and anything in the way of it. Can't say I understand the math. But of course Draka could."

"Wow …" Jonathan James finally whispered. Edward felt JJC's struggle. His programming flickered. He fought the confusion and sought pure Wounded reason, but then came the thought of home. Mom, Dad, everyone. *Suzette Borman.* Only three days ago he'd been in the Arm. Suzette was *there.* She was the human enemy, she and the entire Orion Arm blocked the way of the Wounded, but he loved her.

Edward saw Amy figuring out what held Jonathan James up. "Of course the Orion Arm has to go," she declared. "And *all* humans. It's the only way."

Edward could feel Trotter reluctantly accepting Dr. Amy Nortel as a new force in his *Garthah-/yuu* brother's soul. The Beagle understood the Wounded logic building in Jonathan James, though the dog ached at the idea of his ancient Milky

Way so easily blasted apart.

"Well, maybe. But it's a moot point anyway," JJC said. "If Draka really did plan this place, he obviously screwed it up. We've killed off every robot, we're the last ship, and everything's dying. We're done for."

"There's got to be a way to make it happen. I was *fated* to come here. You and I were *fated* to join up. Somehow we've got to fulfill Draka's dream."

JJC turned on his back, brain surging with images of naked Suzette Borman. "I don't see it. It's not going to happen."

"We'll do it. We have to." Amy came back to JJC and lay beside him, but couldn't bring herself to stroke his flat belly. Her images of Suzette were less precise, consisting of holographic photos in Sol database records she'd plundered during her archivist work at Iota Persei. But her urge to rebuild Draka's weapon redoubled. Edward watched her strain through the executor documents Draka had transferred to her Wounded circuits just as a Martian shattergun bolt rendered him into a billion pieces of glass. The files had never fully compiled. Amy raged at her inability to piece it all together, but all at once Edward grasped the full account.

Dr. Amy Nortel had it all wrong.

It all had to do with the ancient Kjurian map on the lower level of this ship, and its uncanny nine-inch sphere perched on the coordinates for the sun Wiioryvel. Edward had found the map chamber on his first mental tour of the ship and had verified it as an authentic Kjurian artifact. Neither Sol nor Centaurian archaeologists had ever discovered it.

But Draka Sortie, *Typhoon IV* physician/engineer and amateur tomb hunter, had. He'd stumbled upon the chamber on one of his field trips to Kjur in November 2074, but had told no one. At the time he was still unaware of his Wounded nature and had assumed he'd someday write an account for publication and modest fame.

He'd pushed the map out of mind until the moment M'rrpla's shattergun ray struck his temple on July 10, 2075. In his final seconds he flashed that the black sphere poised on the

Large Magellanic Cloud must certainly represent the ultimate Wounded weapon. In fury and desperation he summoned his final Trans-Simultaneity to uproot the entire Kjurian chamber and sling it to the Cloud along with a million Wounded soldiers.

In following the map's directions, he'd thought he was fashioning the ultimate revenge for his death, a final, omnipotent Dyson sphere to wipe out the entire Orion Arm. But nothing happened. Ailyuae stagnated. A crew of ignorant Wounded eventually built Balloon Ship *Armageddon* around the map chamber. A religious cult arose along with 124,400 years of war.

Draka hadn't created Wiioryvel or Ailyuae. He hadn't created anti-dark energy. He'd created nothing.

And only a dysfunctional robot dog had any idea how dangerous this non-electrical solar system really was.

Edward copied the star map down to the last detail along with all the inscriptions in the chamber. He used it as Figure 1 in his new paper, "Towards an N-Dimensional Understanding of an Abrupt Termination of the Universe."

CHAPTER TWENTY-FOUR
Disintegration
May 16, 2076

"Unusual electromagnetic anomalies, Captain!" Laurie cried from the copilot seat. "Recommend breaking off pursuit!"

"No!" Jack shouted. "We can't be more than a few seconds behind the *Frankston*. Ywer! Prep Arkonsky fields to seize her!"

"ArkonskyTrans not responding," the Martian spoke from the console at the rear of the Control Room, where he'd resumed light duty. "I'll try Auxiliary."

"*Typhoon VII* is in fact *one second* behind *Frankston*," the Marsport Automated Transport System spoke. "I corroborate electromagnetic fluctuations emanating from approaching system, consisting of yellow dwarf star and one planet orbiting at one AU. Correction: the star appears to be fluctuating between--"

"Forget it!" Jack said, consulting his own screen. "There's no system there."

Then a sun was right in front of them, blazing through the canopy glass.

"Where did *that* come from?" Amav groaned from the chair behind them. "Veer! Veer!"

Jack was briefly irritated that his non-USSF wife dared issue a command on the bridge of the *Typhoon VII,* but he let it pass. Laurie shouted: "Dropping out of Star Drive!" She was correct to disengage the Drive so close to a solar mass. How did it get here? His screen plotted the *Typhoon's* course relative to the new gravity field ahead. "Robot, where's the *Frankston*?" he rapped out, still finding it difficult to refer to his copilot as "Laurie."

"It's out of Drive, aiming for that planet on the other side of the star. At least I think. My console just went. Wait, I can power to Auxiliary Nine." Jack saw her Auxiliary Mode come up, though her console writhed with spiky blue snakes. "We're still on *Frankston's* track. But, sir, that star's readings are *not normal.* And we're *not* dropping out! We're still under Star

172

Drive!"

Jack's screen showed jagged red streaks. His stomach turned and he fought to keep from blacking out. "Dammit, robot, can we disengage?"

"I--I don't know!" Her main screen went black just as they shot by the star. Jack was struck by the alarm in the copilot's voice. Could robots feel fear? Would that hamper her robotic control of the ship? Should he relieve her of duty? "I can't believe it!" she said. "Trying all Auxiliaries! I think Eleven--" Her screen came up briefly and Jack watched her stab her way through a complex series of dim wavering panels. "Thank God! We're out! Star Drive down! We missed the star by thirty million miles. It's still intact."

"My console's out, too," Ywer grunted. "Miss Laurie 283 is correct. There are unusual electromagnetic disturbances."

All lights cut off, casting the Control Room in lurid shadows from the light of the star they'd just passed. Jack's chair crumbled beneath him and he sprawled on the metal floor. But as soon as he scrambled up, he found himself floating amid surprised groans from the others. Ywer's outradiance was like sheets of torn notebook paper covered with scrawled equations.

"Gravity out. Inertial dampers out," the Marsport Automated Transport System warbled in a deepening bass tone. "MATS cannot offer more than a conjecture at this time. Electrical activity seems to be ceasing aboard this ship in increasing waves of quantum probability so that--so that--excuse me, rerouting memory--so that--so that--"

"So that *what?*" Jack demanded.

"That--that the nature of electricity itself, in this entire solar system, appears to have gone *haywire!* I *am* electricity, Captain Jack! I cannot be without it! And so am I dead! Goodbye!"

There was a long silence as shadows twisted in the Control Room with a slight roll the *Typhoon* had picked up. "God! Is MATS *gone?*" Amav gasped.

"Who cares?" Jack said. He scanned the last tiny flickering readout to Laurie's left. "Dammit, robot, how can we still be going *three hundred million miles per hour?*"

"That's not *possible!*" Laurie said. "I set SD to exit us at fifty thousand!"

"Well, it obviously didn't! We're doing almost half-light speed!"

"Nav has us on course to collide with that planet!"

"Distance?"

"Three million miles! We have thirty-six seconds! God, I can't believe it! No, wait!" She yanked a manual keyboard from under her console and routed it to the surviving panel. "SD Exit's offline, but I've got contact with Aux Thirteen. Maybe I can reprogram it to manually brake--" Her fingers flailed on the keys. "Got it! Somehow! Yes! We're down to fourteen hundred! And look, Aux Fifteen took over and programmed us a rough reentry trajectory!"

"Oh my God. Good work, whatever you just did," Jack gulped, just as if she really *had* been the human Laurie thinking her way through an impossible situation. How had the *Typhoon* come out of Star Drive twice as fast as its highest possible exit speed? At least their particle sensors must've been online to keep dust grains from rupturing the ship at that velocity. If the robot hadn't figured it out, they would've simply punched a good hole in that planet coming up.

To his astonishment a gray, cloud-covered sphere filled the canopy.

"Inertial dampers just went. And we may not have any thruster maneuvering for a landing," Laurie noted, punching at her black screens. "Now I don't have any auxiliary routing. MATS was right! There's no electricity!"

Jack stared at the planet's broad curve and what seemed at first glance like an excellently programmed reentry. A suggestion of red energy flared outside the windows, and the ship seemed to jolt with atmospheric contact, though that was difficult to ascertain when they were all floating. Jack wondered if Amav and Ywer were as dizzy and stomach-sick as he was. Faint gravity built, but even then Ywer had to drift over to Jack, grabbing the disintegrating chairs as Amav reached to steady him. "Are the shuttles operative?" Ywer grunted as chunks of plastic came off the main console under his claw.

Laurie 283 shook her head. "I saw them go offline. Trying to revive one may or may not work. We could try the escape pods."

Jack winced at the idea of shoving them all into the tiny pods that had little chance of surviving an atmospheric descent. He pulled out his comm to check the condition of the pods, but it was blank as well. Strips of plastic wafted off the device. He jabbed the screen and the comm burst into a gray cloud of wires and wafers.

Jack felt the first sickening atmospheric bump. "Dammit, there's really no electricity! The pods would never work!"

"There's no way off this thing?" Amav cried.

"No! I mean yes!" said Ywer. "We have parachutes in locker AE-35!" His outradiance ballooned with the specs for the *Typhoon VII's* six emergency manual parachutes, stored by the lowest airlock, port side, behind the shuttles and beneath the wing for ease of exit. Nobody had thought anyone would ever need a manual parachute, and no *Typhoon* crew had ever practiced for this eventuality. Definitely a training oversight, one Jack would remedy as soon as possible.

But it began to dawn on him that there'd probably never be a chance to remedy this oversight. Yet the parachutes were the only way. He could see that Amav had pulled the solution out of Ywer's mind as well. The robot couldn't, of course, but she'd surely memorized the *Typhoon* specs and knew what had to happen.

"Okay. Four of us," Jack said. "Everyone gets a parachute. Ywer, you've got the procedures to fasten them, and how to use? And they have oxygen bottles and helmets, right?"

"Yes, Captain, absolutely."

They were about to jump at high velocity into an unknown atmosphere. Maybe it was total poison out there. Jack met Amav's eyes and they shared the entirety of their marriage in that glance. This was the end. They both knew it. "We have to try," she finally said.

Jack lurched as the *Typhoon* slapped hard against the

thickening atmosphere. Gravity rose. "Right. Let's get down to Airlock 1."

They clambered down the stairs to Level 2. Jack was gratified to see that emergency ladders had popped out down the length of the fuselage when the inertial dampers had cut out, although the crew yanked several rungs from the walls as they stumbled in the meager planet light from the Control Room behind them. Sections of the floor jerked loose. Plastic and metal were coming undone all over the ship; screws and rivets floated before Jack's face. The ship was plunging like a bullet. Any second now they'd start whirling out of control.

In complete darkness and increasing gravity they found the airlock. Light flared from the floor as the Laurie robot stamped on a pad that glowed like a kid's Halloween safety stick. Jack hadn't even known this airlock had anything like this. Could he possibly have read all the *Typhoon VII* manuals himself? Hell, no, that was what he had crew for. In any case he was pleased to see Laurie stamp eight of these floor pads into yellow-green light and then four larger ones on the walls.

In the new glare she opened storage compartment AE-35 and dumped all six parachutes on the trembling floor. They had real gravity now, and it was climbing above normal. Laurie and Ywer fastened Amav's harness, helmet, and dual oxygen tanks even as bits of plastic and leather peeled off. There were no pressure suits and they had no idea how high they were.

This was suicide and they all knew it. But they all went about their work tight-lipped. Jack accepted his harness but decided to keep the increasingly opaque helmet visor open until they were ready to jump. He could see through the crazed glass of the inner airlock door, then through the outer airlock porthole, that the *Typhoon* was slipping into its fatal wobbling spin. Battering shocks came up through the glowing floor.

They all stood in their parachutes and helmets. Laurie had left her own visor open and turned to locker AE-34 next to the first one. Why in God's name was she wasting time opening the clearly labeled Coffin Storage? They had their parachutes, and there was nothing to do but open the airlock and jump. Jack felt himself slammed into the wall as the ship whirled harder. He felt his left boot spring apart, rubber and plastic strips curling off in the greenish glare. He stared at his right boot cracking open.

Laurie hauled out a glossy white coffin and let it bump to the floor, shards of white plastic snapping off.

"What on earth are you *doing?*" Jack cried. "Let's get the airlock door open!"

"Quiet!" the robot barked. "I need to check the lid seal." She snapped open the upper coffin lid to reveal--

"Oh my God! *Laurie!*" Jack moaned, backed away from the beautiful red-haired woman in the coffin. "*L-Laurie?* She--she *killed herself?* She was so upset that--that--*she killed herself?* And you brought her *along? Why the hell would you bring her along?*"

"I said quiet!" the robot snarled as Jack gaped at Laurie Lachrer's open, glossy dead eyes, the bright blue faded to battleship gray--and the white pallor, the sunken cheeks, the stiffened neck, the once lustrous red hair framing her chin like dried straw. Nobody had even respected her enough to close her eyes. But Jack couldn't bring himself to do it. Was this some sick joke? This robot *animal* had just hauled her around like some obscene trophy?

"Oh my God! Laurie *died?* She died for *nothing?* Just because she couldn't come? Oh my God!"

"C'mon, get a grip, Jack," Amav said. "We've all got to be calm for the jump."

He whirled to his wife. "*You?* Are you all *crazy?*" Meanwhile the demented Laurie contraption secured the lid and dragged over the two unused parachutes.

"Goddammit, what are you *doing?*" Jack shrieked. No one heeded him. He was the captain, everything was coming apart, and nobody cared about this *horror*. Laurie was dead. He was about to watch everyone die. He was about to watch Amav die.

The Laurie robot expertly wove the two parachute harnesses through the coffin's grommets and from some dim shred of rationality Jack noted that she'd fastened the ripcords so that after one parachute deployed, it would open the second. "Yes, she has to be buried with full honors ..." he babbled.

Amav and Ywer bent over the coffin with Laurie, and all three dragged it to the inner airlock door. When Laurie twisted the door handle, it snapped into pieces that clanged on the floor, warring with the increasing whine from outside. Then she dug her hands into the sides of the door and wrenched it back with Ywer's help. Jack stared at the metal floor of the airlock, each atmospheric bang popping out twisted mesh squares.

"This--this is *insane!*" he gasped as Laurie next went to work on the outer airlock door. Its handle wouldn't budge, but as Laurie and Ywer banged on it, the entire door loosened and tumbled into gray chaos. The roar of the twirling ship ratcheted into unbearable thunder. *Typhoon* air blew out and outside gasses flooded in.

Amav clutched a twisting scrap of inner airlock frame. "Cut it, Jack, I'm telling you, it's okay!"

"No! Someone has to take charge!" Mouth agape, Jack stared into Amav's brown eyes through her blurring, melting visor. How couldn't read her at all. How could she be calm? How could she be so courageous in the face of extinction?

To his shame Jack Commer realized that he was the only one out of control. He gazed in wonder as Laurie, Amav, and Ywer, buffeted by the roaring air, shoved the coffin loosely draped in its black parachute harnesses across the disintegrating airlock floor. The robot had to be affected, too, Jack managed to think, as he knew a HAVOTT robot could normally toss that coffin out with one hand.

He only now registered that the outside air wasn't searing them at thousands of degrees, but was distinctly chilly. The atmosphere and the spin had to be slowing them. God, was there any way they'd really make it?

The coffin twirled madly into the void. Amav clutched the top of the airlock and jumped effortlessly. He knew his wife had just killed herself.

Ywer hesitated before the dense rotating clouds. His outradiating thoughts were feverish nonsense. Jack saw only incomprehensible ruminations on Splintering, Conversion,

Quark Energy, Dark Energy, and Complete Reversal of All Basic Particles. It made no sense, but that didn't matter, because Jack's mind was also splintering and in this state he wouldn't have been able to read Ywer's thoughts if they'd all been sitting in a parlor, sipping tea.

If only we could be in a parlor, sipping tea!

If only Amav would come back--

Whatever Ywer had been holding onto snapped off in his little pink claw and the Martian was blown out with a whimper. Jack had had enough. Go do it, then. He defiantly flipped his helmet visor closed only to watch it snap into a dozen pieces.

Jack whirled to the robot. "Goddamn you, you wasted so much time fooling with that stupid coffin when we're all going to die! I could've jumped two minutes ago with a working visor!"

He met her unfathomable blue eyes but before he could bitch any further he took a kick in the stomach that hurled him clear. "Get out, fool!" his copilot yelled as he flailed into space.

CHAPTER TWENTY-FIVE
Quiet Death

The parachute jerked him so hard Jack thought his spine had snapped. The deploying canopy was tattered. Some of its ropes had frayed, but most were doing their job. High above, the white *Typhoon VII* tumbled end over end, wings snapping free, sides peeling, the ship cracking into big black chunks. No flames.

Within seconds the *Typhoon* was a smudge of charcoal drifting in the sky.

Beneath Jack a gray ocean came up fast. He could breathe fresh air and his head cleared. This was the end. No use denying it. He was dead, they were all dead parachuting into this ocean, but somehow it was all calm and dignified, and he was ashamed of his earlier panic. Why, this was all so easy. So he'd screwed up being a ship's captain, or a supreme commander. So what? Hadn't he earned a quiet death here on this unknown planet?

It had been so tempting to think rejuvenation would make him immortal. Of course, he'd known he wasn't, but all the same he'd thought he might have four hundred years to work on his life themes. But they all knew accidents or serious illness could kill anyone at any time, and most USSF officers figured that extending their lifespans just exposed them to the increased probability of the fatal spacecraft accident. Jack had thought he'd go out in style, then, not in a hospital bed. It had kept him somewhat wary and focused. But had he ever really expected this moment? Even after all the other close calls he'd survived across five decades?

No, it was peace. Maybe there was a *Garr/thahg* after all, maybe a human version of the Alpha Centaurian afterlife, a military heaven for humans, he would join Amav there, and Jim and John, so long dead on the *Typhoon I*.

Yes, there she was. His wondrous wife. A parachute with a distinctly blue-clad female twirled far to his left. And that awful coffin had survived as well, floating down further off on two black parachutes.

Something else was moving out there, and fast. A speck

grew into a dark bumblebee churning across the sky, and Jack blinked to see that it was suspended under three huge balloons. The craft's design indicated it should be floating leisurely, but its red, purple, and green balloons slanted back in high acceleration.

The airship maneuvered under the drifting coffin and snatched it out of the sky. To Jack's surprise two figures gathered in parachutes and ropes, and the craft shot forward to grab Amav. But Jack was distracted by an inflating plasti-rubber raft bursting beneath him, forcing his legs apart. As dark rough waves hurtled up, air whined through dozens of holes in a bright yellow raft he'd had no idea existed. Off to the right two other rafts churned on the ocean, dragged in the wind by loose black parachutes.

He hit hard. The raft went sideways and he flew overboard. He swam back for the increasingly limp yellow fabric, righted the raft and scrambled onto it, knees sinking in water. He found a knife and cut the ropes away. They parted like strands of wet spaghetti.

His entire body felt aflame. "Don't touch the water!" he yelled to Ywer and Laurie 283. "There's something acid about it!"

The *balloon ship*--for that was all he could think to call it-- dove from the sky and hovered above the Laurie robot's raft, then Ywer's, dropping netting and pulling those two up as their rafts dissolved.

Finally the ship came for him, and Jack was struck by the immense shadow it cast. What he'd thought was a small vessel was a monster, bigger than the *Typhoon*. A net fell from the starboard side and Jack eagerly clambered into it as his raft sank. To his surprise he found himself dangling with Laurie 283 and Ywer as buckets of water poured down over them from the gunwale above.

"Trotter's not happy we're using his drinking water to wash you folks off!" came the merry call from above. "Looks like Dad got the worst of it, but there shouldn't be any serious long-term hassle there. Okay, Amy, let's get 'em up!"

Jack was pulled over the gunwale. He balanced unsteadily on the rocking deck. *That voice.* He could hardly make sense of what he was seeing, but there was Amav, and so everything was all right. Ywer was there and robot copilot Laurie. And then the tragedy, the Laurie Lachrer coffin on the deck by Amav, its lid open, a suggestion of red hair blowing in the breeze. So insanely final and unbelievable. Jack fought to get his bearings. Despite all the horror he had to come back. He'd lost it, he'd had something like a fast plunge into his own death, and yes, it had been a pleasure, but whether he wanted it or not he'd been sent back to a world of decisions and deadlines, tasks and commands.

That voice.

"Jonathan *James!*" he gasped, noting a grin on his son's face he'd never seen before. Somehow Jonathan James was here, hauling up wet netting along with that simpering Wounded Amy Nortel woman. Amav backed away from them, eyes wide with shock, hand to her mouth.

To Jack's further astonishment Edward was there, but the robot dog just squatted motionless. And the Beagle Trotter barked, broadcasting doggie thoughts Jack couldn't grasp. They were riding a drifting airship. How could this be? Nausea rippled through him, then cut off. He grabbed the gunwale for support.

JJC noted his unease. "Quick update, Daddo. You've been transformed. There's no electricity in this solar system. Every atom in your body's been converted to anti-dark energy. Including what's left of your clothes after your dunk in the water. All your clothes are gonna disintegrate in this air anyway, but the water speeds that up. Gonna have to get you all some new Wounded uniforms." He indicated the tight black suits he and Amy wore, red stripes down the outside of trousers tucked into glossy black boots.

Jack surveyed his ragged flight suit. "Anti-*what*? What's going on here?"

"Bio-beings can transform, why we don't really know. Amy says it's only been three days for her. A couple minutes for you. Deal with it, Daddo."

Jack dragged his mouth back together with difficulty. "You

separated out of that pyramid? You're okay?"

JJC shrugged. "Yeah, but now I'm sort of Lord Wounded. Master of this planet."

"Exactly," Amy Nortel said. "Why did we bother hauling these creeps up, Jonathan James? We should've just let them rot in the sea." But she beamed at Jack. "Though I'm overjoyed to see my star pupil again, of course!"

"Aaah, we need to see what's going on with 'em," Jonathan James said. "Hey, Daddo, we Wounded really aren't so bad once you get to know us. We saved your asses, you know. That ocean would just *dissolve* you."

Jack fell back against the gunwale. "You ... are Wounded?" JJC nodded.

"*God* ..." Was this all a hallucination? But another glance at the coffin behind the inert Edward jolted Jack back to his senses. He took in the white face, the filmy slate-blue eyes. "God, she *died!* She had to *die!*"

"I know, I know ..." JJC managed. "I mean, *Laurie. Again.*" Jack had no idea what this meant. Jonathan James looked back and forth between the live robot and the dead woman in the coffin. "Hard to believe, I guess."

"The poor boy's had a rough few days," Amy laughed. "I think your Lauries must remind him of some old sex toy who bought the farm!"

"Sir, I need to check on Laurie's status," the Laurie robot broke in, bending over the coffin.

"No! Belay that!" Jack ordered as the robot inexplicably put her hands on her twin's unmoving chest and pumped vigorously. "Robot, this is nuts! She's *dead!* You brought a *dead body* here! You've reverted to Runaway Programming Disorder!"

"No! Idiot!" the robot cried, pounding on the dead Laurie. "I can't believe she's gone! No response at all! I thought we'd saved her! Oh my God!"

"Humans," Amy Nortel snorted. "Is this enough of an interrogation, Jonathan James? I'm bored. I suggest we consign your fetching redheads to the ocean along with all our other guests."

Jack unbolted his blaster holster but found it contained only a few shards of crumbling metal. The holster belt itself slid to the wooden planks in a cloud of black dust. Jack was left scratching at his right thigh and saw his fingers scraping away loose fabric to reveal his naked hip.

"Really, all that stuff mostly falls apart in this environment," JJC said. "But you humans transformed pretty well, I think." He pointed to Edward. "These Sol robots with Ywritt tech don't seem to decay. They just deactivate."

"Don't try to jump us," Amy cautioned. "This place messes with our Wounded capacities, but we're still fifty times stronger than all of you put together. Jonathan James, are we going to dispose of these characters now, or not?"

There was an extremely long silence. Wind buffeted the balloons above them in deep rhythmic slaps.

Commander Ywer's outradiance had been jumbled for quite a while, mirroring the death stress all the parachutists except the damn Laurie robot had just gone through. But Ywer was stabilizing and Jack knew the Martian was fighting to control his thoughts. Neither he nor Jack could be certain whether these Wounded robots could read his mind, but Ywer certainly didn't want their captors to know about the Ywritt-enhanced Martian shattergun in his side pocket.

CHAPTER TWENTY-SIX
Team Commer

The air smelled like rotten eggs. Amav tensed for the robots to charge, wondering if she'd vomit on the spot. Backing up against the gunwale was a poor move, but she hardly cared what happened next. She was still stunned by the *Typhoon's* inexplicable ruin, by the mindless jump into frigid, barely breathable atmosphere. Her back was twisted. Ywer's jumbled outradiance about various models of Martian shatterguns only added to her confusion. She picked up his chagrin about his Amplified Thought abilities, which were apparently offline. He was an AT teleportation adept, but he'd been unable to teleport out of the crashing *Typhoon,* or off this ship, for that matter.

"Hell, these guys aren't going to give us any trouble. Right, Daddo? Mom?" Jonathan James sneered. "Are you all properly grateful for us saving your precious asses?"

"There's no reason to waste time chitchatting with these losers," Amy said. Amav wondered where Jack's pompous AP English teacher had found the time to change into that form-fitting uniform. They'd been right on her tail as she followed JJC to this hellish world.

"C'mon, Amy," JJC said, "we need to find out what other plans the USSF may have for heading out here."

"Oh, don't listen to your *contamination,* dearest! We Wounded need to be *ruthless.*"

JJC smirked. "The lady's marvelous on her back, but forgets I'm Lord Wounded now, and captain of this ship. Welcome to Balloon Ship *Armageddon,* folks. The last ship on this planet. I won the final battle a couple days ago. Not that it's doing me a hell of a lot of good, but hey."

"Lord Wounded!" Amy snorted. "Sheesh." She poked him. "How was I on top?"

JJC cocked his head. "More than adequate, I would think." He picked up Amav's grimace and shrugged.

Amav certainly didn't care. Why wouldn't two nasty Wounded robots screw each other? They looked so proud and

185

smug in those black and red naval uniforms. Amav considered her own fraying garments, shocked at how much flesh was coming on display for her sociopathic son and, if she guessed correctly, her future daughter-in-law. That is, if Amav were invited to the wedding and not tossed thousands of feet to the ocean in the next minute.

Why should she be surprised by this kid insolence? JJC was still just an overgrown teenager, after all, no matter his chronological age of twenty-eight. Why would anyone bother listening to the same bombast he always prattled? Despite the apparent reprieve he offered his victims, Amav couldn't bring herself to take a step towards this foul caricature of her son.

"We need to be *ruthless,* baby," Amy repeated. "They're always plotting. Remember how your father got Draka so off-balance that a stupid Martian robot could kill him?"

"Aw, hell, Dad knows he's out of options. Out of spaceships, too." He glanced at a faint line of black against the high cirrus clouds. "That the *Typhoon VII,* Daddo? I was able to see some of its schematics on its way down."

Jack nodded grimly at this demonstration of Wounded awareness. "Yeah. So we just lost another expensive ship. Have to talk to the Ywritt about a new one." Amav saw how much Jack had calmed himself. He was certainly assessing the situation better than she was. She'd been afraid he'd really snapped on the *Typhoon.* At the first shock of the unknown Jack Commer tended to veer straight into hysteria, then at the last second accept whatever circumstances were in front of him and start working with them. And bring everyone out alive. He was really quite endearing that way.

"Guess your damn Sol Council will have a fit about you trashing another ship," JJC laughed. "Or did have, eight hundred years ago. Or whenever it was. It gets very confusing." He pointed at the morning sky. "Milky Way's not up yet. Too bright now to see it anyway. Sometimes you can see it in daylight, though. Took me a while to realize how much ADE warps time. Amy here figured it out."

"Just simple arithmetic, dear ones," purred the unhinged

archivist spy from Myndar. "There's serious time dilation going on here. You were one second, or 1.69 Ailyuae days, behind me."

"That gave us time to travel here, where we calculated we'd intercept your ship," JJC went on. "A little after ten AM local time. I really thought you'd launch a shuttle we'd have to fish out of the water."

"That was *gutsy,* taking to parachutes, dear Jack!" Amy added. "But we really don't have a second to waste. For your information, I'm Draka Sortie's executor, and JJC and I need to set up one hell of a Dyson sphere here."

"Ah, really forget it, hon. We don't have the resources for that sort of crap anymore," JJC drawled. "Not to mention any sailors to help build it. I say it's time to relax. We'll just cruise around here a few years, maybe have a few parties till we drop into the goddamn ocean. End of story."

"No, we can do it! We can convert these guys to Wounded and restock your crew." Amy turned to Jack with a leer. "We're going to blow the whole thing, dear Jack. It's been standing in the way of the Wounded."

"*What* has?" Jack snapped.

"The Orion Arm! We're going to blow it! It was all Draka Sortie's invention. Based on anti-dark energy down to the lowest quark level." Then she giggled. "Oooh, shouldn't have said that! Top secret, top secret!"

Jack jammed his hands to his hips. "You've got some weapon trained on the Orion Arm, is that what you're saying?"

Jonathan James shrugged. "All theoretical, Daddo. Amy thinks we can build a super-Dyson sphere here. I don't know. Maybe we can, maybe we can't. We've got plenty of time to think about it."

Amav let them gabble. She was content to let Jack handle it. She caught Laurie's eye and saw her doing the same thing. But grief welled up as she turned to the shaggy frozen Edward. Was JJC right that the Sol robot wouldn't decay? He looked alive even though she knew he wasn't. It was so wrong. Robots were living things. They deserved respect. So why couldn't

Amav extend that same generosity to this Wounded sculpture of her son?

Ywer's Martian outradiance was muted. Most of his bandwidth seemed engaged in Martian telepathy with Trotter. The Martian frequencies Trotter had long ago mastered were comforting to both, but their exchange went too fast to follow. Amav could still pick up a jumbled undercurrent about thousands of Martian shattergun models developed over the centuries, all interlinked on five-dimensional mental spreadsheets. Whole encyclopedias of Ywritt robotic coding flooded through Ywer's pink skull, taking ingenious places on the spreadsheets and posing abstruse theories on the nature of HAVOTT robots, Ywritt upgrades to HAVOTT robots, and quantum computing algorithms for enhanced Sol/Ywritt tech.

"Okay, you have this airship," Jack said, craning at the giant balloons above. "Excellent work as far as I can tell. But I was wondering how it can move so fast. Seems more like a dirigible than anything else."

JJC smiled at the compliment. "We don't normally expel that much ADE all at once, but we can jet it out the rear of the ship and really accelerate when we need to."

"That's right," Amy added. "Jonathan James and I are going to use this ship to fulfill the will of Draka Sortie!"

"Well, let's just say I haven't decided," JJC said. "We might just use it to fulfill *my* will."

"Dammit, Jonathan James!" Jack shouted. "This is just like the crap you pulled last year! Just like trying to be emperor of the Alpha Centaurians, or that SolGrid nonsense. It's disgusting! What the hell is wrong with you? You always have to be the top dog. And then you find you can't handle it and you come whining back to us!"

JJC's face drained. "You--you can't talk to me that way!"

"Whoa, watch what you say about our captain!" Amy laughed. "He's *contaminated,* you know! But I confess I'm just fascinated by it!"

"You stay out of this," JJC ordered, then whirled to Jack. "I won't have you guys showing up, totally uninvited, and *screwing* with me like this! For your information, being a Wounded lets me do whatever I want, without guilt. I can handle this, believe me. If Amy and I build a goddamn Dyson sphere and blow the whole goddamn Orion Arm, we do. If we don't, we don't. I won the goddamn war, I'm captain, and what I say goes!"

"Goddammit, I've had it!" Amav snarled. "Jack, what on earth possessed us to try to find this evil little *jerk?*"

"Wow, mom, have a cow, why don't you?" JJC sneered.

"Shut up! I've wasted *forty years* on all your idiotic *crap!*" She shook a finger in Lord Wounded's face. "So last month your father and I vowed to finally *deal* with it! What *idiots* we were! Like we were supposed to fix some stupid *unfinished business* with you! Screw it! Like you were really ever our son! And now you've turned into a totally corrupt goddamn *robot!*"

"Well--well--screw you!"

"Amav, *please*--" Jack said. "Didn't we agree we were going to find him no matter what he was? Robot or whatever? I mean, this is our *son.*"

"The hell with that! This whole stupid trip has been superficial *crap* about Team Commer! Admit it, Jack, we were just looking to patch up the holes in our marriage!"

"Whoa!" Amy laughed. "Secrets come out!"

"Mom, just shut your stupid hole, okay?" JJC said.

"Zip it!" Jack yelled, raising a fist. "Amav, look, yeah, I admit, but really, there was so much *more.* I mean, a fresh start, it was like we were finally *confronting* some important stuff, you know."

"Right, right, all that anxiety's supposed to magically disappear!" Amav shouted. "Well, screw it, it'll never be gone! He's always had this seed of Wounded in him!"

"That's not true! Not when he was a baby! The Alpha Centaurians *brainwashed* him!"

"That's right!" JJC said. "Cut me some slack, dammit!"

"Oh, this is *fantastic!*" Amy laughed. "Is this really my new mother-in-law?"

"Shut up, bitch!" Amav yelled, mortified that she and the

Amy whore had shared the same concept. "He never recovered! This whole *crap* is just more of the same goddamn ego trip! Now he wants to blow the Orion Arm! I'm so sick of this!"

"Shut up, Mom, or you're going over!" JJC shouted, advancing on her.

"Damn you, stop it!" Jack yelled, shoving him back. "She's right! Stop being a stupid *monster!*"

"Screw you! Screw you! I'm Lord Wounded and we'll build the goddamn Sphere!"

"That's right!" Amy cried. "We'll build the *Ultimate Sphere!*"

"And you're all gonna be *slave labor* for the mother!"

"The hell with you, Jonathan James!" Amav screamed. "I'm *done* covering up for your stupid *evil!* All your *damage!* I can't stand it! I'm done with it!"

Mother Amav, please, Trotter interjected, *give me credit for keeping Jonathan James at least partly sane in our ancient Alpha Centaurian bond. I too have been uneasy at my comrade's apparent cruelty towards the Orion Arm. But he goes deeper than you think and he does listen to me.*

"So *you're* the contamination!" Amy yelled, aiming a kick Trotter easily scooted away from. "God, I should've known! A stupid dog! You've been keeping JJC from *committing* to the Sphere!"

I am his remaining Garthah-/yuu! *I bear his soul! Mother Amav, share it with me!*

Amav reeled. JJC's lifelong horror flooded full force from the Beagle, driving miles deep inside her. Her son's agony stretched further than she'd ever dared suspect. She relived the shock of his kidnapping by Centaurian stormtroopers, his childhood years of exile, captivity, and indoctrination, and the mind-ripping terror of twenty trillion Alpha Centaurian souls merging inside him as their demented emperor. She felt his stunned shock at the incomprehensible suicide of Captain Clopt, his Centaurian *Garthah-/yuu* brother. She shared his panic at SolGrid's relentless, invasive pseudo-telepathy, and his reckless glee at fomenting an armed revolution against that foolish replica of the Centaurian Grid. She endured the dismay of being shattered to death by Rick Ballard, the claustrophobia of being trapped in the tetrahedron with Ballard and that cold T'ohj'puv entity, and the hot sharp grief of his permanent separation from his soulmate Suzette Borman. Amav knew every moment of eight hundred meaningless years of exile and warfare on this barren planet. She knew the shame of debased sex with a wooden Laurie robot, and the endless psychic warfare with a similar wooden version of Rick Ballard. JJC was drenched in sin and despair and malevolence.

"Oh my God …" she gasped.

Sorry, Mother Amav!

Trotter had patiently borne this gruesome load for thankless centuries. Now it was Amav's turn. To her shock she realized Jack would never comprehend any of it. Amav had inherited it all as Mother to the Monster. Her feeble protest against it meant nothing. She backed into the hull and twisted, staring blearily into tiny cold waves thousands of feet below. She raised a naked thigh atop the gunwale and straddled it.

Yes, so sorry, Mother Amav!

CHAPTER TWENTY-SEVEN
I'll Explode, Damn You!

Edward could hardly bear the scene. There was nothing he could do. His mistress Amav had miraculously followed him to this ADE world, but she was lost in agony, unaware what her splintering mind was proposing. But to Edward's relief the redheaded Laurie sprang to her and yanked her off the gunwale. "No! Absolutely not!" Laurie shouted, dragging Amav to the center of the ship.

"God, Amav, are you okay? Are you all right?" Jack cried.

"I just can't *handle* this!" she moaned. Edward's Empathy Module doubled in storage size. He'd had no idea his mistress could manifest such despair. He'd definitely focus much more attention on her from here on out.

Amy turned to JJC and smirked. "C'mon, Jonathan James, Mommy's rather unfit to become a Wounded robot, don't you think? She knows she needs to go overboard. Let's finish the job for her!"

"N-no ..." JJC stammered.

"Dammit, don't you dare touch her!" Jack shouted.

"The prisoners are rebelling!" Amy laughed, running for Amav only to be knocked flat by a swift kick to the forehead from Laurie.

"Get back, so help me God!" Laurie said. Edward was amazed Laurie had ever learned such a martial-art move. And she'd delivered it barefoot as the last bits of non-transforming garments whirled off her with the force of the kick. She finished in an alert crouch without any embarrassment at her nudity.

Amy sprang to her feet. "Well, damn you, bitch! Don't you dare touch a Class J Wounded! I could stop your crappy mechanical heart with a *thought!*"

"Get back!" Jack screamed. "Or 283 here will tear your head off!"

"You--you disrespectful *swine!*" Amy snarled as Trotter's outradiance informed everyone that while Class J's were still extremely powerful in this ADE environment, many of their functions simply didn't work. Amy must've just discovered that stopping the opponent's robotic heart was one of these. Edward wasn't sure Jack was right about a contest between an upgraded Heroes and Villains of the Thirties robot against a crippled Class J Wounded, but Amy was evidently taking it all into consideration.

Jack held his naked wife in his arms. The last of Jack's flight tunic melted away to reveal powerful pectorals and biceps, a firm belly, and powerful hips. Edward had never considered what magnificent physical specimens humans were. The Martian Ywer stood, also without a trace of self-consciousness, in his dissolving dark blue commander's uniform. Although his outradiance was high, it was full of static, and Ywer seemed to be calculating something on the order of *wishing for a shattergun, if only I had a shattergun, consider all the shattergun models developed over the past thousand years, the Goouik was a classic, my father had one of those antiques but its interface was so primitive, I remember my first trip to Mercury and he let me shoot it, what about that Harri McNarri HAVOTT robot who somehow came up with an improvement for the Jorquih model that eventually led to OmniShatter capability? Imagine a robot coming up with that, of course the human McNarri was a genius, but was it the Ywritt tech combining with HAVOTT algorithms, what about J'siy's theory of quantum decoherence as related to--*

"Okay, everyone," Laurie finally spoke. "It's time to consider what I've been able to figure out about this system."

"Forget it, robot!" Amy snarled. "I'm Draka's executor! I'm going to build his damn final Sphere and that's that!"

"No!" JJC said. "I haven't made my decision!"

Amy snapped her fingers at JJC's mouth. "Silence, dear wimp captain. I'm taking command of this operation."

"*No ...*"

"Jonathan James!" Jack said. "Tell this idiot to stand down!"

"Look, Dad, the goddamn decision's really out of my hands, you know. I mean, none of this matters anyway. This ship is doomed. Sooner or later it goes down. So if Amy wants to launch this Sphere, well, we're Wounded, that's what we do! So why shouldn't we?"

"That's right! I have all the plans in my head!" Amy laughed.

Amav jerked loose of Jack. "It doesn't matter that Suzette dies too? She's at Groombridge, right now! She's back *there*. You had all that karma with her, and *this* is the way it gets resolved?"

JJC's eyes bulged. "Let--let her experience it! Let's all those who resist the Wounded experience it! It doesn't matter! I know it's insane! Mom, Dad! I know it's *insane!* But who cares? Who cares?"

Master, no! Trotter thundered.

"After eight hundred years of *pure suffering!*" JJC wailed. "That Suzette was *the one!* Oh my God!"

There was a long silence as Jonathan James Commer worked it through.

"I'm *human!* Of course I am! I'm not Wounded! I've never been! The goddamn Alpha Centaurians *contaminated* me! I've had their damn seed in me all this time! You all know I could never do it!"

He went sobbing into his father's arms.

"No!" Amy shouted. "You stupid *bastard!* You think you can go back to that Suzette bitch and just lay her left and right? What's that compared to the Draka Equations? Can't you can feel them in the air?"

Everyone stared back blankly. "Yes, I've got them," Laurie finally spoke. "They're a mess, but I've got them."

"A *mess?* Why, you little slut! With your dinky boobs and your scrawny little ass! What do you know?"

Laurie shrugged. "Let's talk Wounded to Wounded, girl."

"You--you--" Amy sputtered. "What the hell would a stupid robot know about the Wounded?"

"First of all, Draka screwed the whole thing up. He thought the sphere on the Kjur's map was some super-Dyson sphere in higher dimensions he could use as a weapon. That assumption corrupted all his equations."

"Forget it! I'm going to make a Draka Sphere that'll rip the Orion Arm to shreds! I don't care if it takes the whole goddamn galaxy with it!"

Laurie pushed her long hair behind her neck and stood with a hand on her hip. "This talk is wearying me, Dr. Nortel. I see your wireless is out so we'll do it the Martian way, okay? And it'll have the revised equations."

The n-dimensional sphere represents contradictory and annihilating forces left over from the beginning of creation: forces the Kjur's physics postulated, and which they called the Uninhabitable. They wanted to map the sphere's countless nodes so they could be avoided by sentient beings, but they found only one of them, close by in the Large Magellanic Cloud.

Everyone jumped. Edward would've as well if he could.

"Oh my God!" Jack gasped. "You have *Martian outradiance?* A--a *robot?*"

Laurie grinned. "Just picked it up in the last couple minutes. The Trans-Simultaneity is strong in this environment."

"This is stupid!" Amy cried. "I won't have it! Just won't have it!"

Draka thought he could use this node as his final revenge. He sent the entire Kjurian map chamber here, but by then he was shattering and in full panic. The million Wounded he sent got no instruction. His last moments were cascading glitches and incomplete data. For instance, you, Dr. Amy, inexplicably failed to transport here, and you were unaware of Draka's fragmentary directives until three days ago.

"No!" Amy screamed. "Damn bitch robot!"

The nine-inch sphere on the map started the myth that Draka was creating some ultimately destructive Dyson sphere. Nobody understood that the Kjur sphere represents forces scattered throughout the universe that dwarf the Wounded's standard Dyson sphere weapon by countless orders of magnitude.

Anti-dark energy is just a byproduct of all that leftover crap from the beginning of the universe. Anything entering this system is transformed, but each transformation contributes a small destabilization to the node. Over a couple hundred thousand years it adds up to the point where the system turns into an ADE quasar. Our arrival on Ailyuae has brought us very close to that point. Attempts to deconstruct this planet to build a Dyson sphere will push us over the edge.

"So what? So what?" Amy shrieked, eyes glittering. "We'll do it!" Edward saw she'd absorbed and understood every equation. She also began to realize that for Laurie, this was all first-grade math.

"You're saying this will turn into a *quasar?*" Jack said. "That'll take the Milky Way with it?"

Laurie's smile was thin. "More equations for us all."

An ADE quasar will expand forever. Any matter, any stray hydrogen atom between galaxies the quasar encounters, is transformed. The quasar grows into infinity. Run the revised Draka Equations. He didn't see it, but you can. Any further interference with this node is like pushing a button to destroy the universe. Essentially, instantaneously.

Amy stared. "I'll do it! By damn, I'll do it! This has all screwed up so horribly! Damn you all!"

Right, honey. The central Draka Equation always comes down to: Who gets to push the button? Yeah, what a fantastic ego boost!

Equations described generation upon generation of universes rising and falling, each ending when some son of a bitch invented a button to wipe out the cosmos.

"Don't you laugh at me, robot whore! I'll press the damn button! Yes I will!" Amy whirled to Jack. "You can understand that, can't you, dear boy? Remember your senior paper on Keats? You got A-plus on it! '*Now more than ever seems it rich to die / to cease upon the midnight with no pain.*' You were in *love* with that poem!"

Jack folded his arms. "Hell with it. I just scraped something together to pass. I hated that class."

"Oh my God!" Amy laughed. "So the truth comes out! Don't think *that* will get you extra credit, dear Jacko!"

"Oh, c'mon, just can it, you two," Laurie said. "Listen, Captain Jack, extra credit or not, Trans-Simultaneity does point to a weird solution to all this."

"Look, robot," Jack said, "I don't know where you're getting all this, but--"

"Oh, shut your pretty mouth, Jacko!" Amy snapped. "Can't you see what your damn robot's doing? She's *trespassing* on Class A Trans-Simultaneity! Usurping Class A powers!"

"If you've figured out that much," Laurie replied, standing effortlessly nude and composed, "you understand that I'm quite higher than you in the Wounded hierarchy at this point."

"W--*Wounded?*" Jack gasped.

"No! I'll *explode,* damn you!" Amy cried. "Standing orders! Explode! Take out renegade Class A!" She furrowed her brow, clamped her eyes shut, and shivered.

Edward noted that he and Laurie were the only ones who didn't flinch. They'd both calculated that Amy had never known that Class J Explosion Mode was mandated in the presence of any higher-class Wounded who went berserk. But she was now discovering that this function was also offline.

"Dammit!" she groaned. "You bastards!"

She turned to stare down Ywer's shattergun barrel.

I'm quite interested in whatever weird solution Miss Laurie may have produced concerning our predicament, came his serene outradiance. *Please cease this aggressive activity immediately.*

CHAPTER TWENTY-EIGHT
The Grazing Shatter of *Kl'alp'lor*

"Not on your life, finback!" Amy snarled, jerking the gun out of Ywer's claw, whirling to Laurie, then taking another kick to her nose, this time from JJC's mother of all people.

The loose shattergun whirled so high it struck the main balloon. As he leaped for it, Jonathan James marveled that the whole USSF seemed trained in this martial-art stuff, even his non-USSF mom. Despite eight hundred years of ship-to-ship combat, he'd never been curious about it. Well, maybe someday he'd have time to learn.

Concentrate on the shattergun, fool!

His own mother, so agile. Both parents unclothed before him, barging in on his crumbling empire. How could this possibly happen? As for the Laurie robot, Jonathan James had fought to keep his eyes off that naked reproduction of his own efforts in wood. Laurie was a slightly older version but infinitely more real: superb, flawless, and untouchable. *Mocking* him.

The dead human Laurie in her coffin was also more lifelike than the wooden gadget he'd made. That lifeless decaying body, its light-blue USSF uniform also dissolving in the ADE-laced air, had been transported here to proclaim the final result of all his brainless fantasies.

Why was everyone so naked, so honest? Why were they tormenting him? As a Wounded none of this should matter, but *contamination back to the human* was surging. The inner Ballard and T'ohj'puv partitions spasmed. Billions of raw feelings vomited up from the depths.

Concentrate on the goddamn shattergun!

Bouncing off the balloon, it spun in the air, veering to starboard as James shot higher. And now Amy Nortel rose from his right. JJC knew she was as certain as he that the Ywritt-enhanced weapon could deliver its full deadliness even in this ADE environment.

Their Class J leaps had taken them 36.876 feet off the deck. Their arms outstretched, legs tangled in each other, JJC couldn't figure out whose limbs belonged to whom as they floated directly over the edge of the ship, with flat ocean 2,186 feet below.

Amy grabbed the gun, her mouth a wild howl as JJC seized her wrist and forced the gun into her face, prying at her fingers on the barrel, both of them squeezing the trigger handle where a tiny blue light indicated OmniShatter activation.

Amy twisted her head and yanked her arm free. The blue-purple ray sang down in a wide spray that washed right through the mainmast 10.455 feet from the deck.

A three-foot-wide chord of the mast exploded, glass shards in a million colors bursting in a flat circle. Everyone on the deck threw themselves down. Pressurized gray ADE gas shot free, blowing off the top of the mainmast and the balloon, rocketing the ship down. Stunned, JJC saw the deck further receding from him.

It's all over! It's all over!

He met Amy's shocked wide eyes as she kicked at gray clouds of ADE. But even as he could see *Armageddon* sinking minus its largest balloon, he realized gravity still worked on this cursed planet and that two were finally coming down. JJC's boots clumped to the deck and his head cleared. The mainmast was gone, along with primary ADE storage for all three balloons. It had all vented out. Where could they possibly limp to for repair?

Amy hit, collapsing to her knees. "You--you *bastard!*" Ywer's shattergun clinked on the boards and she scooped it up.

JJC found he didn't care. His mother was screaming. He whirled. "Mom! God, are you hit?"

Amav pointed past the ruined mainmast. JJC followed her gaze and it seemed everyone else did too. The dead robot dog Edward had been grazed on the tip of his right ear. Everyone held their breath as the cracking ascended the big floppy ear. Amy shrieked along with his mother.

Dead robot dog Edward stood up. He raised his left hind leg and balanced on the right. He positioned his left front paw atop his head and stared straight ahead.

"Oh God! Edward!" Amav and Amy wailed in eerie harmony.

The cracking ear joined the fuzzy St. Bernard forehead and then blue light blazed from between a thousand jagged cracks over his entire body.

Ywer bowed. *The Grazing Shatter of* Kl'alp'lor *shows the truest courage.*

A canvas shredding directed JJC's attention to the mizzenmast at the stern rupturing in a ball of fire. He could see where the pressurized ADE gas from the mainmast had ripped through the side of the rear balloon. He'd seen that happen in combat a few times.

The ship lurched backwards, held aloft only by the foremast balloon. They were slipping into the sea just as *Archer* had, only stern-first this time.

JJC grabbed the gunwale as both Amy and his mother rushed past him on the fresh downslope. Edward was toppling, bouncing up the now reversed stairs to the appallingly angled quarterdeck, his shatter surging in blue, purple, and magenta.

Amy shoved Amav so hard that his mother rolled twenty feet to clunk into the stairs. Jack ran for her, stumbling, going down, sliding.

"Edward! Edward! Oh my beautiful dog friend!" Amy screamed, raising Ywer's gun to her temple and squeezing the handle as she blundered into the toppling, exploding dog. White light blinded JJC and then came the roar of shattering glass. But instead of the usual high-pitched tone, a deep bass thunder reverberated way too long.

Wild rough woofing issued near the warped mizzenmast as the rear balloon blew off in flame and smoke. JJC looked for Trotter, but the Beagle had glued itself to his shin. Clutching the gunwale in one hand and Trotter with the other, JJC stared at the tableau of his naked mother and father grappling with a furry, intact, barking St. Bernard, all three seizing any hold they could get on the ruined, ADE-spurting mizzenmast.

"Get back! Not too close!" the dog shouted. "Amy Nortel and I have combined! It's not safe yet!"

"Edward! Edward! You're alive!" Amav cried, hugging him.

"Some sort of ADE reaction with Wounded tech and Martian shatter," Edward grunted. "I warn you, Mistress Amav, I'm riding this--this *Amy force!* Rerouting to Interface 336-B!"

"I love you, Edward! I love you!"

Edward yapped. "There! Sorry for the drama, Mistress Amav, Master Jack. It took a few more nanoseconds to bind her completely. She's safely locked away now. I can report that I love both of you exceedingly well in return."

"That Wounded spy's *inside* you?" Jack said. "How can that happen? How can you even be alive?"

"Oh, very simple, master," Edward said. "Something I saw in Ywer's brain a few minutes ago when he was reminiscing about hunting on Mercury."

"Oh, right! My first Mercurian Pheasant!" Ywer called from above, grasping a stanchion as the ship continued to pitch backwards. "My father took me there for target practice."

"The giant glass birds on Mercury that turn into meat when they're shattered," Edward said. "A puzzling anomaly to basic shattergun principles. I added that to the revised Draka equations everyone's been talking about. Under certain circumstances an apparently dead robot, but one retaining sentience, can resume normal life upon receiving a shattergun graze. The addition of a shattering Amy caused me to revise some of the algorithms at the last second."

"Wait! That Amy thing's really under control?" Jack said.

"Absolutely, Master Jack! Interestingly, I've grabbed the sum total of all her experiences and can now put them to use on your behalf."

The heavy Laurie coffin slid back and crashed against the quarterdeck stairs, flipped, and banged against the hatch to officer's quarters. Robot Laurie scrambled to it.

"Crap!" Jack said. "What are we going to do? JJC, is this ship going down?"

Jonathan James saw his father already had the answer. He just nodded.

"Hell, we're gonna lose that map, too. I saw it in Trotter's mind."

"The map!" JJC groaned. And with the map, with his entire ship, the chamber beyond the chamber. The sacred bedroom, his ultimate work of art.

Or was it art? Wasn't it all just a dream? A fantasy? A nasty, numbing addiction? Hadn't he spent eight hundred years on this evil ship encased in fantasy and addiction?

"Let it go! Let it all go!" he bellowed.

"Damn, we could've used it," his father said, misunderstanding. "To maybe locate these nodes the robot was talking about."

"No problem," Laurie said, hanging onto the white casket which had snapped apart, its limp redhead half-sprawled out, decaying strands of blue flight suit whipping free in the wind. "Edward made a complete copy of the chamber. Now can everyone just stop panicking for a second? I need to concentrate on Trans-Simultaneity."

"Oh, forget it, robot! I'm so sick of your stupid *ego trip!*" Jack said. "We've got to figure a way out of this!"

"That's what I'm *trying* to do, idiot!"

"How can you know this Trans-Simultaneity crap anyway? Only the real Laurie could do that!"

"Goddammit, Captain Jack, you haven't you figured that out yet?" she snapped, crouching over the body tangled in coffin shards. "Edward, I need some help here. Merge your mind with mine. Anything we can pull from the Amy records might be useful."

CHAPTER TWENTY-NINE
She's Your Best Physician/Engineer

"Haven't … figured out *what* yet?" Jack grunted, holding Amav at the mizzenmast which was still venting foul gray gas. Edward slid down the deck to the coffin.

"C'mon Jack, you really don't know?" Amav said. "Of course Laurie's the one who knows Trans-Simultaneity!"

"What are you saying? *Our* Laurie's dead! That robot there stole something out of her, I don't know what!"

"Please accept my resignation, Captain!" Laurie yelled. "Give me a couple minutes on this Trans stuff and we'll be set!"

"*What are you saying, robot?*" Jack raged. "Laurie *died,* and you brought her along to *mock* her!" The ship lurched even further backwards, and he jerked his head at a metal whining behind him. The foremast was bending impossibly, its giant balloon shuddering. There were probably just seconds left before it ripped free. But all he could do was yell: "That's *Laurie* there! She's *dead!*"

"No, she's not! That's the Laurie *robot!*" Amav shouted. "The real Laurie is right there in front of you! It was the only way we could smuggle her past MATS!"

Jack whirled to the figure working over the body with Edward. "*You?*" He jabbed a finger at the wrecked coffin. "That's not *you? You're* the real Laurie?"

Laurie's nude back jerked but she didn't turn. After an excruciating pause, she nodded. "I'm sorry, Captain, the deception was necessary. You already have my resignation on file."

"Oh my God! Oh my God!" Jack moaned. "*Then who's in the goddamn coffin?*"

"That's Laurie 283, I told you!" Amav said. "We were going to activate her once we found JJC. But it looks like she didn't make it!"

"We're trying to revive her!" Laurie shouted. "Edward figured a possible workaround when Amy piled in on him. If we just can recompile the software!"

"Yes! I have it! I have 283's kernel!" Edward barked.

"I can't believe this!" Jack said. "This ship's going down, and you're--you're--"

"I'm trying to *fix* it, fool!" Laurie screamed back. "I mean, sir!"

"I can't *believe* this! You--you give me all that lip the past three days, you do all that--that *stuff!* Oh my God!"

"Sorry, Captain, but it really was necessary! I had to act the part!"

"It's obvious MATS would never understand why we needed her," Amav said. "But we all knew she understood the Wounded in a way Laurie 283 never could. It was 283 who volunteered to stow away in the coffin so we could have her as backup."

"No ..." Jack said. "*No ...*"

"And that sealed her from MATS," Ywer called from twenty feet above. "It was fantastic luck that MATS demanded no direct electronic contact between itself and your copilot. MATS never suspected."

Jack turned to Ywer above him, hanging onto ropes tangled around the broken mainmast. "*You* knew too?"

"I wasn't sure until after I'd rested, but then I saw why this might be necessary. Please forgive the clumsy temporary blocks I inserted into my outradiance about this, Captain."

"Colonel Lachrer, please explain yourself!" Jack ordered.

"Sir, I need to concentrate on the Trans--"

"I don't care! By your own admission you've been totally insubordinate the past three days, and you've been--you've been--" He couldn't bring himself to add: *coming on to me like a sex addict.*

"Jack! Let her concentrate!" Amav shouted. "Our lives depend on it!"

"Sir, you--you may or may not accept this," Laurie stammered, "but we all knew that whatever I could remember of the Wounded Trans-Simultaneity equations would be vital to this mission. And once we were here, and I was in that Amy thing's presence, well, they kept *expanding.*"

"She had to act out a completely different role!" Amav went on. "Why can't you understand that?"

"You have my resignation, sir!" Laurie repeated, naked back still turned to him. "Just let me save our asses! Uh, I mean, save *us!*"

"I never did accept it!" Jack yelled back. "What is going *on* here?"

"The 283 kernel is stable," Edward spoke. "Are the final Trans-Simultaneity equations ready to roll?"

"Yes!" Laurie said. "Got 'em! Now we have to integrate everything! Laurie 283 memorized the specs for the *Typhoons*. On my count--"

"Look, Jack," Amav said, "I didn't know Laurie had studied 283 *that* well! But she's your best physician/engineer and she must've probed every aspect of her. I mean, when everything's on the line, you just do what you have to do!"

More ripping from above. The final balloon spewed a jet of dark ADE gas, and the ship dropped sickeningly.

"Oh, God!" Jack moaned.

"Hey, no problem, Jacko!" dead Laurie Lachrer 283 laughed as she snapped through her cracked coffin. She was fully clothed in a navy-blue USSF commander's uniform, all proper regulation except for the big oval 283 above her right breast. She pointed to a shadow blocking the sun.

"Into the lifeboat!" cried Rick Ballard.

CHAPTER THIRTY
Not Supreme Commander Yet

Balloon Ship *Armageddon* jackknifed into the dazzling, sun-refracting sea. Splintering boards burst a hundred feet into the air. Jack had trouble believing such a massive ship could be so fragile.

"God, I've done it *again*. I've done it *again!*" JJC wailed. "I can't believe it! God, you're right, Dad, I just can't handle it! I've doomed everyone! *Again!*"

"It's okay ... it'll be okay," Jack said, meeting Amav's stunned eyes as he clutched their Wounded son under three small orange balloons. Jack's chest was damp from Jonathan James' tears, but he was only mildly surprised to find himself clothed in an immaculate if soggy navy-blue USSF uniform, complete with supreme commander epaulets.

"Side effect of the Trans-Simultaneity, sir," Laurie Lachrer spoke. "It was easiest to put us all back to where we were. I don't know how we got to dress instead of flight suit, though."

Jack blinked. She wore a navy-blue colonel's uniform. Aside from the Air Force versus Navy designations and the robot's silver 283 badge, she and 283 were indistinguishable. Amav wore her blue tunic complete with enticing yellow pull ring. Ywer had his navy-blue commander's uniform with its optional Martian regalia.

Jack let out a lot of air. "Well, you screwed up on one thing. You happen to be out of uniform, Admiral Lachrer."

Laurie blinked. "Admiral?"

"Haven't you ever heard of a battlefield promotion, Admiral?"

"Uh, thank you, sir, but in my branch, I believe that would be general."

"Yeah, but it's definitely time for you to finally consolidate all our branches into one USSF. The damn service rivalries have never died. Have to say I've just kicked that can down the road for forty years now."

"Sir, I'm not sure what you're saying."

Jack's head hurt; there were now three Lauries onboard. At the prow a polished wooden redhead huddled with a monstrous version of traitor Lt. Richard Ballard. Jack could hardly remember how all ten of them had gotten onto the lifeboat, but the mutineer had hauled Jack's wife to safety, so Jack wasn't going to complain about last month's treachery to the USSF.

"I'm so sorry … I'm so sorry …" Jonathan James wept.

"It's okay, son … all okay," Jack said, then to Laurie: "More later, Admiral." He turned to Ballard at the prow. "What now, Captain?"

Ballard shrugged. "Well, we used up all our propellant on the way back. We saw an explosion and hauled ass back here. We decided we couldn't let JJC go that easily. Then we find all you guys here."

"There should be some dried biomeat and pure water I stored in the boat for Trotter," JJC said. "It'll last our biologics a few days, at least. I doubt we'll ever drift to an island, though. There's only a handful left. God, I'm so sorry it turned out like this." He indicated the balloons over their heads. "Without replenishment those'll give way in a day or so, especially with all this weight onboard."

"It's no problem," Laurie said. "The Trans-Simultaneity was able to incorporate this lifeboat as well."

"Yeah, I saw it heading this way right as I initialized," Laurie 283 put in. "Laurie was able to integrate that and Arkonsky us. Those balloons are regular helium now."

"We're actually inside an Arkonsky force field forty feet wide," Laurie said. "Everything inside is now normal matter."

"What? We converted back?" Jack said, watching his son pat himself in wonder.

"Inside this field, yes," Laurie said. "No ADE here. All ten of us are normal."

"And my wife and I apparently came through fine," Rick Ballard said, caressing the white-clad robot beside him.

"Unbelievable!" she laughed.

"No way Sol scientists could've figured that out in a thousand years!" Laurie 283 crowed. "But the real Laurie here did! Wooden robots built from ADE, transformed to normal matter! Aren't you glad she came along, dear Jack?"

"This isn't *possible,*" Jonathan James muttered. "*Suzette* ... oh God ..."

"Well, then, Admiral Lachrer," Jack said, "the question is, can you move this Arkonsky field somewhere useful? Is there any way we can contact Sol and have them send a rescue ship?"

"We don't want to do that, sir," Laurie said. "The time dilation effect would still have us waiting on this boat for twelve hundred years."

"Ouch," Amav said from beside Jack.

"My Trans-Simultaneity is fading pretty quickly, sir," Laurie went on, "or obviously I would've just transported us all back to Sol right now. I hope what I *have* been able to do will be sufficient."

"So what are you suggesting, Admiral?"

"Sir, really," Laurie said, "I guess I still don't understand how you can just promote me, and into a different subservice at that, sir."

"I hope 283's insubordination patterns haven't rubbed off on you too much, Admiral. Please just answer my question if you can."

Laurie reddened. "Oh! Sir! I didn't mean--of course I wouldn't. I mean, nothing would really rub off, you know. But I'm just completing my calculations now, and, I guess I'm pretty exhausted by it all, but they should be coming into play about *now.*" She pointed up.

Jack shielded his eyes from sunlight surging through clouds. "Oh my God."

Two white ships drifted in bright blue force fields. Both had the standard triangular wings, but the larger of the two was close to saucer-shaped.

"I told you Laurie was needed for this mission," Amav laughed. "No one else could've done Trans-Simultaneity."

"Yeah, I get that. God, do I get that ..." Jack said.

"Guess I should explain," Laurie said, pointing to the right vessel. "I made the *Typhoon VII* not only from the detailed specs

Laurie 283 memorized, but also because I've gotten so familiar with it I was able to tweak the settings for maximum efficiency. It should get you all home safely. A three-day trip again. And Know-How has been fully upgraded and interfaces perfectly with the *VII's* Nav12 system."

"Know-How?" Jack winced.

"Yes, sir, porting over a MATS interface would've required all sorts of semi-political stuff, MATS declaring an emergency, messaging the United System with its intent to assume command, and so on."

"I ... see. And the *VIII?*"

She shrugged, pointing to the left ship. "Laurie 283 and Know-How had all the specs on the *Typhoon VIII* as well. Between the three of us, I was able to make a fully functional spaceship as far as version 5.6.33 goes. And we have the Ywritt tweaks to Star Drive 4 ported over from the *VII*. I know we never even started construction on it, but this version of the *VIII* will be stable enough so just one crewmember is needed. It also has Nav13, which is the latest Ywritt development."

"Hmm ..." Jack said. "Excellent work, Admiral."

"Thank you, sir. The reason for the force fields should be obvious. Each ship is normal matter and normal electricity hovering in an Arkonsky field like this one, separating it from this ADE environment. I have enough energy left to transport us off this boat, through this Arkonsky and into the others. We'll fire up Star Drive 4 from here, something we'd definitely never do near a planetary surface, but in this case the Arkonskys will hold just long enough for us to be on our way in the Drive. We won't have a single ADE particle touching us."

"And from there?" Jack pressed.

Laurie took a breath. "Well, here's the thing. Basically, I now have a course set in *Typhoon VIII's* Nav13 program that'll take it to the Kjur's n-dimensional sphere. Which of course can be understood in one sense to be exactly right where we are at the moment, but also--not. Because it's in n-space, with manifestations all over the universe."

"I see. Very interesting."

Edward issued a soft bark. "No matter the time scale involved, that sphere needs to be dealt with," he said. "Or sooner or later the universe ends prematurely. Civilizations won't develop at their own speed and work out their destinies. Someone will start fooling with an ADE node and press the final button."

Jack nodded. It was only a matter of time before someone tried that stunt again.

"Probing the Kjur sphere involves flying the ship straight into Wiioryvel," Edward continued. "I see the results of Laurie's equations. Theoretically the course will translate the *Typhoon* to higher dimensions and take the ship to the n-sphere. It has to be the *VIII,* because only the new Nav13 system can handle the calculations. A good side effect is that going into the sun in Star Drive will supernova this entire solar system and convert all ADE to normal energy."

Laurie swallowed. "That's why I rigged the *VIII* for a single crewmember. I'll fly it in, and the rest of you will be going home in the *VII.*"

"Really," Jack said.

Laurie nodded. "It's the only way, sir. Frankly, I'm exhausted from this Trans work, but I think I'm the only one that can bring this off, before I start forgetting, or get too tired, or whatever. I know I'll be drained soon. But the equations point to the *Typhoon VIII* getting right to the heart of the n-dimensional sphere."

"Another possibility," Edward said, "is that the ship might also shift through higher dimensions to one of billions of other sphere loci in normal space. If we can perfect this technique, possibly over eons we could discover others and map them. Quantum computerization from the Ywritt might extrapolate other locations, and we slowly remove the crap."

"That's the scenario I call *rewriting the universe,*" Laurie said. "But it might take billions of years. Either way, I'm ready to take the *VIII* in now, sir."

There was a long silence. Jack let it sink in. "Well, Admiral Lachrer," he spoke, "I think it's quite possible that a little too much Laurie 283 really has rubbed off on you after all. She could order me around, but I don't think you can. You're not Supreme Commander yet."

"Sir!" Laurie's face went blank. She'd never received a reprimand in over forty years in the USSF. Her body quivered, fighting the urge to come to cadet attention. "I--I didn't intend-- I mean, I was just charting out the most logical--"

"So what are you going to do when you arrive at the sphere in your multi-dimensional *Typhoon VIII?* Fire a few multi-dimensional Augmented Xons at it? Do you have a plan for first contact with that thing? I say we send a team there capable of figuring out the problem once and for all."

"I ... I ..."

"Well, you won't be the first supreme commander to draw a blank. I do it all the time."

"S-sir?"

"Just keep in mind that you're not supreme commander *until* you get back to Sol."

"*What?*"

"Of course I want you for SCUSSF. Have to admit your little acting career back there threw me, but what the hell. I guess it shows the kind of flair a supreme commander needs."

"That's--impossible, sir!"

"That's impossible, *fool!*" Laurie 283 laughed. "Get your diction straight, girl!"

"You didn't tell me this," Amav said. "I admit it's a great idea, but what about Joe?"

"Joe knows he's acting SCUSSF back at Sol," Jack went on, "and at my resignation in a few minutes, he'll be in command until Laurie gets back and he gets all the Council paperwork through."

"Forgive me, sir," Laurie said, "but I have *no* idea what you talking about."

"What I'm really doing is assigning crews to those two ships up there. Admiral Lachrer, you'll captain the *Typhoon VII* back to Sol."

"Sir? What about--"

"You're badly needed as the new supreme commander, and you're about to have your hands very full dealing with the United System Council and how it interfaces with the Wounded robots throughout the Orion Arm. And you can investigate all those new civilizations in the Arm we heard about through your equations. A lot on your plate."

"Well, that sounds like a wonderful honor, but the *VIII*--"

"No problem. We have your navigational program on the *VIII,* and Edward fully understands it. Congratulations on your appointment, Admiral Lachrer."

"I ... I ..." Laurie gasped into the silence.

"Congratulations, Laurie!" Amav said. "It's brilliant!"

"I finished my side of the paperwork before we took off," Jack said. "Joe has a copy of it. You know he's never wanted the top job, and said he'll retire when I do. So I wanted your promotion done, especially if we didn't come back. It's actually been in my personnel files for months now. Just needed a few updates."

"But, Captain," Laurie protested, "I mean, after the way I've acted the past three days ..."

Jack was amused how deeply the new supreme commander of the United System Space Force could blush. "The United System Council won't be a problem. Senator Lee's on our side on this, and he'll get your appointment through. And Trotter will supply the full telepathic account."

Absolutely, father of my master and in a way included in our Garthah-/yuu *group!*

"Thank you, sir. I don't know what to say."

"Okay, Admiral, here's the rest of your crew. Jonathan James, to interface with the Wounded and with other civilizations in the Orion Arm, and with the Ywritt. We still have a lot to straighten out with them. They're going to big a major help as we explore outwards."

"Dad, do you really think ..." Jonathan James began.

"Son, you're obviously needed back in Sol to represent the Wounded and where it can go from here. We have to have someone who knows the territory, who can interface with any

Wounded in hiding."

"Well, really, Dad, you know, maybe I should be the one on the *VIII*. I mean, look, we can all admit it's a suicide mission, but someone's got to do it. You all have lives back in Sol. I don't. And I mean, I can learn how the ship works in a few minutes, really. The Class J programming and all."

Jack shook his head. "Thanks for the offer, son, but I need you more at Sol. You've been through this Wounded stuff and you've bounced back. We need you dealing with the Wounded who're still at large in the Milky Way."

"Well ... maybe, but--"

"And just maybe you don't need to be *top man* anymore. No glorious suicide mission. Maybe step back, just be *of service* for a change."

JJC nodded, though Jack saw that he was dazed by the concept of being *of service* to anyone or anything. "Maybe. I don't know. All the Wounded spies there are really all normal biological robots, you know. But you think maybe I can get to them and talk somehow?" He frowned. "Actually, it'd be my *contamination* talking to them."

"Right. I think that's the key. I picked that idea up from Trotter. Here in the Cloud, your contamination was too isolated to affect the Wounded. I think the Wounded are just going to come around whether they want to or not. And I think you do have some business back in Sol after all. Looks like you need to find Suzette Borman."

JJC blinked. "Oh my God. If I haven't screwed things up too much."

"I'm sure Trotter will help you with that and everything else."

Certainly, Trotter radiated. *That's what I'm here for.*

"My first captain said you could never go back," JJC mused. "Never reconfigure back to normal electricity. Guess I took that to heart, figured I could never get back."

"Definitely not true," Laurie put in. "You're standing here in normal electricity. We all transformed fine."

JJC emitted a faint smile. "Yeah. Going back. Got some

stuff to do there, I guess."

"Mr. Ballard, and Ms. Laurie 1014," Jack continued, "I'm assigning you to the *VII* as well."

They nodded. Jack was grateful that the Ballard robot didn't spout back any of his usual insolent guff.

"The Ywritt will be able to get them some great upgrades," Laurie said.

"That would be lovely. Thank you all," Laurie 1014 said.

"But look, Dad, I can't be with the *robots* anymore," Jonathan James cut in. "I mean, we've had this very complicated thing ..."

"Very complicated!" Laurie 1014 laughed. "But Rick and I worked all that out while we were floating off. We're all just going to have to start all over, especially once you find this Suzette creature we've heard so much about over the centuries. It looks like it's your karma to know us. You've still got parts of us in you. There's no escaping that. There's got to be a new way of looking at all that."

"Karma ..." JJC muttered. "Oh my God."

Everyone paused to let that sink in. Jack could only guess at the complications they referred to. He had a feeling Amav would be able to fill him on that and much more. He shrugged. "Questions, any of you? All right then. My resignation as supreme commander takes place the instant the *Typhoon VIII* enters Wiioryvel. By that time I'll be unrecallable by the USSF and I suppose you could define the *Typhoon VIII* as a pirate ship from that point on. But I'll be captaining her in any case, and I'm bringing along a team to investigate the n-sphere. First up for the *VIII,* we have Commander Ywer as copilot."

"Yes, sir!" Ywer chirped in English, radiating Martian fractal patterns of enthusiastic assent.

"Next, Edward will be our navigator, interfacing with Laurie's course for the sphere."

"Really?" JJC blurted. "Doesn't he still have Amy Nortel inside him?"

"She still here," Edward said. "I've been integrating her more and more over the past few minutes. She has some fascinating background on Draka Sortie and the Wounded which should be a great help."

"Is she really secured?" Amav asked.

"Oh yes! Although she's quite distressed that she can't press a button to end the universe. She was programmed all her life to destroy everything. Now she knows she needs to reevaluate all that. I can synthesize her voice if you like."

"No, I think--" Jack began.

"*God, what am I gonna do?*" wailed Amy Nortel out of Edward's St. Bernard muzzle.

"Oh!" Amav gasped.

"Now you're *sure* she's secure, right?" Jack said.

"Absolutely," Edward said. "Believe it or not, everyone, we must have Amy Nortel along on this ride."

"Of course. That's why I wanted you on the *VIII.*"

"I've reassured her that we'll all support her as we go along. She still loves me, so that's a start."

Jack smiled, shaking his head at the prejudice he'd harbored against the robot for so long. He could no longer disdain Edward as merely a servant or a mechanical pet. He was a fully developed, independent being. And the damn thing was just liable to save the universe in the next few minutes. "And if you haven't guessed," Jack continued, "Laurie 283 will be our physician/engineer. She'll interface with Know-How and keep the ship running as it translates into higher dimensions."

Ditto on all the ill will he'd harbored against 283. He turned to Amav. "Amav will be our planetary engineer. She'll have tremendous insight on the sphere and she'll keep us together."

"And I'm resigning all that Dictator of Sol crap," Amav said. "I think Sol has had plenty of time to get its act together without me. But thank you for assigning me to your ship, dear Captain Husband."

Jack grinned. "We both knew you were coming. I need you on this."

CHAPTER THIRTY-ONE
The Star

"Out of the first Star Drive, Captain!" Ywer called. Jack grunted in surprise to find himself standing in the Control Room of a *Typhoon VIII* that had been a vague set of plans just a few minutes ago. Now the daunting work began and he had to focus. He checked Amav and Ywer, blinking and balancing themselves. Edward barked happily from the rear of the room, and Jack turned to Laurie 283, on her feet and grinning.

Ywer settled into the copilot's seat. "I suggest navigator and physician/engineer take up their posts."

"And ex-Dictator of Sol," Amav said, seating herself behind Ywer as Edward scampered out the Control Room door and Laurie 283 headed for Engineering.

"Know-How is engaged," came a feminine voice from the ceiling.

"Fine," Jack spoke. "Know-How, maintain constant contact with Laurie 283. Run continual self-diagnostics. Also don't override Edward's Nav13 program."

"Certainly, Captain."

"I do hope you trust her," Amav said.

"Sure. Just checking," Jack said, seating himself in the command seat, surveying the console. "It's so strange to be here. The *VIII*. It seems so much like the *VII*, but different somehow. Maybe it's the Ywritt tech. This room's a little bigger maybe." He looked out the port windows at the much wider white saucer shape. "Hard to believe. Where are we, Edward?"

"Star Drive took us a little over two hundred million miles from Wiioryvel, then shut off," Edward reported over the ship's intercom. "Ailyuae has been destroyed by our two ships initiating Star Drive, though its ADE fragments are expanding outwards."

"We have a residual Arkonsky field protecting the ship from any ADE particles this far out," Laurie 283 announced from Engineering. "By the way, *Typhoon VII* is en route to the Milky Way."

"Right," Jack said. "I figured Laurie wouldn't disobey me and fly in after us."

"She wouldn't," Amav said. "She knows what needs to get done back there." She pointed out the canopy. Ywer had muted the filters so the glare of Wiioryvel wasn't blinding, but the Milky Way blazed nevertheless, a lovely spiral, slightly warped over the eons from contact with its neighboring dwarf galaxies.

"Course ready?" Jack said. He pointed to the sun in front of them. "We're sure we'll supernova that thing? And that'll wipe out all ADE in this system?"

"Affirmative," Edward replied from Navigation down the fuselage. "We must strike at the equator, at exactly ninety degrees. Course laid in."

"Course accepted and transferred to command console," Ywer said. "The star is 201.318 million miles away. *Typhoon* motionless in respect to object, aimed to insert at ninety degrees to the equator. Star Drive 4 ready to engage." He turned to Jack. "Captain?"

"Wow …" Jack said. "I can't believe we're doing this to a brand-new spaceship."

"It's time, Jack," Amav said. "This is the only way." Her hand came to his shoulder.

Jack's fingers hovered above the red and blue squares on his console. "Guess we're ready? Ready to see about this sphere?"

"Ready," several crewmembers called at once.

And Jack Commer shot his spaceship directly into the sun.

About the Author

Michael D. Smith was raised in the Northeast and the Chicago area, then moved to Texas to attend Rice University, where he began developing as a writer and visual artist. His Jack Commer, Supreme Commander science fiction series is published by Sortmind Press. In addition, Sortmind Press has published Smith's literary novels *Sortmind, The Soul Institute, CommWealth, Akard Drearstone,* and *Jump Grenade.* All titles are available from Amazon.

Smith's web site, https://sortmind.com, contains further examples of his novels and visual art, and he muses about writing and art processes at https://blog.sortmind.com/.

Amazon author page
https://www.amazon.com/author/smithmi/

The Jack Commer, Supreme Commander Series

The Martian Marauders
Jack Commer, Supreme Commander
Nonprofit Chronowar
Collapse and Delusion
The Wounded Frontier
The SolGrid Rebellion
Balloon Ship Armageddon

www.ingramcontent.com/pod-product-compliance
Lightning Source LLC
Chambersburg PA
CBHW060921180626
46817CB00004B/1337